Melissa Cunningham

Clean Teen Publishing

Reluctant Guardian
Copyright ©2013 Melissa Cunningham
All rights reserved.

ISBN: 978-1-94053-414-5
Cover Design by: Marya Heiman
Typography by: Courtney Nuckels
Editing by: Cynthia Shepp

For more information about our content disclosure,
please utilize the QR code above with your smart phone
or visit us at
www.CleanTeenPublishing.com.

Prologue

ALISA

I should have realized that suicide was not my best option. But, like most teenage girls, I hadn't planned ahead. I never pictured my parents and brothers picking up the pieces of my broken life, or the empty hole I would leave in my wake.

I honestly didn't think anyone cared that much.

Medication hadn't helped either. It made things worse. When my best friend, Natasha—or Natty, as I'd always called her—died from a brain tumor, nothing could have shattered me more. Not just because Natty and I were closer than Siamese twins, but because we shared a dark, horrifying secret.

Something I'd never told anyone.

Not even my parents.

Once she was gone, I didn't know how to shoulder that weight on my own. I was drowning in sorrow. I'd fallen into a dark pit and I had every right to take that antidepressant. My parents thought it would help.

I should have been more open about my feelings. I should have confided in my mom and dad and explained that the medication wasn't working. But I didn't. I didn't realize the drug was affecting me adversely... until it was too late.

The only thing I wanted that night was to *not* feel anymore, to not have my heart ripping in two, and to not cry so hard that my whole body ached.

Would it be painful if I rammed my car into the tall pine at the curve in the road? Would it do the trick or just turn me into a vegetable for the rest of my life?

I gambled.
I took a chance and got what I wanted.
Death.

1

Paradise Lost

ALISA

The headlights of my car shine brightly into the woods, pulsing with an eerie glow with each swipe of the windshield wipers. Deep shadows stretch past the foliage, the seat-belt sensor dinging in the solemn silence.

I'm alone, staring at my motionless body as blood drains from a large gash on my forehead. The crimson rivulets drip down onto my shirt, spreading like blossoming roses. For a moment, I wonder if I've made a mistake and remorse tugs at my heart. Maybe I shouldn't have done it. Maybe I shouldn't have given up yet.

But things will be better now. I'm sure of it. No more nightmares, no more panic attacks, no more medications. And, definitely no more curious glances from friends, neighbors, or even my own family.

They had all gossiped behind my back, and no one had truly cared. At least that I noticed. My family loved me, sure, but I'd been a drain on them, exhausting in my need for constant reassurance. The last conversation I had with my older brother had ended in a fight, and even my parents were fed up.

Just this morning my mother had lost her temper and yelled at me, saying she was tired of my self-pity, tired of my complaining, tired of my crying, and if I didn't clean up my act, they'd resort to more serious measures. I'm not sure what those measures would be, but it didn't sound good.

So, here I am, freeing my family of the endless annoyance of *me*. They'll be sad at first sure, but they'll get over it.

People always do.

I look around in the quiet stillness, wondering why no one is here to meet me. All my life I've heard that loved-ones will appear and take my hand to guide me through the pearly gates of heaven. Maybe the stories aren't true after all.

Maybe my atheistic theory is true—that there is no God, no heaven, no angels, and no afterlife. I am just experiencing a lack of oxygen, my brain creating fanciful scenes of a heavenly occurrence.

A strong tug pulls at my chest. I grow anxious, wondering what is happening. The world around me dims and I move forward, feeling drawn toward a strange pinpoint of light. It draws me as though a string is attached to my body, like a doomed fish being reeled in.

At first I resist, afraid, digging my feet in, but then I give up, and I move with it.

Recognition dawns. The light. The pull. This is it! There is a heaven and I am going there. It's all true! Relief floods through me in a wave of happiness. Deep down, I hadn't wanted to completely disappear. I'd wanted the pain to end, yeah, but I also wanted— no, *needed*—to know that death wasn't final, that my Gram who had already died and my best friend, Natty, lived on. That their radiant lives hadn't been snuffed out completely.

Any minute now, the heaviness in my heart would dissipate and I'd be free, dancing through daffodils on heaven's hillside. I'd be in the arms of my best friend and grandmother. I'd be assigned my own silver-lined cloud. I raised my face to the sky.

Any minute now...

It doesn't happen, so I follow the light, curious, and after floating for what seems like forever, I realize that the rush of bliss— that blanket of warmth I've read about, isn't going to come. I don't feel any different than I did before I crashed my car. I still carry my grievous burdens. I still ache over the death of my friend and the loss of my grandmother. The memories breathe inside me, alive and tormenting.

With one last glance over my shoulder, I gaze at my surroundings. The woods and broken car are far behind me like a distant dream.

I step forward, leaving behind the world I long to forget. Before me is a beautiful meadow of wildflowers. Many of the blossoms are varieties I've never seen before—the colors, vivid and bright, and some, blindingly white. Reveling in the glorious scent of their fragrance, I forget for a moment why I am even here.

On the other side of the meadow lies a wide, glittering bridge embedded with diamonds, complete with silver handrails. I move through the swaying flowers, running my fingers along the tops of their velvety petals.

Wonder fills me.

This world is so big, so bright, and so beautiful. Hope blossoms like a helium-filled balloon, lifting my weary soul. I can be happy here. I can release the heartache of my old existence. I won't have to think of the misery Natty and I endured for so many years.

A lazy smile spreads across my face. I am free.

Other disembodied people enter the meadow and head in the same direction. They pass by me, their eyes glowing with happiness, their hands reaching out to the souls on the other side of the bridge. I don't see anyone familiar yet, but surely, they are waiting.

I hurry to join the throng, but as soon as I place my foot on the bridge's glittering surface, an unseen force repels me backward. I lose my balance and land hard on my behind. Sparkling dust poofs up around me.

People glance my way, but no one stops. Embarrassed, and not wanting to attract attention, I try again. But like the wrong side of a magnet, my foot won't move over the edge of the bridge. I try again and again, barely controlling my urge to let loose a string of four letter words.

Something here is really messed up.

I watch the others cross. They make it look easy as they enter the beautiful city on the other side. A city of brilliant light, filled with golden cathedrals and towers that sparkle in the distance. I yearn to go there more than anything. I *have* to go there. I *killed* myself to go there!

But I can't cross.

I was supposed to rest for eternity on pink clouds and fly on golden wings without a care. What is with the stupid barricade? Why are others crossing without a problem? Why am I blocked? It doesn't make sense.

That's when I see her. She exits the city's gates in a flowing white dress that swishes about her bare ankles. A smile stretches across her familiar, loving face.

"Gram!" I forget the bridge, forget my frustration, and forget my inability to cross. I barrel forward, eager to throw my arms around my beloved grandmother, who championed me my whole life, who loved me in spite of everything.

I ricochet back, falling to the ground in front of everyone.

Again.

Now they do stop to watch. Hot shame flushes through me. There is something wrong with me. I'm not wanted here. A tight fist closes around my heart, and the burning sting of tears scalds the back of my eyes. I pull myself up, keeping my head high, not meeting anyone's gaze.

Not even Gram's.

She crosses the bridge and envelopes me in her arms, kissing my head, smoothing my hair and gazing into my eyes. "My sweet Alisa," she says, without even moving her lips.

My embarrassment disappears as her thoughts flow into my mind like a river. I raise my eyes to meet hers. Gram speaks in a tone of love and acceptance, but it's all inside my head.

I'm so happy to see you, but you shouldn't be here!"

And then it hits me. I'm a mind reader! I have magical powers!

This is awesome!

I bask in the warmth of Gram's affection, feeling loved and safe for the first time since I left my body. She knows me. She understands me. She'll get me into that glimmering city, come hell or high water.

But instead of taking my hand and leading me across the bridge, she pulls me in the *other* direction.

2

My Mansion on High

ALISA

*J*ust to be clear, the other direction isn't hell—thank heavens—not that I know where hell is, but I am relieved anyway. I certainly don't think I deserve to go there.

With a blink of Gram's eyes, she takes me to a place she calls *Idir Shaol*, which she says means "between worlds" or something like that. It's a hamlet compared to the teeming city across the bridge, but at least it doesn't have leaping flames and groaning souls reaching from its wailing depths.

"This will be your home for a while," she says, gazing lovingly into my eyes. "Remember how much I love you, and that I'm rooting for you, dear. Now go and show everyone how strong you really are." She shoves me forward.

I turn to face her and then look over my shoulder at the quiet village behind me. "Aren't you coming?"

She shakes her head slowly, her eyes saying goodbye.

An awful tingle spreads through me as I realize what this means, but she won't really leave me here... in this *between worlds* place, trapped and alone. I don't know anyone, and I don't want to be alone.

"Come now, Alisa. It'll only be for a while." She smiles as her words enter my mind. "You'll learn things that will help you, and before you know it, we'll be together again."

I argue automatically. I was a fantastic debater before I died, and I loved a good fight, perfecting the art with my parents. I have a feeling if I don't argue my case just right, Gram will really leave.

I think carefully. "Umm, that does sound great, and I totally want to do that later, but I feel like we should stick together. At

least for now. I'm here to rest and be happy. Not to... learn things."
I give her a wide grin, knowing she won't be able to resist. But
watching her face and waiting for a reaction makes the light go
out in mine.

My words—and I can tell they *have* affected her—have not
changed her mind.

"Alisa, that's not how it works." She shakes her head and cups
my cheeks between her palms. The familiar fragrance of apple pie
wafts up around me.

I search her eyes, because I know that look—her look of...
disappointment? In me?

"Don't worry. I'll be back," she says. "Learn as much from
your time here as you can. You're in for a *wonderful* experience.
I promise." With a kiss she steps back, waves goodbye, and then
leaves me standing inside a set of high, wooden double doors,
like doors to a fort. I stare at the empty space where she'd been
standing.

A man wearing a deep green robe approaches, looking right
at me. I turn my back, hoping he'll pass by. I don't want to talk to
anyone when my heart is so heavy. He nears, the air growing static.
A strange power emanates from him, with a brightness I've never
seen before. I look away, but it's not long before I feel him right
behind me, like a sure knowledge of a monster under the bed. His
presence presses against me and I swirl around to find myself face
to face with his perfectly chiseled face.

Long, dark hair falls around his shoulders and a glow pulsates
around him as though a piece of sun rests beneath his skin. Even
his eyes shine with emerald brilliance. His lips turn up into an
amused smile and I stare, unable to form any coherent thoughts.

He sticks his hand out. "Welcome to *Idir Shoal*! I'm
Raphael." He says this out loud, his deep, rumbly voice reminding
me somehow of Rocky Road ice cream. Rich and chocolatey.

I shake my head, trying to clear the fog, and take his offered
hand. I gasp and pull back in surprise. "You have a body!" I peer
more closely wondering why he got to keep his.

"Good gracious! You're right!" He pats himself down, looking confused. "How did this happen?"

I feel a moment of panic before his teasing sinks in, and I give him a wry smile, wagging my finger at him. "Good one. You must say that to all the dearly departed."

"Nope." A wide smile spreads across his tan face. "You're the first."

I could like this guy. Cute, funny, and nice. But way too old for me. "So are you in charge around here?" I glance around, wondering if this is a corner of hell I've never heard about. It's not bright like that golden city across the bridge, but there isn't any weeping, wailing, or gnashing of teeth. I start to wonder if hell is really a quiet place that slowly drives you insane with the need for sound. *Any* sound. My illusions of what death is have been flushed down the toilet, so what do I know?

"Come, I'll explain as we walk." He drapes my arm through his. The heat of his skin permeates through my robe and he pats my arm as though I am just as corporeal as he is.

We move over the path at a slow pace, and the cool, flat stones feel smooth beneath my feet. I soak in the vivid colors and try to remember everything Raphael says, but there is too much. Too much color, too much to focus on, too much stimulation. Nothing sticks in my mind, and I'm too embarrassed to ask him to explain it all twice. His informative speech pours through me like water through a sieve.

He continues as though he doesn't notice. "You will live in a cottage with three other souls who also took their lives. You'll attend classes to learn your new role, and then we'll take it from there. How does that sound?"

"Wait. Classes?" I'm able to focus on that word without difficulty. "Like school?" With a sinking heart, I search his face. I'd hoped to dwell for eternity with loved ones, not strangers in this unfamiliar place. Doesn't he realize I have no loved ones in *Idir Shaol*? And the idea of living with other suicide victims is *not* what I had in mind when I ended it all. "Is there an option C?"

His warm chuckle resonates like the soft strum of a bass guitar, and he pats my hand. "Nope. No option C. Sorry."

Raphael leads me to a bungalow with rounded walls, a thatched roof, wooden shutters, and a red front door. Very Hansel and Gretel. I wouldn't be at all surprised to find a witch inside, stirring a pot of poisonous stew.

"These are your quarters." He pushes the door open. "We try to make things as homey as your home on earth." He hands me a box that is sitting on an empty mattress with miscellaneous items inside. "Everything you need is in here, and then take time to familiarize yourself with *Idir Shaol.* You can explore wherever you want. My office is located down that path." He points to a large, white, marble building in the middle of town. "You can't miss it. I'd like to talk with you again as soon as you're settled."

"Okay."

He squeezes my arm and then leaves me standing in front of my mansion on high. I enter my new home. There are four beds—one against each wall, like in a dorm room. Three of the beds are obviously taken, as they've been made up with quilts of varying color, and personal items have been placed on small tables next to each one.

Why are there beds? Do we need beds? Do we sleep? I *am* exhausted and could use a nap.

Placing my box on what I guess is my bed, I search the quiet emptiness. This is my life now—this place, these people. I fall to the mattress, completely disillusioned and yearning to cry. The ache is still there.

I've ruined my life—*completely* ruined it.

Things were supposed be better after I died.

How could I have been so stupid?

3

Drifting Alone

BRECKEN

The days lengthen as spring approaches, and the darkness of winter fills Brecken's heart. Nothing feels right in his life. He's just a performer, acting out a part, and the performance never ends. He drifts through a timeless space.

Since the drawn-out illness and death of his mother, his dad has been distant. No. More than distant—nonexistent. He's never home. He's always taking out-of-town jobs. Not that Brecken minds that much. He and his dad have never seen eye-to-eye. Their moments together are a series of arguments that Brecken always loses. But with his dad gone, he has total freedom, and also total responsibility for his two little sisters. That responsibility weighs heavy. Bills need to be paid if they want to stay in this stupid little house, and groceries have to be bought.

Brecken doesn't have a job, and he knows his only way out is to stay in school. In the afternoon, he helps his sisters with homework, makes dinner, and does the laundry.

The constant complaining of his sisters weighs him down. They don't want him to replace their dad, let alone their mother. They don't want to be told to clean their rooms, help with chores, or anything else by their dumb older brother.

He doesn't blame them.

There are many nights he lies awake in bed wishing he could talk to his mom, that her ghost would appear and comfort him. She never does though. Nothing is more acutely disappointing.

His grades are dropping and he has gotten in a few fights at school—nothing he started, but ones he finished.

The only light on the horizon is Jill. Beautiful, kind, wonderful Jill. Always there like a balm of happiness, ready to cheer him up at the end of each dark day. She is the miracle he needed, and he plans to hang onto her as long as he can.

4

Roommates

ALISA

I have no idea how long I lie on my new, unfamiliar bed—which is made with a quilt that looks exactly like the one on my bed at home. Weird. I miss the tick-tock of my clock, the pictures on my walls, my closet full of clothes. And let's not forget the ability to judge the passing of time.

No shadows move across the walls here, nor does anyone call me for dinner. When is it time to go to bed? When are the classes held I'm supposed to attend? How do the people here stand it? How will I? I'll go crazy if I stay, and I wish more than anything to turn back time.

Within a few moments, my new roommates show up, barreling through the door. The front-runner is laughing, and when they see me, they freeze, stiff smiles appearing on their surprised faces. It's easy to see they have already become friends and that I'll be the odd one out.

My death is turning out to be as wonderful as my life. What a nice surprise.

"Hi!" the laughing, boisterous redhead exclaims when she sees me. She plops down beside me on my bed and gives me a one-armed hug. "It's great to meet you! I'm Shana." She takes my hand and pumps my arm up and down with a firm grip.

"Hi." I pull away slightly. She smells like buttered toast. Weird. Gram smelled like apple pie. I wonder what I smell like, if anything.

"That's Cinder," she says, pointing to the sullen girl whose long, black hair hangs over one eye. Cinder doesn't brush it back or even tuck it behind her ears, but carries her aura of sorrow like a heavy shroud. I feel depressed just looking at her. She may have brown eyes, but I can't tell. She walks slowly to her bed and sits, keeping her chin tucked to her chest.

The third girl, who is at least six feet tall with the shoulders of a linebacker and thick flexing hands, towers over the rest of us. She glares, animosity radiating from her in palpable, threatening waves.

I have to live with these people? Okay, I can deal with Shana, Miss Happy Cheerleader, but people like Miss Muscle terrify me. The jury is still out on Cinder.

"That's Deedre." Shana points to the giant who lies on her bed with her hands intertwined behind her head. "She's... not as bad as she seems. She just needs a smoke."

"You can do that here?"

Shana leans closer slowly shaking her head. "That's why she's so ornery. Just stay out of her way."

I stare at Deedre's spiky blonde hair and muscular body. Staying out of her way won't be a problem. I have no desire to get close.

Deedre's head whips around and she stares at me hard, her dark eyes cold and hateful. A river of hostile thoughts plows into my mind, along with pictures of Deedre's hands around my neck, her yellow teeth gritted above my face. The image will be forever imprinted on my mind. She shakes her head slowly, never taking her eyes from mine.

I shuffle back on my bed in stunned surprise, my hands automatically raised over my face to protect myself from the mental onslaught. I feel pummeled and, to some degree, violated, which somehow leaves a bad taste in my mouth.

Deedre laughs and the attack stops.

I look up to see Cinder and Shana staring. Deedre snickers, a make-believe cigarette held between her fingers. She brings her hand to her mouth and takes an imaginary puff, then blows the pretend smoke toward me. "Dweeb."

"Be careful who and what you think about," Shana whispers, leaning in. "If you think about someone, they'll know. Good thoughts or bad."

Great. A shiver runs over my shoulders, and I straighten out on my bed. I don't even know Deedre, but her thoughts—which run along the lines of murder—totally freak me out.

This is not going to work. I cannot live here.

"How 'bout a tour?" Shana says, interrupting my thoughts. "I'll show you around." Her peppiness and undisguised gaiety rouses me from my paralyzed state, and I let her lead me out into the bright light of day. Or what looks like day. I feel lighter and happier instantly.

Shana takes me through town, points out the sites, and even shows me the library. I had no idea they had libraries in... wherever I am, but I'm not going to complain. The library is one place I'll happily explore when I get the chance. Getting lost in a good book sounds like heaven. And if I can't live in heaven, I'll live in la la land instead.

After my brief tour, Shana and I stand in front of the white, marble building where Raphael's office is located. "I have to go inside," I say, remembering he wants to speak with me.

"Oh, right. Well, I guess I'll see you later then." She leaves reluctantly and doesn't seem happy to go back to the cottage alone. I feel sorry for her. I wouldn't want to be alone with Cinder and Deedre either.

With a sigh, I take a moment to prepare myself for the coming interview. What will Raphael want to talk about? Will he ask about my suicide? Will I have to explain? Can I request new roommates? That thought is enough to propel me through the double doors in search of his office.

He is all smiles once I enter, and gestures to a chair across from his desk, where I sit down. "How do you like your new place?"

I have a feeling he already knows. "Uh, about that."

"I know, I know." He raises his hand to stop me. "The beds

are the most confusing. Why beds instead of tables and chairs? We get that a lot."

"Um, it's not the beds. The beds are fine."

"Oh. Good. Did you find the quilt inside the box I gave you?" A bright light radiates in his eyes and his lip twitches in anticipation.

"Yeah. I got it. Thanks."

Leaning forward, he clasps his hands on his desk. "Did you notice anything special about it?"

I scowl, picturing the quilt in my mind. "It's like the one I have at home?" I couldn't care less about the stupid quilt, or *The Spirit's Guide to Immortality* book that had also been in the box. If it had been my *real* quilt, that would have been something. But it's not. It's only a look-alike. A cheap copy.

"Yes!" he says, excited. "We do that on purpose, you know. To help you feel more at home here."

It doesn't work. I don't feel at home. I feel lost, hovered over, and frustrated. Everything is different and weird, and a quilt doesn't matter in the grand scheme of things. "Actually, it's my roommates I want to talk about."

"Oh?" He leans back.

"Well, I wondered if I could get different ones. Shana is okay, but I really don't think I should hang out with Cinder or Deedre."

"Really?"

"Deedre wants to kill me. That kind of bothers me even though I'm pretty sure she can't do it."

Raphael sputters. I smile, because this is such a ridiculous conversation. I'm sitting in an office asking for new roommates, when I should be flying free through clouds of snowy white. Where is my harp? My golden wings?

With an exasperated sigh, I lean forward. "Listen. I'm not sure what I'm doing here, but I'd really like to get on with the rest of my life."

After regaining his composure, he becomes serious again and leans forward until our faces are only inches apart. "This *is* the rest of your life."

Needless to say, I feel completely disillusioned. All my dreams of rest and happiness have slipped through my fingers. Not only that, but the aching hurt of missing Natty and Gram is now replaced with missing *everybody.*

And now I have to go to school? My first session in class is one to be remembered though. The classroom is an expansive area with high windows. Bright light shines through the crystal clear glass, and I can smell that strange, musky aroma I associate with high school. Like old paint and worn carpet. It's funny how smells affect me here and bring back memories... good and bad.

The only thing to do is go along with their silly routine, to attend the classes—which let me just say—make me miserable. I hated school—well, at the end anyway—and now I have to endure it after death too? Sitting at a desk, listening to angelic teachers ramble on about things I'm not interested in, and living with depressing people, makes me think this isn't *Idir Shaol* after all.

Make no mistake. It's hell. Just without the flames.

Shana, who is with me on that first day of class, wants me to sit on the front row. Everyone stares as I step through the door, like I have a big, red "A" glued to my chest. They watch me with accusatory glances even though they're here for the same reasons I am. I sweep the room with a cursory glance, then turn and face the front. There are about twenty people in the class, and we all look pretty much the same age.

Our teacher stands before us, her golden hair falling over her slender shoulders in waves. The light around her is bright, and I find myself studying her pink robes. I was never a pink girl myself, but the hue, one I've never seen before, takes my breath away. Her small feet are bare, and her hands fly through the air as she speaks.

"Welcome to *Idir Shaol*, class. I will be your instructor during your brief time here," she says in a lilting voice.

Brief? My time here will be brief? Am I going somewhere

else? Oh, I hope so. Thoughts of escape swirl through my mind until I realize I'm not paying attention, and the teacher has stopped talking. She looks directly at me, her gaze intrusive, piercing. She can see inside me, I just know it—to my whole life, to my inadequacies.

Her eyes narrow and she frowns at me even though I didn't do a thing to earn her disapproval. After a second she turns back toward the rest of the group. "I am Anaita. I will be your instructor for this course. This class may be the only one you need, as some of you will move on more quickly than others. As most of you know, *Idir Shaol* is a waiting place for those who need to redeem themselves in some way. A place for those who were too ignorant, stupid, or selfish to change during their mortal lifetime. Most of you took your own life. The reason you're here and not already in Soul Prison is because someone up here thinks you deserve a second chance."

Wow. Someone needs a coffee. Her tone does not match her angelic appearance, and I wonder if anyone else gets that same feeling.

She glances in my direction. Did she just read my thoughts? Her pretty pink lips purse, her creamy skin resembling Raphael's. I'm willing to bet hers is a body of flesh and bone.

How do they get those?

5

The Funeral

ALISA

At the start of my second day—at least I think it's my second day. There are no clocks here—I receive my first assignment. It begins the next stage of my progression, but it includes doing something so terrible and so dreadful, that I debate running away. I have no idea where to go, but there has to be somewhere to hide. It's not like I'm in Soul Prison... yet.

Up until the moment I see my grandmother at the entrance of *Idir Shaol*, waiting to guide me on this exciting adventure, I had decided to rebel. I don't need to move on, I don't need roommates and school, and I certainly don't need difficult assignments I can't pass.

"Hello, my sweet Alisa," Gram says, cupping my face. "Are you ready?"

"No."

Chuckling, she draws me close, and I smell the tangy scent of apple pie on her robes again. The taste of her pies coats my soul's tongue with longing for one bite of apple sweetness.

"I'll be with you every step of the way," she says. "Everyone who takes their life has to do this. It's a requirement. Committing suicide is serious business, and can't be taken lightly. It affects everything and everyone around you. Forever."

I know she's right, but dread fills me. Gram takes my hand and with a wink, we disappear from *Idir Shaol*—the waiting place of wounded souls.

An organ plays the familiar hymns I grew up with, and the unmistakable doors of my neighborhood chapel rise up before me.

I squeeze Gram's hand for support. With vast reluctance, I step through the entrance and feel the cool breeze of air-conditioning waft past me. Over a hundred people fill the benches, sniffling and dressed in black. Familiar faces sit in row after row of the little chapel, and the high windows allow rays of light to filter through onto the tear-streaked faces before me.

"Should we sit down?" I ask Gram in a terrified whisper.

The aroma of flowers fills the air. I can smell them but not in the same way I could smell the blossoms in heaven. My senses here feel muted and slightly dulled. But for the most part, I can smell everything, hear everything, and *feel* everything.

I hate it.

"We can sit if you want to," Gram answers with a pat on my hand.

I take a seat at the end of a pew just as the doors at the back open. Everyone stands. Gram takes hold of my arm and pulls me up too. For a spirit, she's pretty strong.

Three guys from my school, my two brothers, and two of my cousins enter slowly, carrying a gleaming mahogany casket. Clutching my throat, I freeze as it rolls by. I can't stand seeing the tears that drip down my brothers' faces, staining their clean, white dress shirts, their red, swollen eyes, and their white knuckles as they clutch my coffin. I try to turn away, but some unseen power forces me to watch.

The casket comes to rest before the pulpit. My family sits on the second row. Friends and relatives fill up the rest. I can't believe how many people have come; people who I didn't think even knew I was alive or cared that I had been.

Everyone carries an aching heart, and I *feel* it, heavy, like iron, weighing down my soul in despair. Their pain rips through me like a rusted, jagged saw, opening fresh wounds, slicing, slicing, slicing. I feel rent in two, and pulled into the depths of unexplainable misery.

I turn to Gram, my panic building. I have to get out of here.

She puts her arm around my shoulders, and holds me. "I know, honey. I know. Let it out. Let it all go."

I tremble in her arms as we follow the casket to the front. She leads me to the second row where my family waits.

"Sit down, dear."

I lower myself into the space at the end of the bench.

"All these people," Gram motions over the crowd, "are here for you and your family." I see kids I knew from school, and I stare, shocked. Why are they here? They never cared about me when I was alive. I can't even count the times I walked down the hall at school feeling totally alone, no one talking to me. Maybe they just want to see a dead body roll by.

But their mournful feelings of despair wrap around me like a suffocating blanket, telling me otherwise. I can't understand their feelings. All this time, I thought I'd had no one.

Then, as if a dam has broken, memories of these very people come rushing to mind. A soft pat on the shoulder, a smile of sympathy. They *had* been there trying to befriend me. I just hadn't seen it, hadn't wanted to see it.

My mother's head bows as she presses a hanky to her eyes. She wears a beautiful black dress I've never seen before, and not even makeup can hide the paleness of her skin or her sleepy, red-rimmed eyes. My dad sits next to her, his face stoic, his eyes swollen too. My brothers, who are usually laughing or teasing each other, are silent, staring straight ahead.

I was sixteen years old, and now I'm dead. This isn't a dream. My brain isn't making this up. I'm really here, watching my family mourn over my wasted life.

A hard wrenching grips my stomach, and I feel sick, like I'm going to throw up, but I can't. I'll never be able to rid myself of the corrosion churning inside me. Emotion wells hot, black, and fighting for a way out. I realize with horror how selfish I've been, thinking only of *my* pain.

Oh, how I want to turn back time—to go back to that moment in the car. I should have stuck it out longer. I might have been happy again, living the rest of my life, getting married, having kids. Now I'll never get the chance.

Wracked with guilt, I cover my face, hiding from the terrible emotions that overwhelm me. I don't even try to be quiet as I sob. My shoulders shake as an agonized moan tears from my mouth. "I need to go." My voice is raspy with desperation.

"It's not over yet," Gram answers, staring straight ahead. Her mouth is in a tight, thin line, like a cruel taskmaster, and she makes me stay to witness the agony I've caused.

I groan again, glancing over at my mother. I can't do this. I can't watch the people I love hurt so terribly.

Gram smiles sadly. "I'm *so* sorry."

The minister stands, and the music stops. "My dear friends. I welcome you to the funeral services of Alisa Kristine Callahan."

He goes on to tell stories about my life. Stories from my early childhood to my preteens. I'd quit going to church when I was thirteen, and I'm surprised he has any memories of me at all. I decided at a young age that since God didn't seem interested in me, I wasn't interested in Him. My mother tried bribery to get me to go, but she quickly gave up. She wasn't about to embarrass herself by dragging a screaming teenager through these sacred double doors, and I wasn't about to get dressed up for religion.

The minister continues. "I remember when Alisa was about ten years old. She came running in one Sunday morning and ran straight into my arms, begging me to perform a marriage ceremony between her and Stephen Keiths right away. She'd fallen in love and didn't want to lose him to anyone else. Poor Stephen didn't even know he was engaged."

Stifled chuckles erupt from the audience, along with strangled sobs.

I remember that conversation. I also remember Stephen with his hazel eyes, his lovely smile, and sandy-blond curls. Is he here now? Oh, I hope not. I turn in my seat and search for his face, finding him eight rows back. He's seventeen now and on the football team. He sings in the school choir, and is still as beautiful as ever. My chance with him is gone.

When the minister finishes, my aunt Karen stands and gives

the eulogy. I haven't seen her in a long time, but I'm glad she's here today. She keeps her speech short and tells about my birth, about me growing up, and how much she loves me. She talks about my talent in music and how sad I'd been when my friend Natty died of cancer.

My mother sobs, her shoulders quaking as she hides her face behind her hanky.

I move over to kneel at her feet, gazing into her tired, blue eyes. "Mom, I'm sorry. I'm *so* sorry." I rest my cheek against her thin, cool fingers, and breathe in the smell of her. So familiar, so soft. Like lilacs.

She can't hear me, but she lifts her head. Tears swim in her eyes, along with a look of surprise. She glances toward my dad, then back at her hands, and smiles through her tears.

"I love you, Mom," I say fervently. "I'll fix this. I *swear* I will. Please don't be sad." I place a kiss on her tear-streaked cheek. Her blue eyes sparkle, and I know that somehow she knows I'm here. I move over to my dad and do the same thing, getting a similar reaction.

Then I kneel before my brothers. I take Tyler's hand first. He's the youngest. Only twelve. Tears stream freely down his cheeks, and he doesn't bother to wipe them away. He's combed his hair neatly to the side, and his tie is remarkably straight. I wonder who helped him. That was always my job.

"Tyler, I love you," I whisper. "Don't be sad." I stroke his cheek, and memorize his face, the color of his eyes, the cowlick in his bangs. "I'm gonna miss you, and... and I'm really sorry I did this. I wish I could go back." I kiss his head and squeeze his hand. He doesn't act like he senses anything, but I hope with all my heart that he does.

I take a deep breath and turn to my older brother, Derek. He's almost eighteen. A man. He and I look the most alike with his dark, golden hair and his chocolaty eyes. His mouth, set in a rigid line, and he doesn't even twitch when I touch him. He keeps his arms tightly crossed, his gaze hard.

I whisper that I love him, that I'm sorry, but he is totally unresponsive. I can't get through no matter what I say. Maybe it's because we always argued during my life. Maybe it's because I said hateful things to him the last time we were together, and he told me to quit being a baby and feeling sorry for myself.

The guilt is a hard, jagged rock resting firmly in the pit of my stomach, but I deserve that misery. I altered my family's lives, and I can never fix it, no matter what I promise, no matter how hard I try. I killed myself, and I can't go back.

I tell Derek goodbye, and then back away, my heart ripped, shredded, and lying at his feet.

A limo takes my family to the cemetery and I ride with them, holding my mother's hand. No one says a word. I stand by my grave. A dark, muddy, gaping hole. Actually, it's covered in fake green grass, but I can imagine the dirt beneath where my body will lay forever. Cold. Alone. Rotting. I hate cemeteries.

Holding back a sob, I beg God to perform a miracle—to let me live again. I stand there—raw, open, bleeding, and no one can stop the flow. I'm forced to hear it all, feel it all, and experience it all.

Finally, Gram turns to me, places her hand on my arm, and closes her eyes. Two seconds later, we stand before the entrance of *Idir Shaol*.

6

Secrets

BRECKEN

recken holds the phone to his ear. It's after midnight and he'd been asleep when his cell rang. Jill's voice pushes back the darkness of his basement bedroom. He isn't the least bit irritated by her call.

"I missed you, baby," she says. "I had to call and tell you so."

Brecken's eyes are heavy, and he is still half-asleep, so he answers in a soft whisper. "I always miss you." He keeps his eyes closed and rests the phone on his pillow.

"I figured. Want me to come over?"

"Naw," he says, rolling over on his mattress. "I'm too tired tonight. I'll see you at school tomorrow."

"Oh, I won't be there." Her voice dips and he can picture her bottom lip jutting out in a pout.

"Why not?"

There's a slight pause and then a breathy laugh. "Well, I'm going to a conference thing, but I can't talk about it right now. It's kind of a secret. It's supposed to be super cool though, so if it is, I'll tell you all about it when I get home."

"Why is it secret?" Brecken asks, annoyed that he'll have to spend a whole day without Jill to distract him. "What's the big deal?"

"I don't know, silly, but I promised not to talk about it, so I'm keeping my promise. Well, I better go before my parents get home." She kisses into the phone and tells Brecken she loves him.

A wonderful feeling of warmth envelopes him and he knows he will never care about anyone as much as he does for Jill. "You too. See you later." The reflective light of the screen darkens, leaving him to ponder the strangeness of a secret conference no one can talk about. A thread of nervousness tickles his mind, but he pushes it away. Jill is smart. He doesn't need to worry about her. She isn't usually so secretive, but... whatever.

He's too tired to think about it.

7

A Way Out

ALISA

Emotionally drained and totally exhausted, I fall onto my bed in *Idir Shaol*. How is it even possible for a spirit to be so weary? I could sleep forever. Unfortunately, that is not an option. Instead, I lie in my Hansel and Gretel cottage and stare at the swirling blue ceiling. It looks like Earth's sky, and as serene as it's supposed to be, it doesn't help me feel any better.

I face the wall and try not to think about my terrible, hopeless situation. Raphael told me I would feel this way when I returned from my funeral, that I would be worn-out, restless, and unable to feel at peace, that I would need rest. But all thoughts of rest and relaxation fly away the moment my roommates come through the door.

"Yeah, he's leaving. I can't believe it! I'm *so* jealous." Shana exclaims, all excited, gesturing wildly as she speaks. "Oh man. What a dream!"

I sit up. "Who's leaving?"

"Anthony Wiser. He's going to Earth." She plops on her bed and opens her manual.

My mind begins to spin. Someone is leaving this place. He's going back to Earth. For good? "To be born again?"

"Man, what an idiot," Deedre mumbles as she drops down on her bed. "There's no such thing as reincarnation, stupid. Not like people think."

"He's going to be a guardian," Shana says, closing her book and studying me with a serious expression.

With narrow eyes, slitted and cold, Deedre watches me, her

mouth turning into a sardonic grin. "You don't even know what that means, do you?" For some reason, this gives her undeniable pleasure.

"Oh shush, Dee," Shana says before turning back to me. "Anthony finished his courses and now gets the chance to pay back his debt. He gets to be a guardian. You know, to help someone on Earth. If he succeeds, he'll get to live in Elysium."

"Elysium?" I've never heard of it, but if that's where Gram lives, move me in!

"Yeah," Shana answers. "You know. Heaven? Paradise?"

"That place you couldn't get into?" Deedre sneers.

I ignore her. I don't care what they call it as long as I get live there too. "Can anyone be a guardian?" Hope blossoms in my chest.

"No." Cinder states with finality. These are the first words I've heard her utter. Her total lack of enthusiasm makes me wonder if she is one of those unfortunate souls missing out.

"Well," Shana says. "It all depends on your situation, but I bet if you talk to Raphael he'll tell you if you qualify. We could go now if you want."

A moment later, we stand in the airy hallway outside Raphael's office. Bright light shines through the high windows, reflecting brilliant color off the marble tile. If *Idir Shaol* is this beautiful—and it is slowly growing on me—how much more wonderful will Elysium be? I can't wait to go there, and I am willing to do anything and everything to make that happen.

I take a deep breath and knock. The door opens.

"Well, hello girls. What can I do for you?" Raphael waits with his hands clasped before him, his feet bare. Once again, I'm shocked by his overpowering brightness, his beauty, and the love he radiates. I want to hug him like a puppy and tuck him in my pocket.

"Alisa wants to know if she can be a guardian," Shana says before I can even open my mouth.

I glance at her with an irritated frown. She shrugs and keeps smiling.

"Is that so?" His eyes search mine, and it feels like he can see right through me. "Come in, Alisa, and we'll discuss it. He shuts the door on Shana, and I am on my own.

Raphael shows me to a chair and from the look on his face, I'm sure he'll tell me I don't qualify. I mean really, who wants someone who killed themselves to help them out of a sticky situation?

"So, Alisa. Tell me. How are things?"

"Fine." I plaster a fake smile on my face, determined to act my way through this little charade, but if he can really see inside me, he'll see a damaged, broken, miserable soul. I'm not really fine at all.

"Any problems?"

"No."

"You have an interest in becoming a guardian?" He reclines in the armchair, the curve of a smile barely lighting on his face. His green eyes focus on mine, and it feels like he can see my heart, my sins, my weakness, and especially my desperation.

For a moment, I just sit there, realizing how stupid this is. I wish I could crawl inside myself and hide my shame. I don't qualify to be a guardian. What was I thinking? "To be honest, I'm not even sure what a guardian is."

He nods in understanding. "It is a grave responsibility. You are given charge of a person on Earth and you're to help them through a very difficult situation. You are not told what their obstacle is beforehand. You must figure it out through inspiration and meditation. Then you must help them overcome the obstacle. If you succeed, you are allowed to pass on to Elysium. It is more difficult than it sounds."

It actually sounded really hard to me, but I'm willing to give it a try, because the thought of being stuck *here* for eternity is not an option.

"I'd like to do it. I know I have a lot to make up for, and I want to help someone else so they don't make my same mistakes." One of the first, truly honest things I've said since I got here. Since my funeral experience, I realize with terrible clarity the gargantuan mistake I've made.

With a sad, loving smile, he says, "We'll discuss it at our next board meeting and see what everyone thinks." He squeezes my hand and the heat from his touch sears me. All the guilt I've ever known feels dredged up and on display.

My heart sinks, and I pull my hand away, not wanting him to discuss me with *The Board*. Anaita is probably on that board and she certainly won't let me go. She'll relish the thought of torturing me in her class forever and ever.

After my conversation with Raphael, time—which is hard to judge anyway—moves slower than ever before. The torture of waiting for the board's decision eats at me until I want to pull my hair out... which I can't really do.

I am sure they'll say no.

I go about my usual schedule, another class being next on the list. I amble along beside Shana as we make our way down the path. Cinder and Deedre follow behind. When we step into the classroom, I head for the back row. Shana always sits at the front, but she doesn't put up a fuss when I pass that row and keep going. I find a seat as far from the teacher as possible and slump down, hoping to become invisible.

Anaita stands at the front like an avenging angel, light and power radiating from her very fingertips. During class, she locks eyes with me, and I pray she can't hear my thoughts. I make every effort to keep my mind blank, which really isn't hard. There isn't anything of consequence in there. I'm lucky enough that she doesn't pick on me today. Small miracle.

When class ends, I hurry to the door, determined to be free.

I'm not fast enough.

"Alisa, may I speak with you a moment?"

I wince, but I try not to show any feeling when I turn to face her. Dread spreads through me like slow moving tar as I see her eyes harden. I make my way back across the room to where her ivory desk rests under a wide, bright window. She leans against her desk, pink robes fanning out around her.

"Raphael spoke to me about your desire to become a guardian. I think it's a little too soon." She doesn't smile, but cocks her head as though trying to figure me out. She'll have no success in that area. I can't even figure myself out.

"Well," I answer finally. "You're wrong." I fight the urge to cover my lips, blocking the escape of any other errant words.

Her eyes darken and she crosses her arms over her chest. "I see fire in your soul, Alisa, and that is a good thing... sometimes. But if you are to succeed, you'll need more than just fire. You'll need unwavering confidence. Your charge will rebel at every turn. He'll try to escape your influence. He... well, it doesn't matter. You're sure to fail."

"Does this mean I *can* go?" I ask in surprise.

She sighs and walks around her desk. "We discussed it and the vote was mostly in your favor."

She must have voted otherwise. Not a big surprise.

8

Learning in the Library

ALISA

I float all the way back to my cottage and can't wait to share the good news, especially with Deedre. I feel a tiny desire to rub it in just a bit. She got here before me after all, and now I'll be the first to leave. Take that!

I open the door with all the drama I can muster and... no one is there. I stare at the empty, quiet room, deflated, but then a spark of excitement begins to glow inside me. This is the perfect time to visit the library! I have nothing else to do. Slamming the door behind me, I race toward downtown *Idir Shaol*. I pass a few buildings, not remembering what they are for, and easily find my favorite place in the entire world.

The library.

It looks just like it should. Red, glittery brick, tinted windows, cement steps leading inside. And there are people everywhere. Their voices carry easily as they visit, bustle about, or sit at desks, working at what look like small, compact computers. I move slowly, completely absorbed and baffled by this strange, new experience.

A group of people sit on carpeted risers in the corner of the large room. They stare at a movie screen, so I make my way over, curious about what has captured their attention. They watch the film with determined focus. The small-scale amphitheater seems cozy, so I sit on the edge next to a friendly looking girl.

"What's going on?" I whisper.

"Shh." She glances at me, and then turns back to the movie.

"But what are you watching?"

"A training visual. Be quiet."

"For what?" I ask.

She turns and faces me fully, a frown pulling on her lips. "A training visual is instructional media on how to be a guardian."

"Oh."

"Shh!" The group turns to stare at us. My mouth snaps shut, and I fight the instant desire to leave, but I'm curious, so I stay and watch. This is what I'll be doing after all. Being a guardian.

Because I'm watching a movie, an instant yearning for hot, buttery popcorn comes to me, but since they don't have hot, buttery popcorn here, I feel empty and deprived, hating myself for what I am missing on earth. There's no way to curb this craving, so I sit there, depressed that I'll never taste my favorite treat again.

The video continues with a spirit guardian tagging along behind his charge, who is battling a desire to enter a bar. The guardian hovers behind him, whispering frantically into his ear. They stand on the street corner, the man's eyes glued to the door. He wears a leather jacket and seems about the same age as my dad. Probably in his late forties. His hands clench and unclench as his Adam's apple bobs up and down.

"He's an alcoholic," the girl next to me whispers. "He just finished AA."

"Oh," I whisper back. "So why is he at a bar?"

The girl scowls at me like I'm an idiot. "That's the whole point. His guardian is trying to talk him out of going inside."

I have the feeling she wants to add *duh* to the end of her sentence.

The scene plays out and I lean forward, my toes clenched and my eyes straining even though the picture is crystal clear. I'm spellbound, holding my breath. Will the guy screw up months of success for just one drink? Will he throw all those torturous hours of AA away?

Just when I'm sure he'll lose the battle, the man turns and hails an approaching taxi. The people sitting next to me jump up and cheer. I find myself jumping up too, hugging the girl next to me in celebration of the man's success. A thrill of excitement rushes through us.

Will my charge have temptations like this? Will people here watch my work? As cool as that sounds, I'm not someone who wants an audience. I'm sure to screw up if I know people can see me in a movie like this. "Do you watch these training visuals all the time?"

"Oh sure," she says. "Especially if there's a special situation where the task is difficult and the guardian is successful. They want us to learn from one another's achievements... and failures."

"Right. Got it." I'm sure to be in lights someday. Probably to show what *not* to do. When the group disperses, I meander to a different part of the library, anxious to see what else this fascinating locality offers.

I pass some high bookshelves and stop to pull a book down. The pages are thick and appear very old, crackling with a musty odor when the pages part. The words are in a strange language. One I don't understand, so I put it back and pull down another, only to find the same thing. What is this section? Where are the romance novels? The suspense thrillers.

"Are you lost?" a voice behind me asks.

I turn to see a small woman in white carrying a large stack of ancient tomes. Not unlike the one I'm holding.

"You work here?" I feel an instant liking for this woman. She seems sweet, motherly.

"Yes. I do. Are you lost? Most people don't wander aimlessly in this section," she says with a smile and a wink. "You must be new. Can I help you find something?"

"Well, I came to read, but there's so much to see." I look at all the different people watching videos, conversing, or in discussion groups. I can't see one person just lazing around enjoying a good book.

"This isn't a library like you'll find on Earth if that's what you mean. Everyone here has a job to do, or is in training."

"Oh. Well, I don't have a job since I'm leaving for Earth soon to be a guardian."

"That says a lot about you." She places her hand gently on my forearm. "You must be an old soul. Wise, to be sent back to earth so quickly."

Old soul? Wise? She definitely has me mixed up with somebody else.

"I have some time to visit if you'd like." She smiles with a warmth I can't ignore, and I'm so lonely that I take her up on her offer.

"My name is Annabelle. I've worked here for a long time. Over a century in Earth time." She sits down at a nearby table, so I sit opposite her.

"You've worked here a hundred years?"

"Yes. Time doesn't move the same as it does on earth, but I love my job. I chose to come here, to help souls like you." She sits back with a serene expression. "What is your name, dear?"

"Alisa. Alisa Callahan." This lady reminds me of my grandmother, which is actually kind of wonderful. She has the same oval face and twinkly blue eyes. Even their smiles are similar. She makes me feel wanted and comfortable. Something I've been craving for a long time.

Annabelle leans forward, her countenance open and peaceful. "I died of natural causes in the late eighteen hundreds. After I died, I learned that all spirits continue to work, to help out in some way. There's a lot to be done in every area of existence."

Will I have to work for eternity too? Actually *work*? Did Gram have a job? Did Natty? I close my eyes in despair. I don't want to work forever. I want to rest. I'm tired. That was the whole point of killing myself. I shake my head and glance down at my hands.

"What did you imagine people do after death?" she asks kindly. "Float on clouds of happiness all day?" She places her hand over mine and gives me a couple of squeezes. "That would get a little boring after a while. Don't you think?"

Actually, no. I don't think it would. It sounds wonderful.

"I know it's a lot to take in, but once you return from your guardianship, you'll be able to choose where you'd like to contribute. That is, if you succeed."

I glance back at her. "*If* I succeed? What happens if I don't?"

She pauses and slowly raises her eyes to meet mine. "You go to Soul Prison."

9

A Bad Deal

BRECKEN

*B*recken sits across the kitchen table from Damion, a kid he knows from school. He's not a friend, just a means to an end... kind of. Their business arrangement is new, but more and more often, Damion has told Brecken to do things he doesn't like, things that cross the line, but how else will he get the extra money he needs?

He can't call his dad. Those conversations always end in an argument, with his dad telling him what a crappy job he's doing paying the bills and saving the money he left them. Doesn't his dad realize they need food too?

Anger at his hopeless situation sprouts anew, and his resolve to go along with Damion's latest scheme strengthens.

"They're gone by eight in the morning," Damian says, his dark eyes intense. "They have a dog, but it's little and can't do any damage. Kill it for all I care. They're crappy neighbors anyway. They leave their bathroom window cracked open. Idiots. Anyway, there's a screen on it, but you can easily push it out. Go for the master bedroom. Jewelry, that kind of stuff. All I want is a third of what you take."

"A quarter. I'm the one taking the risk." Brecken gazes into Damion's muddy, brown eyes with disgust. The only reason he is still here is because their phone will be disconnected tomorrow if they don't pay the dumb bill. Brecken needs ninety-five bucks, and if he's late paying, not only will his cell phone be turned off, but his dad's too. It's a family plan, and his dad needs his phone for his business.

"Fine."

Brecken grits his teeth and looks down at his hands, shame blossoming in his chest, making his heart feel as dirty as the grime under his fingernails.

He leaves with not only regret, but a raw dose of fear too. How can he continue to live like this?

10

First Glimpse of Hell

ALISA

"Soul Prison?" I repeat, staring into Annabelle's eyes in horror. "Like a penitentiary?" I don't want to be punished forever for one little misunderstanding. That doesn't seem fair. I want a shot at redemption, to be with my family, with Natty. I can't go to prison!

Annabelle continues to smile as if it's no big deal, like it happens every day, and maybe it does for some, but not for me. I'm not the jail type. I've never stolen, done drugs, or anything else illegal. Okay, I did try alcohol once, but I didn't like it. That has to count for something. I've never even made out with a boy... officially. Nothing past first base.

I killed myself to be free!

"There are areas of Soul Prison that aren't so bad," she says. "Some people even like it there. Other parts though..." She shivers. "You don't want to know."

She is right about that.

She twists away and closes her eyes, becoming quiet and perfectly still. "One moment, please," she says putting her finger up for silence. "I'm getting a message."

A message? I frown, waiting. "Annabelle?"

She is still for a moment longer and then turns back to me. "Raphael... I assume you know him?"

"Yes."

"He knows you're here with me in the library."

Of course he does. There is less privacy here than on Earth. What a surprise.

"He says I should take you to visit Soul Prison so you can see firsthand what it's like. That the experience will help you. It's not one of my normal duties, but I would be happy to be your guide." She stands and smiles sweetly, then offers me her hand.

I stay in my seat, my hands in my lap. "I don't want to go there."

She chuckles and reaches for my hand anyway. "Not to be imprisoned. Just to see it."

She links arms with me, and I brace myself for what is sure to be torture.

We disappear from the library with a blink of her eyes. It seems to take a long time and I wait to appear... somewhere. Anywhere. I feel suspended in darkness. The landscape looks unnaturally shadowy, and I can barely see Annabelle beside me.

"When will we get there?" I whisper after a moment.

"We *are* here, dear."

She pulls me down a slightly sloping path as a heavy blanket of fear wraps around me. The darkness is heavy and a viscous mist descends, its gummy substance accumulating on my arms. It won't come off and sticks to my fingers like gum. Horrifying screeches, like wounded animals dying in pain, rises on the dank air.

I can't do this. I can't be in this place. "What is this?" I shriek, trying to wipe my arms.

"It's desperation, sweetie. Defeat. Agony. The torment of guilt."

The wailing grows louder, penetrating like a dull knife, magnifying the horror of this evil place. "Can't someone help that poor... whatever it is?" I ask, distracted by the gooey mist collecting on me. It mushes between my toes, fills my hair, and sticks to the roof of my mouth.

This evil place, this dark world, has wrapped its sinewy fingers around me, clinging with the icy chill of dead hands, dead souls, and dead dreams. Not only do I feel physically tormented but emotionally too. Hopelessness, fear, and anger, as though live entities, float in the mist, making me want to lie down and die all over again. This is way worse than my funeral.

Annabelle pulls me further down the path. When I venture

too close to the edge, the razor-sharp grass cuts painfully into my feet. Not in a physical way, but a stab through my heart, with feelings of shame and depression.

"Somebody shut that thing up!" I finally scream, covering my ears, no longer able to tolerate the alarming cries. I've never heard anything so pitiful, so agonizing.

"It's not a *thing*, dear. It's people. Souls."

I stop, frozen to the mucky stones beneath my feet.

"That's right, Alisa," she says, turning to me. "What you hear is the wailing of anguish from people paying for their sins. People who refused to make amends during life."

"You're kidding me." My hands still cover my ears, but my eyes are adjusting. A short way off the path I see thin, dark arms, writhing, reaching upward, raspy voices crying for another chance, for forgiveness. My soul recoils, afraid they might touch me or contaminate me with their filth.

"Please." I grasp Annabelle's hand. "I don't want to stay here."

"But you will if you fail in your mission. You can't stay in *Idir Shaol* indefinitely. You have to move on. One way or another." For someone so small, she seems enormously strong, but I cling to her, desperate not to be left behind when she blinks away.

"There's someone you need to see."

"Here? Who?" Annabelle pulls me further down the path.

I've become a blubbering idiot, terrified, and clinging to her. "Please don't leave me," I plead over and over.

She stops, and a dark *thing*, half crawls, half stumbles toward us, the muck pulling against him like melted tar, holding him to the path. He stops before me, a bent figure carrying an agonized expression. I recognize his tortured face immediately.

"Mr. Roland." I'm breathless and suddenly nauseous.

"Yeessss," he rasps in a hot whisper. "You remember."

Of course I remember. I've tried to forget, to block the memories out, but I haven't been able to. Like a dog drawn to its vomit, they always came back to me.

If anyone deserves to be here, *he* does. It happened so long ago, but the memories are instantly before me again, starkly clear.

He molested me repeatedly, along with his own daughter, my best friend, Natasha, for years.

I shrink back, horrified to see him. He ruined my life. He ruined Natty's. I was only a child—so innocent, so good, so sweet. He took all that away from me, and for a moment, I itch to spring forward, to rake my fingernails down his already marred face, to spit in the dark coals of his eyes. I'm *glad* he's here. Glad he's miserable. I hate him. More than anyone or anything else in the world.

The hot burn of tears—that aren't really there—presses against the back of my eyes as I stare. His crime was discovered, and he went to jail just after my thirteenth birthday. I never saw him again. Every night—after I heard he'd died—I prayed he was burning in hell.

He moves toward me, reaching for my hand. I jump back with a shout. "Don't touch me! Don't ever touch me again!"

He pulls away, scars streaking down his anguished face. "I'm sorry, Alisa. I'm so, so sorry. *Please* forgive me. If only I'd known..." He looks pathetic. He *is* pathetic. He is a wretched creature with no hope of redemption. Ever, I hope.

"I will *never* forgive you," I say in a quiet growl, my jaw clenched. "Do you hear me? Never!"

"Please," he begs again, falling to the ground at my feet, groaning, the muck stretching over his back in a tight cocoon.

I glance around at the inky darkness of this world, the heaviness of the very air. A world where no one glows with light. A world where souls live in darkness because of the terrible things they've done. He *is* getting what he deserves.

"No." I take Annabelle's hand, and we disappear with a blink of her eyes.

11

The Heist

BRECKEN

recken waits outside Damion's neighbor's house. He watches the couple leave for work in their Lexus, and wishes for the kind of ease these people have. How would it feel to have enough money for whatever you want? He doubts he'll ever know.

He waits ten minutes, and then creeps around the corner of the house, keeping behind the bushes that shield him from pesky neighbors. He finds the bathroom window cracked open, just like Damion promised.

With a screwdriver, he pries the screen away and then sets it down with a quiet twang against the bricks. The window is only four feet up but on the narrow side. He jumps, balancing on his hands until he hooks his knee on the sill, then slithers through, almost slipping and falling. His shoes leave a scuff mark on the pristine white toilet seat.

Brecken creeps to the bathroom door and peeks out. The house is silent except for the ticking of a grandfather clock in the living room just down the hall. Thick carpet cushions his feet and he takes off his shoes so he won't leave any prints. He wiggles his toes for a moment, awed by the lushness of something that is so ordinary for most people.

Brecken turns toward the stairs. Light streams in through high windows above the front door and into the living room, reflecting off a chandelier, creating rainbows on the beige walls. So beautiful, so quiet, so peaceful. So unlike his house.

The master bedroom is at the end of the hall. He stops in the doorway for a moment, staring at the four-poster king-size bed.

Satin quilts grace the mattress and ornate dressers stand against two of the walls. There is a tilting, full-length mirror in one corner. He notices marble countertops in the master bath.

How much money do these people make anyway? What do they do for a living? He can't believe the luxury, the wealth, of this house. Shaking his head, he hurries over to the dresser and finds a beautiful jewelry box that matches the rest of the dark, glossy wood in the room.

Brecken lifts the lid, hating himself for what he is about to do. This is not him. He doesn't have the heart of a criminal. He doesn't want to hurt people. He doesn't want to take precious treasures that don't belong to him, but what choice does he have? What is left for him to do?

Acid fills his throat and he almost turns around to run out. Backing up, he rests his hands on his knees, breathing deeply.

He *has* to do this. He has to. There is no other way. His eyes moisten in frustration. He wipes them dry, grits his teeth, and goes to work.

12

A Visit From Heaven

ALISA

*S*eeing Mr. Roland brings up all sorts of memories I don't want to think about or relive, but now I can't get them out of my head. They plague me. Like gnats flying around in my mind, nipping, biting, itching. I long for the sweet oblivion of sleep, which I can't have.

My thoughts turn to Natty. Where is she now? Why haven't I seen her? Is she happy with loved ones? Has *she* forgiven her father? I meander along a path in *Idir Shaol*, the cool stones hard beneath my feet. I'm not in the mood for classes, interviews, and especially my roommates.

I find a grassy knoll and sit down, my long, white robe covering my feet when I bend my knees and wrap my arms around them. I rest my chin on my arms and close my eyes, picturing Natty's almost white-blonde hair, her endearing, crooked front tooth, her bright blue eyes.

I *miss* her. I actually thought I'd be with her after I died. How disappointing. I let the hurt well up inside me and fill me with ache. She is up here somewhere. Does she even know I died? Or worse, does she know *how* I died?

Natty and I were there for each other during and after the abuse we experienced at the hands of her father. She helped me cope, and I did the same for her. When she died, so did that critical support. Everything piled up with no escape. Suicide seemed my only option, my only way to rid myself of the shame and depression. What I wouldn't give to talk to her again, to feel her sisterly support, to feel her quiet strength.

Not two seconds pass before someone sits beside me on

the grass and places a soft hand on my shoulder. Too soft to be Raphael's. Did Shana see me and wander over? Or Gram? At that thought, my head snaps up, hope blossoming through me.

There she sits. Right next to me, as though no time has passed at all. "Natty!" I throw my arms around her, a wave of happiness rippling through me. Radiant light bursts from her face as she smiles. All of our time together rushes through my mind. Natty has been my best friend since I was three. The week after she moved into my neighborhood, my mom invited her mom to join the local bunko group. She came with her mother, and from then on, we were seldom ever apart.

Even as we grew, bunko night was still the best part of the week. We'd lock ourselves in my room, painting our toenails, whispering about boys, and watching movies. She was the sister I never had. We spent every day together... until her headaches began.

It wasn't long before her problem was diagnosed.

Anaplastic Astrocytoma.

Brain cancer.

Inoperable.

A death sentence.

"What are you doing here?" I take her hand and kiss it, holding it tight, just in case she decides to disappear as quickly as she came.

"You were thinking of me, Lis, and I felt it." Her blue eyes sparkle as she squeezes my hand. "I can't stay long though."

"Why not?" I desperately need my best girl beside me. Everything seems right, now that she's here, and I don't intend to let her go easily.

"It's just how it is. I can visit, but I can't stay."

"You live in that big city, don't you?" I ask, envious.

She nods, but her smile is sad as she gazes at me.

"What's it like?"

With a sigh, she looks up, pondering. "It's wonderful, beautiful, and busy. I'm very happy."

"You are?"

"You sound surprised." She laughs and shakes her head. "Dying wasn't a bad thing. At least for me."

"It was for me," I answer, feeling the sting of invisible tears behind my eyes. The reaction is automatic even though I can't really cry.

Again, she nods. "That's true, but Earth-life only lasts a short while. You know that." She watches my face and her gaze feels warm against my soul, like the sun's rays, delicate and soft. I glance at the deep green grass beneath my feet and move my toes through it. It feels alive, and I swear I can hear it singing in happiness, just to exist.

I turn to her. "I don't know anything. Nobody knows anything. I thought I would be with *you*."

"I know," she says, socking me playfully in the arm like old times. "Silly girl. Always jumping before you look."

Instead of chuckling like I would have in the past, I ask her the question that has been plaguing me since I came here. "Are you *really* happy, Natty? Tell the truth. And if you are, why? You left your mom, your home... me."

"Yeah, but I'm still with family. My grandparents are here, and their parents, my cousins. Tons of relatives I'd never met because they lived long before me. It's like a huge family reunion."

She doesn't mention her dad and neither do I.

I wanted a huge family reunion too. I wanted happiness, rest, and beauty, but all I got were scary roommates who don't like me, except for Shana—and a fieldtrip to hell.

At Natty's smile, I feel a twinge of jealousy twist inside me. I want what *she* has. But I was too impatient. I was stupid.

"Don't worry. You'll be a great guardian."

"You know about that?"

"Yep. We all have guardians. Most are guardian *angels*, but sometimes, people like you get to repay their debt. It's totally cool. I'm hoping to be a guardian angel soon, but it will be for my charge's *whole* life, not just a short stint. And for guardian angels it's always a relative, or a descendant."

I hadn't known that. I don't know anything, and the longer

I listen, the more I realize it. "I'm not sure I can do it, Natty. I'm so screwed up. I've totally ruined everything."

"Not everything, Lis. And you *can* do this." She stands up and I stand with her.

"You're not leaving, are you?"

"I have to. I only came for a minute, but I'll keep tabs on you and visit when I can. Don't worry. You'll be just fine. We'll be together soon. Okay?"

I nod and pull her into an embrace, hating the moment we let go. With a blink of her eyes, she's gone.

Just that fast.

And once again, I'm left behind.

13

The Dreaded Call

BRECKEN

*I*t's a cold, rainy spring Saturday and the wind blows with a biting ache. It has rained for the last week and Brecken's sisters have been stuck inside the house all morning, bored and ornery. He finally sends them to their rooms, so he can have privacy to make this call.

He stares at the phone in his hand, dreading the coming conversation. It never seems to matter what Brecken wants, says, or asks for. His dad's automatic answer is always no. He doesn't even listen. Or maybe his dad just doesn't care. The hurt of numerous rejections stings, and Brecken doesn't know how to fix things.

At one time, life seemed so simple. He remembers past fishing trips with his dad, nights they stayed up late doing math homework, one-on-one basketball games of HORSE. Those days are long gone.

He dials his dad's number, almost hoping he won't answer.

He does.

"Hey, Dad," Brecken says, hesitating.

"Hey," his dad answers. "Can I call you right back? I'm kind of in the middle of something."

His dad won't call back. Not because he is a liar or completely unreliable, but because he is *always* in the middle of something. It happens all the time. Brecken waits and waits for the call back that never comes.

"Actually, this can't wait, Dad. We need some money deposited into the account. We have some late bills, and the companies are calling."

There's a moment of silence on the other end of the line, and

Brecken is sure his dad will tell him he's sorry, but that he can't give them money. He's surprised when the reply is, "Okay, Bud. I'll get to the bank this afternoon. I was just paid for my last job, so I have a check. Will five hundred do for now?"

No. It won't. The house payment is due as well as the power bill, the gas bill, and a hospital bill. *And* he still needs to buy groceries.

This should be his dad's job. Brecken should be able to act like a regular teenager, have fun with friends, play lacrosse or basketball, and go to dances. But he keeps his voice flat, neutral, not wanting his dad to know how hard this is for him. Life is hard for his dad too.

"Sure, Dad. Anything would be great." His dad doesn't have a lot of money to send. He lives in their camper when working out of town, and he needs materials in advance for his jobs and money for food too.

Not one word is said about being glad Brecken called, or *I love you*. No questions about school, friends or homework. With a heavy sigh, Brecken places the phone on the coffee table and grabs the keys to his dad's old beater car.

14

Returning to Earth

ALISA

As time passes, I attend my classes, study the handbook, and have regular interviews with Raphael. I've managed, so far, not to have any with Anaita. But that success streak ends abruptly.

Shana comes running to our cottage with a vellum note clutched in her hand. She thrusts the note into my face while I sit on my bed reading boring educational material that is supposed to help me during my guardianship.

"Alisa! You have a letter from Anaita." She watches me as I read. "She saw me on the path and asked me to give it to you. What does it say?"

I take the thick, scratchy paper and gently unfold it. "She wants to see me." My spirit has many of the same reactions as a physical body, except it's more about the emotion that is attached, so the moment I read the note, it feels like my heart races, and then drops into my stomach. A wave of anxiety plows over me, and I struggle to find an excuse to refuse. I come up with nothing.

"Just great." With a sigh, I leave my cottage and plod down the path to the white marble building where my guardian classes are held. It sparkles in the light like a beacon, but does not beckon me forward. It is the last place I want to go.

Once I reach Anaita's office, I hesitate, my fist ready to knock on her door. *I can do this.* I rap on the solid wood. The door opens without a sound and there she stands—gleaming and golden.

"Hello, Alisa. Have a seat." She gestures to a bright, red couch to her right. A wide window gleams crystal clear, and I sit down, glancing through it at the small town of *Idir Shaol*. I won't miss this place when I leave.

"How are you?" she asks, pulling a chair close.

I shift uncomfortably and turn to face her. I'm pretty sure she could care less how I am. "I'm good."

"Have you enjoyed your time here?"

That is a loaded question. She'll know if I lie, so I stick to the truth, trying not to sound like the surly teenager I am. "Not really."

Her laugh resonates through the room, full and rich, but with a touch of sarcasm. "Yes. I know what you mean, but nothing happens by accident or chance."

I nod, but in my head, I think the complete opposite. What kind of loving god would destine me to be molested, or to go through all the heartache I have? No. Even with everything I've seen here, I'm not sure I even believe in God, and if he is real, then he's cruel and uncaring.

Anaita leans back in her chair assessing me, her hands clasped before her, eyes narrowed. "Raphael has decided it's time for you to go."

Because of the cold tone of her voice, my hope sinks. They've changed their minds. My thoughts fly to the prison I visited, automatically assuming that is my new destination. She smiles, but her expression is dark, sinister somehow, and I wonder how that's possible, considering her job and everything. "To Earth, Alisa. As a guardian."

"Oh." I breathe in relief. "You have no idea how good that sounds. I thought you meant that other place."

"If you don't succeed, it will be that other place."

"Right."

"I wanted you to come to my office for a specific reason *before* you discussed your new charge with Raphael."

"Oh?"

"I understand you, Alisa. Whether you like the sound of that or not. I see a lot of myself in you. And although you rebel against authority, detest what you don't understand, and take the easy road instead of the best road—"

"Hey!"

"I don't say this to hurt you, but you need to understand how serious this assignment is. It's your last chance. Your *very* last. Do you understand? You fail here and your soul will rest forever in the bowels of hell, screaming for a release that will never come. Never." She pierces me with her iron gaze, her eyes smoldering with something I don't understand. She's not the least bit heavenly like a teacher should be. She is nothing like Raphael, and it terrifies me.

Wanting to escape as quickly as I can, I say what she wants to hear. "Yes. I understand."

"I hope so. If you need anything, don't hesitate to call in your mind. You know how to do that I assume?"

"Yeah."

"Good. Now go to Raphael. He'll fill you in on the rest."

I hurry to the door and reach for the handle as though it's a life preserver.

"And, Alisa?"

I turn, my hand trembling. "Yeah?"

"Don't ever forget what I said." She shows no emotion, and her words are a threat, not advice.

Paralyzed by her stare, I don't answer. I feel no love, no compassion, and certainly no encouragement emanating from her. After a moment, I pull the door open and fly down the stairs past Raphael's office.

Though her actual words hadn't been cruel, her intent behind them was. Even I am bright enough to see that. What I don't understand is why. She wants me to fail. It radiates from every inch of her perfect, celestial body, and I'm pretty sure she doesn't intend to help me, even if I call. The hardness of her crystal-blue eyes, the tightness of her mouth, even the way she holds her hands, suggests she'd rather reach out and choke me than come to my aid.

Raphael pulls the door open before I make it too far down the hall.

"Alisa!"

I slide to a stop.

"I thought I felt you passing by. Please, come in a moment."

He is all smiles and warmth. The complete opposite of Anaita, and I wonder if he knows what she's been up to. With a steady hand, he guides me to a chair with love and concern in his eyes, a welcome respite.

He sits behind his desk and begins sorting through a small box of crystals that are no bigger than my pinky. The crystals glow in a rainbow of color, some bright and bold, others with pastel softness.

He takes one out, its hue blood red, and places it in a slot at the corner of his desk. He turns it to the right. Within seconds, a life-size movie, similar to the one I saw in the library, appears on the opposite wall, projected from some unknown location. "This boy is Brecken Shaefer. He is seventeen years old."

He is of average height, muscular, and wears a black leather jacket with faded blue jeans. All I can do is stare at the face on the screen—my eyes drawn to his—as though I should recognize him somehow. I squint, trying to see him more clearly. I can already tell—just by looking at him—the kind of guy he is. Apart from being totally hot—I would have to be a total idiot not to notice— he looks dangerous. From his mussed, dark hair to the way he stands, the dare in his dark blue eyes.

A devil without a cause. I don't like him.

Raphael drones on, but I only hear half of what he says. The first words to register are: *arrest*, *fights*, and *suspended*, but I've already made my judgment.

I can't guard this wild, angry, intimidating boy. He is too... something, and he frightens me.

"So what do you think?" Raphael turns to study my horror-stricken face.

"Uh... I... well, he seems nice enough, but I wonder if there is anyone else to choose from. Not that this Brecken kid isn't great, but I kind of hoped to guard a girl. You know, for propriety's sake."

A knowing smile spreads across Raphael's slender lips. I don't like the look at all, and I brace myself for his next words. "There's no one else. The board takes these assignments very seriously. Every guardian is placed with a certain charge for a particular reason. Brecken is the one for you. Take him or leave him."

That's pretty cut and dry. No arguing allowed? No debating? And what *are* those specific reasons for why I've been placed with him? That is something I'd like to know. "So if I choose not to guard this Brecken boy, then I can't guard anyone at all?"

"He's not 'the Brecken boy,' and yes, that's pretty much it in a nutshell," Raphael says, unblinking. There's a touch of humor behind his eyes. Maybe he is more like Anaita than I thought.

Humbled at my predicament, I shake my head at the hopelessness of it all. It's do or die, metaphorically speaking. "I guess I accept."

"Great!" Raphael's eyes are full of newfound excitement. "That's the spirit! Here's how it works. Brecken has a huge obstacle to overcome."

"Yeah, I know that part."

"Let me finish. It's important for you to realize the seriousness of your assignment. It's a life or death situation. Your job will be to help him overcome this immediate hurdle. If you succeed, you will be allowed to move on and continue your spiritual training, which will be more wonderful than you can imagine."

More wonderful than I can imagine? I can imagine something pretty dang awesome. And I also think it's entirely unfair they won't give me a hint at what Brecken's problem is. How can they send me down there completely unprepared? How will I ever succeed without prior planning? It's like taking a final exam and not studying beforehand.

"Alisa, you'll do fine," he says. "You have a brave heart. Follow it. Pray, meditate, call for help."

This will never work. Why would anyone start listening to me now? I'm not sure I want to pray anyway. How has God ever helped me? All I can think of is how soon I'll be returning here humiliated, a permanent resident of the underworld.

Raphael motions for me to take his hand and looks into my troubled eyes. "It won't be as hard as you think. You *can* do this. Believe in yourself." With a blink, we are gone from his office and standing outside a beige, brick building.

I recognize the look of it immediately.

A high school.

Ugh. High school wasn't that great of an experience the two years I attended before I died. Mainly because my grandmother and best friend had died, but also because I'd become so reclusive, had lived so deeply inside myself, that the other students had stopped even *trying* to befriend me. I'd become solitary. Invisible.

"Now that you've been assigned to Brecken, you will always be drawn to him," Raphael explains, guiding me with his hand toward the front doors. "All you need to do is think of him, and you'll know where to find him. Oh, and don't forget about Brecken's special gifts. You need to be careful and be ready."

"Special gifts?" What did that mean? He's telling me this *now?* At the last second? Is Brecken disabled in some way?

Raphael gazes at me with warm concern, his eyebrows pulled down in a frown. "You know. What I told you in my office? About his gifts?"

No, I don't remember. I hadn't really been listening. I'd been too shocked at Brecken's rugged, slightly beautiful, but scary appearance to hear anything. "Oh, right. Yeah, I remember," I lie. "No problem. It will be fine."

"Good. Well, this is where I leave you then. Good luck and Godspeed." He takes one last look at me, gives me a big thumbs up, and then shimmers from sight.

The world dims, seeming dark after being in Raphael's presence. Even *Idir Shaol* radiates with brighter light than Earth does. Shaking my head—because it doesn't really matter—I slip through the doors, not even needing to open them.

Being a ghost has its perks.

15

The Presence

BRECKEN

ath is boring as usual. Brecken sits with his legs stretched out, the laces on his boots untied, and a scowl on his face. He surveys the other kids in the room, not caring one bit what they think of him. He's past bullying. Anyone who dares comment on his black boots, black clothes, or black expression will live to regret it.

His tough-guy exterior serves his purpose, and most people leave him alone. The only "normal" guys he's friends with are the ones on the lacrosse team, and he only socializes with them at practice once a week on Saturdays. He can't afford to be on the team anymore, but they still include him even though he can't play in the actual games. That hurts more than anything else does.

At that moment a strange feeling comes over him, making the hairs rise on the back of his neck. Chills run down his spine. Someone's in the room. A presence. He hasn't felt one for a long time. It tingles around him like jungle mist, warm and humid. He smells cinnamon, suddenly and clearly. It's not the same scent as last time, but he knows what it means.

He sits up, searching the room and gripping his desk. It's too bright to see anything. This can't be happening. Not again. Not now. He can't measure the amount of misery he's been through because of his curse. A curse that has plagued him his whole life. They won't leave him alone. They kept coming and coming.

He knew this hiatus from all things spooky and psycho was too good to last. Glancing at the clock, he prays for the last five minutes of class to zoom by.

They don't.

He hears every tick of the clock, every scuffle of feet, and every droning word from the teacher. On and on the class proceeds. His armpits grow sticky, the room stifling. Perspiration beads on his forehead and his heart races. He can't breathe as he cradles his head in his hands. He has to get out of here, away from the suffocating presence.

Brecken wonders if he really is crazy. Maybe it really is all in his head. Maybe none of it is real.

No.

He can't believe that.

The bell will ring... any second... he has to hang on until the bell...

The room grows dark, and he begins to feel dizzy. He scrunches his eyes closed.

16

First Touch

ALISA

*J*ust like Raphael said, I feel drawn to this mysterious boy. Who is he really? What kind of mess is he involved in? What are his feelings, his desires? What will I experience being with him all the time?

I could have been at his side with a blink of my eyes, but I take the long way. Why hurry after all? I float through the familiar-looking halls, amazed that all high schools are built exactly alike—from the painted brick walls, to the hard, glossy floors.

I let the unpleasant sensation of being in school again wash over me. It prickles the back of my mind, making me feel anxious and unprepared, like I have a missing assignment or something.

I stop at a puce-painted door halfway down the hall. Brecken is inside. I can feel it, and the sensation paralyzes me. I place my fingertips on the door and close my eyes, leaning my head forward. The room will be filled with at least twenty students. They can't see me, and won't know I'm there, but I imagine the pressure of their gazes, as though I am walking in with a real body.

This is it. This is my moment, and I'm not going to let some stupid boy scare me into failing. Closing my eyes, I float through the closed door, letting myself enjoy that slight pull on my soul as I meld with the wood for one second, feeling its aliveness, its purpose. This is one part of being a spirit that is genuinely cool. *Everything* is alive.

Once through, the brightness in the room surprises me. As unexpected as that is, what amazes me even more is that the glow radiates around one person in particular.

Brecken.

He sits sprawled at his desk, his feet clad in heavy black combat books, his ankles crossed. A thick, ratty sweatshirt stretches over his wide shoulders, and even though his hair is a mess, it fits him, making him much sexier than is healthy for a seventeen-year-old boy.

I stare.

Brecken sits up straight, looking terrified. His hands grip the edge of his desk and his head swivels back and forth, searching the room.

I search too. What is he looking for? Maybe he belongs in a loony bin rather than public school. The students sitting closest to him look nervous and scoot further away. I sit down in an empty seat and watch him.

"Dude, what's your problem?" a boy to Brecken's right asks, scowling.

"Shut up," is Brecken's terse reply.

The teacher at the front of the room explains some mathematical theory I don't understand and Brecken is back to slouching in his desk, carving a deep crevasse into the top with a sharp object I can't identify. His fingers are white knuckled, his shoulders high and tense.

Turning to the rest of the class, my gaze falls upon a girl who watches Brecken. Her short, spiky hair and black leather clothes narrow down which crowd she hangs out with.

He doesn't give her the time of day or even glance in her direction. It's as though she doesn't exist for him at all. Poor girl. I know that feeling—liking a guy who doesn't give a crap if you are dead or alive.

I sigh. What do I care? I'll never get the chance to be with a guy ever again. At least this girl still has time.

As soon as the bell rings, Brecken explodes from his seat, practically flying from the room. I actually have to hurry to catch up. The first thing I do is smack straight into a tall, well-muscled jock, who is also hurrying to leave the room. We meld together, my soul filling his body, his heartbeat becoming mine, his muscles filling me with strength, his thoughts becoming clear to me. With a yelp of surprise, I pull away, a humid substance clinging to me. Not unlike the muck in Soul Prison. Yuck.

The boy freezes, a frown appearing on his tanned face. He turns and searches behind him, stands there for a moment shaking his head, and then finally continues on to his locker.

Making my way carefully, I avoid every other person before me. Staying focused on Brecken turns out to be tricky, until I float to the ceiling to follow him. He escapes outside, and flees around the corner of the school. When I catch up, he's bent over, his hands on his knees, practically hyperventilating.

"Who *are* you?" he says in a venomous whisper.

I search the surrounding area trying to figure out who he's talking to. I shake my head, thinking he really is crazy, but then he stands up and seems to look right into my eyes. We're almost the same height. He's only a few of inches taller.

"I know you're there. I can *smell* you."

I look around again. He can't be talking to *me*. He doesn't even know I'm here. No one can see their guardian. And I smell? What the—? How rude. I pretend I didn't hear him say anything.

Other students pour from the doors, hurrying to the buses parked at the curb. Some walk down the sidewalk in front of the school. The rich ones climb into their own cars. Curious, I wait to see what Brecken will do. He just stands there, leaning against the cool, brick building, his eyes closed.

Not knowing why, and not really thinking about it, I reach up and place my hand on his arm. Mostly to comfort him since it looks like he needs it, but also to figure out... something. Anything.

He radiates light—not like Raphael or other spirits I've met—but a brighter light than most living people. What makes him different?

As soon as my fingers touch his skin, a tidal wave of pressure washes over me. Not physically painful, but agonizing in its loneliness and despair. My mind grows dark and dizziness overwhelms me. I crumple in on myself, letting go of him and stumbling to the rough cement. I back away, weakened, and look up at him, holding my fingers, which still burn with the memory of contact.

"You shouldn't have done that," he says with an *I told you so* tone of voice. "I don't know who you are, or what you're doing here, but there's no way you can help me, or change who I am. You might as well leave like all the rest."

He knows I'm here. He felt my touch. That isn't possible. How can I guard a guy who knows I'm here? It won't work. And there have been others? Am I doomed to fail too? A momentary panic seizes me. Closing my eyes, I take a moment to re-focus. Just because others failed doesn't mean I will.

"I mean it," he says again, slouching against the brick wall. "Go."

Just then, a girl rounds the corner. She sidles up next to him. "I thought I might find you here." She slips her arms through his, and then leans in close, her straight, platinum hair flowing like a veil over Brecken's face. As she presses forward, brushing his lips with hers, her short mini-skirt lifting. She moves against him, and I can actually see her hot pink underwear. He wraps an arm around her and brings her closer.

Entranced, but disgusted, I keep right on staring. What will they do next? Right here in broad daylight?

17

First Day on the Job

ALISA

Watching Brecken kiss the sleaze-bucket actually makes me nauseous, and I don't have to wait long to find out what they do next. The girl slides her hands up the inside of his sweatshirt, and snuggles against his bare, muscled chest. For a split second, I want to rip her arms off. I have no idea where the emotion comes from.

Brecken looks around, and then pulls her arms gently from his shirt. "Not now, Jilly."

"What?" She looks around with a sly smile. "There's no one here and it's always more fun when you might get caught."

"Ugh," I say, turning away so I don't have to watch.

Brecken straightens and gently pushes Jill back. She stumbles over her combat boots, and I laugh out loud.

"What?" she asks, confused, her eyebrows creasing.

He takes her hand and leads her down the sidewalk toward the street. "Don't follow me," he says over his shoulder.

I guess he's talking to me.

"Why not?" Jill asks. "I thought we were going out tonight." She gives him a cute little pout that I'm sure she has practiced in front of a mirror.

"Not *you*." He grits his teeth and pulls her along.

Jill's lips pucker and her eyes close to slits. "Well, who else, Breck? There's no one around." She turns in a circle and motions with her hands out. "You're being weird again."

With a sigh of resignation, he shakes his head. "Whatever. Come on." He doesn't say anything more, and I float along behind them reluctantly. At least they are somewhat entertaining. I'm beginning to think this job of being a guardian is not what it's cracked up to be. So far, it's not what I expected, nor am I having any fun. My mood darkens the longer I follow them. If this kid can hear me, maybe I should tell him what I think of this whole situation.

"Your first and biggest mistake is your taste in girls." I walk behind them, my hands clasped behind my back. It makes me feel very therapist-like.

"It's none of your business!" He storms down the sidewalk, Jill's hand gripped in his fist.

"It *is* my business," Jill says, whipping her hand away. "You scare me when you act like this. All paranoid." She folds her arms and cocks her hip. "Look, Breck, I've stayed by you through thick and thin, but if you're going to go all nuts on me again..."

"Jilly, I'm not nuts."

"Let me help you," she begs. "You know I can." Her arms snake around his waist as she presses her body up against him again.

I can't help but laugh, shaking my head. "What a winner."

Pursing his lips, he gently shoves her back. "I can't do this right now. I need to get home. I won't be able to go out tonight either, but I'll call you. Please don't be mad." He pulls her close and kisses her quickly, then jogs away, leaving Jill and me staring after him.

That's it? He's going to run away and hide? What happened to Mr. Tough guy? I glance at Jill whose mouth gapes open.

"I don't think you should go after him," I say, since it looks like she might.

With an angry shrug of her shoulders, she turns and heads the other way, a scowl on her face.

And it hits me. She listened to me! Was that all it took? A little suggestion? A tiny whisper in her ear and she changed her mind? Maybe this assignment won't be so hard after all. Then I remember I can't whisper in Brecken's ear. I don't need to whisper at all. He can hear me loud and clear.

I stand there thinking I should probably go after him. It's

what a good guardian would do, and if I want to succeed at this stupid mission, it will be better to get it over with quickly. I can get out of here and be with Gram, and then I'll never have to see Bad Boy Brecken again.

I blink my eyes, feeling that tug and pull in my belly that is now familiar with spirit travel, and poof, I'm at Brecken's side. Oh, happy day.

He pounds down the sidewalk, his hands stuffed into his pockets, his frown deepening as soon as I appear. "Can't you go away?"

"Go away? I just got here. I *have* to be here, and believe me, you're no picnic." I look the other way, truly wishing I were anywhere else.

He turns toward the sound of my voice. "Excuse me? How did you get this job? They have to recruit from snobville now?" he says with a derogatory laugh.

That's totally rude and certainly not true.

"You *can* hear me. Unbelievable." I can't believe Raphael would send me to someone like this. I shake my head, itching to smack Brecken upside the head. I try to think of a comment that will get under his skin to get even for the "recruiting from snobville" comment. "Why can't you drive home? Did the cops impound your mexi-car?"

"You're an idiot."

"Shut up," I answer, trying not to sound offended.

"*Shut up.*" He mimics my voice.

"You're *so* mature. You argue like a two-year-old," I say, even though I sound the same way.

A sneer twists his face as he goes in for the kill. "How old are *you?* You sound like you're twelve. Did they send a snot-nosed, elementary school kid to guard me? Really?"

I stick my tongue out, tempted to add another gesture even though I'm pretty sure he can't see me, but then decide it won't look good on video at the library... just in case anyone is watching.

With a resigned shake of his head, and his mouth twisting in irritation, he walks toward a neighborhood where all the houses look exactly alike. Small, brick—varying in color—tiny front porches, and peeling paint on the gables over each front door.

I don't say another word until we turn up the walkway to a red brick house. The neatly trimmed lawn has browned, and a couple of little bushes grow on either side of the cracked cement porch. It's obvious right off the bat that the people who live here don't have a lot of money, but at least the house is neat.

"This your place?" I step into the living room behind him.

"No, it's the neighbor's. I'm here to rob them." He throws his backpack in the corner and goes straight to the fridge. He grabs a beer and pops the lid, collapsing onto the couch.

"I wouldn't be surprised," I say, mumbling and looking around.

He closes his eyes and chuckles like he doesn't care.

"Do your parents know you drink?" Maybe this is the obstacle he needs to overcome. Maybe he's an alcoholic. I can deal with that. Get him to sign up for AA. Get him to go to meetings. Get him a sponsor. Easy peasy.

He throws an icy stare, then, with a snort, he takes another swig, not bothering to answer.

His lack of emotion irritates me, and I feel no desire to keep my mouth shut. He reminds me too much of my older brother, Derek, when he's in one of *those* moods.

"What a moron," I say. "I don't have to stick around and watch this. Why should I waste my time with you?"

His expression falls and pain fills his eyes for a split second. A pang of guilt pricks my conscience, because I'm being rude and I know it, but how could my comment hurt a guy like him? Why would he care what I say? He doesn't want me here, and guys like him... well, I just don't know how to deal with this situation other than how I'd do it with my brother, which will end in a big argument. I obviously don't know how to influence Brecken without saying something mean. I already regret the comments I've made so far.

I'm not normally such a brat and I don't know what is wrong with me now. I should apologize, but can't bring myself to do it, and I don't want to sit around and watch him get drunk or hear any more of his asinine comments.

I want only one thing.

The comfortable, familiarity of home.

The memory of my mother's face and her robust laughter calls to me. Maybe smelling the yeasty aroma of baking bread, or seeing my dad sitting at the computer going through *Craig's list* will make me feel better. My little brother's good-humored teasing could pull me out of this funk easy.

All I have to do is close my eyes. The tug and pull begins in my belly and when I open my eyes, there I am in our bright, airy kitchen. I don't know if I've traveled a hundred miles or a thousand. I'm in the one place I love most.

I take a moment to soak it in—the quiet, the familiarity of each piece of furniture, each picture on the wall, and relish the feel of just being here, of being home.

Normally, at this time of day, my mom would be standing against the counter, reading mail or making some treat for us to eat once we get home from school, but silence fills the kitchen and my mother's absence makes everything seem sad and too quiet.

I float upstairs to her room, stopping at mine on the way. The closed door doesn't block me, and I move through it. The unopened blinds and sheer curtains encase the room in shadow. My perfectly made bed—not like *I* left it—stands under the window, and not one poster I put up has been removed from the walls. Not even bare-chested Jacob Black. My mom hates that one.

I quickly grow uncomfortable in my empty shrine, where only crumbling memories remain instead of girl things like ponytail holders, makeup, and rumpled clothes. I'll never sleep in that bed again. I'll never wear my favorite Big Star jeans, or brush my hair with the silver brush and comb set my Gram bought for me before she died. Ache fills me as I look around, heavy, cold, and filled with regret.

Not wanting to deal with it right now, I head toward my parent's bedroom and stop in front of their door. I don't hear anything, but I have the eerie sense that something is happening inside. Uneasiness, like the overpowering stench of rotten potatoes hidden in a dark cupboard—overcomes me.

Taking a breath, I push through the door. Only a sliver of light pierces the room through a crack in the heavy brocade curtains. The familiar cherry-wood king-size bed stands against the far wall, and a stale odor permeates the room.

A form lies on the bed, unmoving. I know who it is immediately and step closer. Familiar dark hair covers half of her sleeping face. A white, dry trail of tears ends in a wet spot on the pillow. She hasn't been asleep long.

I kneel beside her and run my fingers along her cheek. Why is my mom sleeping in the middle of the day? She never used to. She was always the first one up, running on her treadmill, working with the PTA, doing volunteer work at the children's hospital downtown. She would have considered a nap in the middle of the day a complete waste of her time.

I stay by her side and watch her breathe. It's not long before I hear the downstairs door open quietly, and then slowly click shut. I never realized I could hear so well, and I wonder who is sneaking into my house. Glancing down at my mother, I realize she hasn't stirred at all, but lies on her bed completely comatose.

I go to the top of the stairs and see my little brother, Tyler. He throws his backpack next to the wall and slumps onto the couch, grabbing the remote and flipping on one of those stupid Japanese cartoons I hate. A tug of nostalgia fills me. What I wouldn't give to sit next to him and watch TV.

Normally, he gets a snack. He's never been overweight, but he was always a bit on the chunky side—perfect for playing little league football. Now his clothes hang from his shoulders, his pants baggy. He has barely hit puberty and can't have burned off all his baby fat yet.

I sit on the couch next to him and place my hand over his. A rush of loneliness washes over me, and feelings of despair settle in my chest. Is this what he's feeling right now? Is this heavy weight of torment what little Tyler carries around all day?

"Go get something to eat," I whisper.

He doesn't move.

I say the words again, more forcefully this time. He throws the remote down and gets up to rummage around in the kitchen cupboards, pulling out graham crackers and milk.

He comes back with a bowl of soggy crackers, plops his feet on the coffee table, and stares at the TV. With a sigh of resignation I stand, thinking I should go back upstairs to my mom, but something tells me it's time to find Brecken.

Dang.

18

Too Much, Too Soon

ALISA

I close my eyes and picture Brecken—his dark, wind-blown hair, his thick, black eyebrows, and his intensely blue eyes. In a blink, I appear in some sort of basement bedroom—dark, dank, and surrounded by cement walls. A lone bulb swings from the unfinished ceiling.

Brecken sits on the edge of an unmade bed, holding a pill bottle. I inch closer to read the label but his fingers close over it. He grits his teeth and opens the bottle. Maybe he's planning to overdose. Maybe my moment to help him is at hand. I'll be finished with my job and back to *Idir Shaol* in no time! I hurry forward, but instead of swallowing a handful of pills, he takes only one... without water.

Oh gag. Doing that would have burned a hole through my esophagus.

He pitches the bottle onto a small table that holds an old, wooden lamp, and then he lies down and faces the wall.

"Brecken," I whisper, unsure of what to say. Since visiting my family, the desire to fight has disappeared, and I don't want him to be mad at me either.

He covers his head with a pillow.

"Brecken, if you can hear me, please talk to me."

"Go away."

I sit in a chair across the room and watch his still form. "I don't like this anymore than you do." I wish he didn't know I was here. I could work so much better incognito, like I had with my little brother, or the girl named Jilly that Brecken kissed. Slowly, he turns and searches the dim room. "Why do they keep sending you people?"

"How should I know?" I shake my head and cross my arms over my chest. Everything he says irks me. Even the way he holds his mouth when he speaks. "What was that pill you took?" I ask finally. "Are you into drugs or something? Are they painkillers? I want to know what I'm dealing with."

He exhales and turns toward me. "Zyprexa, if you must know. It's a prescription."

I've heard of Zyprexa but can't remember what it treats. Just my luck to be assigned to some psychic wacko. "What's it for?"

"It's for schizophrenia," he says, sitting up on his bed. "Everyone thinks I'm nuts. Okay? If someone claims they hear voices, they're usually given medication or are wrapped up in a long white shirt that buttons down the back."

He has a point there. "Yeah," I say slowly. "What else can you do? Any other amazing talents I should be aware of?" I have a feeling these weird things he can do are the special gifts Raphael was talking about when I wasn't listening.

With a whoosh, he falls back to his pillow. "None of your business. I wish you'd just leave."

"I'd like to, but you see, if I don't finish my assignment here, I have to live in hell for the rest of forever, so a little help would be nice."

A string of obscenities flies from him mouth and he sits up again. He searches for me in the corner.

"What did you just say to me?" I yell back at him. "I don't need to listen to that! Watch your mouth or I won't help you at all!" I want nothing more than to walk out, to leave this doper to his fate, but I know what mine will be if I do. My threat is empty and he probably knows it. He'll do whatever he can to get rid of me.

As soon as that thought enters my mind, I feel strangely relaxed. A calm descends around me like a wooly shroud and I chuckle, which brings a frown to Brecken's face. His ploys won't work. I understand his technique now. I can see right through him. Maybe it's a guardian gift.

"Hey," he says suddenly, leaning forward and squinting his

eyes. "Just so you know, I can see you. What do you think of that, little guardian angel?"

I freeze.

The next second, I disappear back to my old bedroom.

Those four words, "I can see you," rock me in a bad way. More than I would have thought possible. Being able to hear me is one thing, but see me too? It's not fair. I have a harder job than any of the other guardians, and I want to guard someone easy, boring, and not so complicated. I aim my complaints at Raphael, sure that he can hear me, but I get no response. I picture him up there laughing.

This isn't how it's supposed to be, I scream in my mind. A few-four letter words flit through my mind, as I look around my old room, knowing I can't come home every time things get hard. Am I even allowed to visit my family? It's one of those things Anaita surely went over in class, but for the life of me, I can't remember.

With a tired sigh, I close my eyes. I have to stay with Brecken whether I want to or not, so I picture his face, fully expecting to reappear at his side.

Nothing happens.

I try again.

Nada. I take one of my imaginary deep breaths to slow my mind and close my eyes, trying again. Slowly I open them. I'm still in my room. The only explanation I can come up with is that I need to be here at the moment, which seems strange considering I'm supposed to stick to my charge like glue.

I push through my closed bedroom door and out into the hallway, then tiptoe through the quiet house. Downstairs in the living room, Tyler still watches TV, and on the table in front of him rests the empty graham cracker bowl.

A familiar rumbling echoes through the walls. The garage door. Someone's home. Glancing at the clock, I figure it must be Derek. He drives an old rusted, 1971 Ford Mustang that I love and hoped would be mine when he left for college.

That will never happen now.

The back door in the kitchen opens and closes with a loud bang.

Tyler doesn't even turn around. He doesn't say hi, or lift his hand in a wave. Derek doesn't greet our morose little brother either, but hurries down the long flight of stairs to his bedroom in the basement. I hear his door slam three seconds later. When did they all become so hostile?

Here is sweet, little Tyler, sitting alone for the last hour, lonely, forgotten, and hurting—I know because it's radiating off him in palpable waves—and Derek doesn't even stop to ask how he is.

Furious, I stomp down the carpeted stairs to the basement, wishing I could sound like thunder, intending to give Derek the lecture of a lifetime. He has no right to treat Ty this way. His shut door stops me for only a second before I barge through.

He lies on his bed, ear buds stuck in his ears, his iPod resting on his stomach. One arm covers his eyes.

"Derek."

He doesn't move, not that I thought he would.

"Derek!"

Nothing.

"Derek!" This time I scream his name, my hands fisted, my whole soul shaking with fury, but it doesn't matter. He can't hear me. He can only hear the awful pounding of AC/DC from his tiny, black mp3 player.

I can't do anything here, so I float back upstairs, straight through the floor to save time. Ty still vegges on the couch, only now a single tear trails down his cheek.

I kiss the tear, my heart breaking. I don't know what to say or how to help. "Tyler, I love you. I'm so sorry this is happening. I know it's my fault." My death is the cause of all this continuing sorrow. My heart aches, but I don't know what to do about it.

Shaking my head, I begin drawing on his arm with my finger. It's something we always did in the past. We'd stay up late watching movies, drawing on each other's arms or backs the whole time. It was our thing, our tradition.

I hear an intake of breath and he sits up straighter, rubs his arm hard, like it itches, then reclines back against the couch with his arm outstretched. Tears well in his eyes. A smile spreads across my face, and I snuggle into the cushions, once again trailing my fingers up his forearm. One lone tear drips down his cheek, but I feel a small ray of hope trying to shine though the loneliness he feels. It's one of the coolest moments of my life.

It's quickly interrupted by the most horrifying sound I've ever heard.

19

A Second Visit with Death

ALISA

A terrifying screech echoes from upstairs, and the look of horror on Tyler's face says it all.

"Stay here!" I command before shooting through the ceiling to my mother's bedroom.

Her room, still dark, is shrouded in shadow. She kicks off the blankets and lies there panting, sweat beading on her forehead.

"Mom! What's wrong?" For a moment, I totally forget she can't hear me. When she doesn't respond I place my hand on her forehead, but I can't tell if she has a fever or not since I don't feel hot or cold the same way as before. A second passes before she slips her feet off the bed and sits up. Leaning forward on her arms, she rests, swaying from side to side, and then she stumbles to the bedroom door, tripping on a quilt that lies tangled at the foot of the bed. Curse words tumble from her mouth. Words I've never heard her use before. Her eyes are glazed and wild.

This is not my mother.

She was always so loving, so happy, so fun. But this madwoman is something else. She yanks open the door and ambles to the stairs, clinging to the rail as she takes one step at a time, her movements jerky and slow.

"Tyler!" she hollers. "Get your butt up here!" She continues her laborious descent, looking like she'll fall any minute. Not knowing what to do, I rush ahead to find my brother, hoping to protect him from whatever storm is coming.

He's alone in the living room, his face as white as winter frost, his hands twitching at his side. He doesn't even try to hide. I don't think he can move; he looks so scared.

Without a moment's hesitation, I fly from the living room and down the stairs to the basement in search of Derek. He's still on his bed, tapping his fingers to whatever music blares in his ears. I scream for him, shout, and even try to smack his face, but nothing works.

My whole soul cries out for him to hear me until I kneel on the floor at his side, sobbing invisible tears. At that moment he turns, a frown appearing on his already unhappy-looking face. Sitting up, he tears the plugs from his ears.

He leaps for the door, taking the stairs three at a time with his long, athletic legs. I rush behind him, relief soaring through me. Now that he's up and running I have no fear... until I reach the living room.

My mother has Tyler by the hair, screeching at him for not having finished loading the dishwasher. I turn in confusion, noticing the spotless kitchen. Derek hurdles over the couch and grabs Tyler away from our mother. Tears streak down Ty's face and a red hand print covers his cheek.

"What are you doing?" Derek screams. "Look what you've done!" He gestures to Ty's face, his own stricken with disbelief. "What kind of mother are you?"

Everyone stands silently staring at one another, and the only sound in the room is their heavy breathing.

Then, in a quiet, controlled tone, Derek says, "I hate you, and this is it. I'm done. We're leaving." Derek storms back to his room, towing Tyler behind him.

My mother sinks to the couch in defeat and covers her face, but she doesn't cry. Instead, she pulls her legs up beneath her and lies down on a throw pillow, staring straight ahead.

After a few moments, Derek returns to the living room with a duffel bag slung over his shoulder, an empty one in his other hand. He and Tyler mount the stairs, not even looking our mom's way. After ten minutes they return, the second duffel bag full. Without a backward glance, they leave the house, the front door slamming behind them.

I can't believe what I've just witnessed. Nothing like this has ever happened in our home before. Yeah, Derek and mom would argue sometimes, but leaving the house? Running away? Mom slapping Tyler? I don't get it.

After a moment my mom stumbles up the stairs, her feet tangling in her nightgown. She trips and slides down the stairs. After regaining her balance, she hobbles up to her room and goes straight to her bathroom. She opens the vanity and pulls out a tan pill bottle. She shakes a couple of pills into her palm, staring at the white circles. She pours out a few more, then a few more.

"What are you doing?" I come around to stand before her.

She doesn't answer.

"Mom. What are you doing?"

Without water, she pops more than fifteen pills into her mouth. I can only stare, stunned. She goes back to bed and falls on top of the blankets. After ten minutes or so, her eyes glaze over—even more than before—and her breathing slows, her chest barely rising with each inhalation.

"Mom!" I shout. "You can't do this! Derek and Tyler need you!" It doesn't matter what I say, though, because she can't hear me. I fall to my knees and plead to the God I still have yet to meet, to help my mother.

Around me, a light grows from a pinpoint, moving closer. Gram floats beside me bathed in radiant brilliance. She smiles and takes my hand. "Hello, Darling."

"Gram! Something's wrong with Mom! I think she's dying!"

"Yes, dear, she is," she says with a frown.

Why doesn't Gram do something? This is her daughter! She just stands there, watching my mother with no reaction whatsoever.

"But... but she can't die yet!"

"It's a terrible thing to witness, isn't it?" she says, gazing into my eyes. "I felt the same way when I watched you die in your car. I was there, you know."

I didn't know, but I don't want to be the first person to see my mother after she realizes what a terrible thing she's done.

I can't let this happen.

When the loud bang of a door slamming rings through the

house, I jump up. Someone is home. Did Derek come back? I let myself sink through the floor to find my dad standing in the kitchen, flipping through the mail.

"Dad! Hurry! Mom needs you."

He continues to read each envelope and even tears one open, pulling out a bill of some sort. A frown creases his brow and he exhales a loud breath.

"Dammit, Dad! Go upstairs!"

He looks up, confusion in his eyes.

"Yes! Go upstairs!"

He drops the mail, still staring at the ceiling, and hurries up the stairs. Suddenly he's racing to the top, barreling toward his bedroom. He finds Mom on the bed, totally unresponsive.

"Laynie, wake up!" He pats her face, checks her breathing, and then puffs three breaths into her mouth. After a hurried 911 call, he rushes back to my mother and continues doing CPR.

20

A New Plan

BRECKEN

Brecken lies on his bed, staring at the dull, cracked ceiling in his basement bedroom. The sun will set in just a few hours. Lazy rays of light filter in through the tiny window above his dresser.

He lets his mind drift over his earlier conversation with the angel girl. She spoke to him. Actually spoke to him out loud. And she glowed, sitting there in the chair across from his bed. Long, blonde hair down to her waist, and her eyes...

There is something about her eyes that intrigues him, and it isn't just her pretty face. Her aura—the energy that swirls around her—is golden and faintly pink. He's never seen anything like it before, and he has seen plenty.

He'd had other visitors—guardians—and they always glowed white, like he imagined all angels would, but this girl...

What is it about her? Not that he is interested in finding out; surely this new guardian will be no different from the others.

The thing that really surprises him is the fact that she spoke to him. None of the others had or would. As soon as they learned he could not only hear them, but see them too, they freaked out and disappeared, only to be replaced by another. The last one had been over a year ago. He thought he was free of them.

He shakes his head and gets up. He'll get rid of her, just like the others. Show her what he's really like. That's all it usually takes. Once she gets to know him and learns about the life he leads, she'll be gone. It won't take much. It never does.

21

A Civil Chat

ALISA

After a few hours of sitting at the hospital, I begin to feel that familiar itch that tells me I need to get back to Brecken. I ignore it, not willing to leave my mother yet. She needs me more, and I'll stay here as long as I can.

When the feeling becomes so intense I can no longer ignore it, I kiss my mom's sleeping face, so peaceful in her drug-induced coma. She'll be okay. Gram told me so, and I believe her, but I've had a small taste of what I did to my family. It's a bitter, jagged pill to swallow.

Reluctantly, and with a heavy sigh, I picture Brecken, focusing on his sad face, his penetrating eyes. This time I only take a second to appear at his side. He sits at a worn Formica table, slurping up Kraft macaroni and cheese. Two young girls eat beside him.

"Hey," I say, sinking down in the one remaining chair. "I'm back. Sorry I had to leave—family emergency."

Brecken freezes, the fork halfway to his mouth. He doesn't say a word, but looks around, taking a hesitant bite.

"You can hear me, right? I'm back," I say again. "Just so you know."

After a slow, controlled breath, he takes another bite, and I take in the scene. Brecken's eyes are the only things that move other than his methodical eating. The two little girls, roughly the ages of twelve and nine, continue to eat in silence.

"I guess you can't see me anymore since you're looking in the wrong direction," I say, leaning back with a chuckle. "Who are these two?"

The slurping continues until the younger girl drops her fork in her bowl and says, "I'm done."

"Put your bowl in the sink," Brecken says, not looking up.

The girl obeys and not long after, the older girl follows suit. "I'm going outside," she says with a half wave.

"K," is Brecken's only response. When the door shuts firmly behind them, he places his hands on the table and frowns, his lips forming a pucker. "Why did you come back?"

"I'm supposed to help you. Duh." I figure if I am open and honest then maybe my job will go quicker, and I can get out of here.

"With what?" he asks, clearing the table.

"I have no idea. They don't tell us. We have to figure it out ourselves. Maybe your drinking problem?"

He laughs, his eyes squinting, trying to see me. "I don't have a drinking problem."

I laugh right back. "Yeah. Well. Whatever."

He turns toward the sound of my voice. "So who are you?"

I forgot I haven't introduced myself. "I'm Alisa." I'm not sure how much I should tell him, and I can't ask Raphael or Anaita since I'm pretty sure they already explained the rules when I wasn't listening.

"So you died or something?" he says, walking out of the room.

I figure I'm supposed to follow, so I do, floating a foot off the ground. It makes me feel cool and spooky. "Yep. I died."

"How?"

"I really don't want to talk about it."

"And I really don't want you around."

"Touché."

I follow him to the basement, to the room where I saw him earlier when he took his psycho pills. My mother has strict rules about going into a boy's bedroom. It's a big, fat no-no. And I have a hard time wanting to break her rule now.

I stare at him, and he stares at the wall, thinking he is staring at me. "Fine. I'll tell you a little about me, and you tell me a little about you. All right?"

"Fine."

I decide, as his guardian, that it's okay for me to go into his room, because it's not like we are going to make out. I walk in and sit down on the lonely wooden chair that faces his bed. Brecken plops down on this bed, crossing his feet.

"So, ask me anything," I say, ready to deflect questions that get too personal.

He crosses his arms over his chest and contemplates. "I can see you again. Just barely."

This is not what I expect him to say, but I don't leave in a panic this time. "How?" I ask, curious.

"I am a man of many talents." He chuckles, waving his hand through the air. "It's something I've always been able to do. I don't know why. I see auras too, but the light has to be dim. They're hard to see otherwise."

I nod, thinking this over. "I guess that's why you can see me down here in the dark."

These are definitely the special gifts Raphael spoke about. They have to be. And if I want to succeed, I have to be okay with it. I take stock of my feelings and analyze them, realizing that for the most part I'm cool with it. Kind of.

We sit silently for a moment.

"You're hot," he says with a crooked smile. "At least from what I can tell."

I swear I blush, if that's even possible. I've always thought my straight, dishwater blonde hair and dull brown eyes were plain, bordering on boring. I don't know why, but his compliment warms my cold, little heart a tiny bit. "Thank you. Do you see spirits on a regular basis?"

He laughs and sits up, bringing his arms up to rest on his knees. He turns serious. "Naw. But I've seen my grandpa and my grandma a couple of times. Not my mom though. Don't know why."

"Your mom? She's—"

"Yeah."

"Oh. Sorry."

He shrugs and doesn't say anything more about her. "The other people who've come, the ones like you, didn't like it that I could see them, and they wouldn't talk to me. There were three others."

"Really? Girls or boys?"

"Two girls and one guy."

I wonder who they were and what it was that made them give up and leave. "How long did they last?"

"Hanging with me, you mean?"

I nod and he glances at the ceiling, thinking. "Let's see. The first one only one day. That was a girl. The next guy lasted a week, but got totally frustrated when I wouldn't obey him." He laughs and shakes his head. "Idiot. And the last girl stuck around for almost three weeks. I'm still not sure why she left."

"Yeah. That is weird." I wonder where those guardians are now. Did they get to try again with a new charge? I don't intend to bail on Brecken because this might be my only shot. I can't mess it up, and anyway, talking to him like this seems nice. Maybe we could even be friends. Maybe if he can like me, even a little, he'll listen to me.

"No, it's not. You'll see. You'll leave too, but you *are* different. I can't tell what it is, but I'll figure it out." He gazes at me, his eyes steady.

I sit up straight, uncomfortable with his scrutiny. "I'm different? How?"

"Well, first of all, you're talking to me. Second, you kinda have a pink glow around you. None of the others did. They were white."

I hold my arm in front of my face and turn it back and forth. No glow that I can see. "Hmm."

"So, anyway, I need to go. You should probably stay here." He grabs a jacket from the foot of his bed.

"What? Where are you going?"

"Somewhere you won't want to follow."

22

Little Sisters

ALISA

*I*n front of his house, dust blows across the sidewalk, dry and stale. A lone tree grows by the curb but isn't thriving. Neighborhood kids play outside in a grass-less park to the south, dust devils rising on the breeze. A few cars are parked out front, none of them worth enough money to steal.

Brecken straddles a motorcycle and turns the key. It roars to life, the black paint gleaming in the sunshine. It isn't new or particularly expensive-looking, but it isn't rusty and falling apart either.

"Where are you going?"

"Don't worry about it, angel. I'll be back in a few hours." He revs the engine and smiles. As he peels out, gravel peppers me like gunshot.

"Idiot."

I follow my charge. Like he thought I wouldn't? I hold back though, worried he will sense me. If I hide in the background and watch, get a sense of who he is, maybe it will help me know how to deal with him. Technically, it's a good plan.

He drives to a house not far from his and pulls into the driveway. I stay across the street, figuring it's far enough away. He raps on the front door of a ranch-style house with black shutters. When he enters the house, I move closer. Peeking through an open window, I watch Brecken talk to a kid his age. They don't even bother to whisper. And considering their plan, I'm surprised.

"They'll be gone by six," the kid says. "The back window will be open, just like last time."

Brecken nods but doesn't say anything.

"Her jewelry box is upstairs in the master bedroom on a white dresser. That's all we want. Got it? The jewelry box. Nothing else." The boy hands Brecken a white envelope. "You get half now, and the rest after."

Brecken nods.

"Cool, dude."

Brecken turns to leave.

"Oh, and don't get caught," the kid laughs as he shuts the door.

I stare at my charge, my mouth hanging open in disbelief. I have to guard a criminal? If he doesn't care about robbing his neighbor, why would he listen to me? I watch him climb onto his bike and frown. He tucks the white envelope into the waistband of his pants and revs the engine. With gritted teeth, he takes off.

His form grows smaller and smaller. A moment later, I appear behind him on his motorcycle. The wind buffets me, and I throw my arms around him so I won't fall off—a reflex. He jerks in my grasp and the motorcycle swerves. He over-corrects, and I scream in fright, hugging him tighter—reflex again.

The wheels skid to the right. The bike slides in the loose gravel, and Brecken's boot smokes, skimming along the asphalt as he tries to balance us out. My screams echo loud in my ears, and I close my eyes, not wanting to witness his demise. He manages to straighten the bike at the last second and pulls over to the curb, a panicked expression on his face. He turns around on the seat, trying to see me. "What the hell are you doing?" he yells, yanking off his helmet.

"What a stupid question," I say, already hopping off his death machine.

"I told you not to follow me!"

I laugh. "And I'm supposed to obey? I have a job to do, cowboy, and I'm going to do it."

"I don't need a babysitter." He glares in my direction, his

mouth tight.

"From what I've seen, you need a jail cell."

He eases back into traffic and doesn't say anything else the whole way home, which is fine by me. Nothing he can say at this point will matter.

After we arrive at his house, he lifts off his helmet and stares at where he thinks I stand. Totally in the wrong direction. I hover a foot off the ground to his left and he looks to the right. "It's not what you think," he says with a tired sigh.

"Oh really?"

With a heavy shrug, he kicks the kickstand, and then throws his leg over the bike.

I have to be honest here. Watching his thigh muscles bulge under his Levis distracts me... momentarily. His blue eyes sparkle in the bright sunlight, and his full lips curl into a grimace. I can't quit staring. Just because I don't trust boys doesn't mean I'm not attracted to them in other, dysfunctional ways. I've never had a serious boyfriend, but I want guys to like me. I *need* them to like me. I don't understand it, and probably need therapy.

He drops down on the porch and rests his helmet on his thigh. "We're out of money. My dad's out of town. We're out of groceries, and if I don't pay the electric bill tomorrow, they'll turn off our power. I don't have a job right now. Okay? I'm looking, but haven't found anything yet. I *have* to do this."

"Nice. Try the sympathy card." I cross my arms over my chest and scowl. "It's not going to work."

He curses, his hands in a fist, and then stomps inside the house.

"Excuse me? You can't talk to me like that!"

He ignores me and slams the door in my face.

Like it can block me. I slide through to see him standing at the kitchen table, breathing hard.

"I can talk however I want," he says, his back to me. "And I didn't say any of that to get your sympathy." He turns to face the door. "I just thought you might understand." We face off in the small kitchen, neither of us wanting to give in.

"Fine," I say. "Be stupid. Rob someone. Take things that aren't yours, things that are probably precious keepsakes, and give them to your idiot friend."

His expression falls. He holds onto the back of a kitchen chair, his knuckles white, looking like he wants to explain, but then he straightens and gives his head a hopeless shake. "Whatever." He runs down the stairs, taking them two at a time.

I let him go, and I go back outside, wishing I could feel the sun's warmth on my face. I feel warmth, but it's not the same as really *feeling* it. It's the same with cold. It's there. I can sense it, but it doesn't bite my skin or feel uncomfortable.

To my right, I hear the squeal of children and notice the playground nearby. The two girls who ate lunch with Brecken are there. The youngest is on a little merry-go-round with a couple of other kids. Faded red paint is worn thin under their feet. The older girl sits in a swing, barely moving, but keeping her eye on the younger one.

I wander over and sit in the swing beside the older girl, her long, dark hair reaching past her waist. She looks up and the sun catches her blue eyes—deep pools of sadness. Almost identical to Brecken's. She watches her little sister, silent and waiting.

I push back in the swing, but it doesn't move. I always loved swing sets and I ache to feel that roller coaster tug in the pit of my stomach after going too high. Instead, I sit still, bored and frustrated. "So, you're Brecken's sister?"

She doesn't answer. I didn't think she would, but maybe Brecken's talent runs in the family. "Okay. I'm going to ask you some questions. If the answer is yes, push back on the swing. If no, just stay where you are. Got that? Back for yes, stay for no. All right. Here we go."

I pause for a moment, thinking of the things I most want to know. I decide to start with an easy question. "Are you a brat like Brecken?"

The girl pauses and after a couple seconds, pushes back with her foot, setting the swing in motion.

"Good!" I knew it. She has that sassy-britches expression just like her brother. I think for a moment then ask, "Do you like where you live?"

She lets the swing slow to a standstill. I don't blame her. The neighborhood is a dive, not to mention rundown, dusty, and altogether ugly. "Okay. Time to tell me about Brecken. Is he a nice brother?"

The swing moves, but she keeps her toe on the ground as she swivels back and forth. I take that for a *kind of.* "Hmm. Are you two close?"

Again the swing moves, but this time hard. The girl leans back, her face determined. She pumps the swing a few times before letting it slow again. Anger radiates from her, pricking me like darts. What is she so angry at?

"Okay, okay. I get it." I don't know the details, but I can tell this girl is hurting terribly.

The other little girl runs up to the swings, a wide smile spreading across her dimpled cheeks. "Heidi. Will you push me?"

Hmm. Heidi. Cute name. "Heidi, say your sister's name for me, please."

Heidi stops swinging and frowns. "I'm not really in the mood," she says to the little girl.

"Please. Just once?"

"Fine, but you have to make my bed for me."

The little girl's expression dips, a frown taking the place of her smile, but she climbs onto the last swing in line and waits.

"Say her name, Heidi," I say again.

"Come on, Sophie. You don't have to pout." Heidi gets up from her swing and gives Sophie a half-hearted push.

"Good job! Thank you."

The two stay on the swings for a few minutes more, and I watch them interact. I always wanted a sister and luckily found one in Natty. Thinking of her brings a smile to my face. We loved going to the local park and sitting on the swings. A rush of memories comes to mind. All of them good.

Soon, Heidi and Sophie became bored and run off to play on the sun-faded big-toy across the field, dust puffing up around their feet as they race. What a crappy, depressing park.

23

The Break-in

ALISA

After Brecken's sisters run off to play, I decide to take the easy way back instead of walking. I close my eyes and concentrate, but I don't appear in Brecken's house—which is what I expect—but in a dingy, smoke-filled living room. Not his.

Sunlight filters through the ratty, brown curtains and onto a dark, shag carpet. I can't tell what color it was originally, but now it's throw-up, orangish-brown. Brecken sits on a couch with large holes in the worn, tangerine fabric. His feet are propped up on the scuffed coffee table, and his arm is draped around a girl—Jill. A joint dangles in his other hand.

How did he leave his house without me knowing? Sneaky little devil.

He brings the joint to his lips, taking a long inhalation, and then laughs when someone tells a stupid joke. He seems strangely relaxed with the four other teens who laze around the room too, puffing away. Loud music blares from a stereo in the corner, and empty beer bottles lay scattered over every surface. I definitely should have stayed with his sisters.

I march over and stand before him. "This place is disgusting. Why would you even *want* to be here?" I cross my arms over my chest, hoping he can see me.

He freezes, the butt halfway to his mouth. With narrow eyes, his lips tighten and he clenches his jaw, leans forward, snuffs out the joint and grumbles.

"If you have something to say, just spit it out," I say. "What exactly are you doing here?" I stare at the homemade cigarette in his fingers. "You're smoking weed? Are you freaking kidding me?" I am fully aware that some kids in high school smoke marijuana, but I never did. Not that I was a goody-goody—as if that's a bad thing—but compared to Brecken, I was the freakin' pope.

"Great," he growls, rising from the couch.

"Aw Brecky, don't leave," Jill whines, snuggling deeper into his side. "We're just getting started." She pouts, her lips turning down at the corners.

"I know. Sorry, but I need to go."

"Where?" a boy across the room asks. His sandy-blonde dreadlocks haven't been washed in a month. Neither have his jeans with holes in the knees. His feet are bare just like his chest. He takes a swig from a dark bottle.

"Just somewhere, Jeff," Brecken answers, grabbing his helmet beside the front door.

"Get me some too!" Jeff calls with a chuckle.

Brecken hurries to his motorcycle and turns the key, ignoring his friend.

I hop on the back, not about to be left behind, not that I would stay here, but whatever. This just seems easier and like Anaita said, I like the easy road best.

He peels out and automatically my arms go around his waist. I pull back, not wanting to sit close enough to touch him. "Where are we going?" I yell into the wind.

If he hears me, he doesn't answer.

"I need you to leave," he says, pulling into a deserted parking lot. "Get off."

"You want to dump me here in the middle of nowhere?" I can't believe he's kicking me off his bike. I shouldn't take it personally, but I do—like I'm defective in some way.

Rejected, I get off. He smiles and takes off down the road at break-neck speed. Then it hits me. He's going to commit his crime. I don't know how I know it, but I do. With frightening clarity.

The sun descends and brilliant colors of pink and orange paint the early evening sky. It should be a beautiful, peaceful moment. Instead, an intense, jittery feeling consumes me, like I've had too much caffeine. I feel sick, like I've already failed.

I close my eyes, hating the fact that I have to go chasing after Brecken. I hate following him like a pathetic, lost puppy, begging for his master's attention, but I have to try one more time.

Just like always, I feel that tug in my center and immediately I appear at his side on a backyard porch.

A pool glistens behind us, reflecting the pastel colors of the radiant sky. A fenced basketball court sits off to our right surrounded by wide, green lawns, and a wrought iron table and chairs are situated left of the door. The morning paper still flutters in the late afternoon breeze.

"Brecken, please don't do this."

He stops, his hand on the brass handle. "Go away."

"I can't." I'm not sure what else to say.

"Then wait here." He pushes the door open and steps inside. I follow him into a wide, open kitchen with stainless steel fixtures and white cupboards.

It's one of the most beautiful kitchens I've ever seen. "Wow."

Brecken ignores me and hurries to a long staircase. He runs up to the first floor and pushes open a bedroom door.

That's when the rumbling starts. He freezes, and I try to pinpoint the source of the familiar sound. "Garage door," I whisper in horror.

Brecken hesitates momentarily, then turns and flies down the stairs, ready to tear through the front door, but seeing someone's distorted form through the beveled glass, he runs back toward the kitchen. I follow him, fearful of getting caught as though *I* am the one performing the robbery. My mind races, thinking only of escape.

The front door opens behind us. A mother's voice rings through the halls all the way to the kitchen. "Take off your shoes, Chloe." She sounds happy, full of energy. The way my mother used to sound. She has no idea we are there, no idea she should be afraid, that a thief is in her house, her haven, her safe place.

I glance at Brecken. Instead of the angry, guiltless expression of a seasoned criminal, I see dread, remorse, sadness, and terror.

He doesn't hide or search for a weapon to hurt the woman with. He doesn't grab anything valuable.

He runs.

Runs like the hounds of hell are after him. He pulls open the back door with lightning speed, barrels across the backyard past the pool, and then amazingly, he vaults over a six-foot vinyl fence, tearing through a side yard where his motorcycle waits. He straddles the seat and turns the key. The bike revs to life, and Brecken drives away, his dark hair whipping around his horrified face.

I don't go with him, but study the house where his bike had been parked. It takes only a moment, but I quickly realize that it's the same house where he got the envelope of money.

Nice neighbor.

24

Despair

BRECKEN

he theft is a complete bust and Brecken is beyond embarrassed and ashamed. His stomach twists and his heart aches as he drives up to the campground at the mouth of the canyon and turns into a small parking lot. He pulls off his helmet with an exhausted sigh and sets it on his knee.

Searching his surroundings, he decides to take a walk down the deserted path, and stops at the third picnic area on the right. He stares at the scenery. The familiarity of the trees, the fire-pit, the shallow stream. Without warning, tears spring to his eyes. His family used to come here every Sunday. Every weekend before...

He remembers holding a hotdog over the fire on a flimsy Willow branch. His sisters were little and had to have help. He felt so big and important, and proud that his parents would let him do it alone. Those peaceful, sunset-filled nights are over, never to be relived except in his mind.

What does his mother think now? Does she know how lost he feels? Is she the reason the guardians keep coming?

At first, he liked the "guardians", as they call themselves. They would play games with him when he was little and make him laugh. His parents thought it was sweet that he played with invisible friends. When he grew older, it wasn't funny anymore, and over the last few years, the guardians started driving him crazy. He hated having them watching over his shoulder, and all they did was criticize, correct him, and tell him what a loser he'd become.

Sitting on a bench, Brecken stares into the water. He'd give anything to go back in time, to be able to change the future, to save his mom. But that isn't possible, and dreaming about it won't change anything. He clenches his teeth and wipes his cheeks.

He doesn't know where to turn or what to do next. If he gets caught stealing, he'll go to jail. He knows that, and he's old enough to be prosecuted as an adult. Who would take care of his sisters? His aunt lives nearby, but she's busy with her own family. Brecken's dad makes everything sound fine to friends and relatives.

Well, they aren't fine, and Brecken is at the end of his rope.

25

A Raging Heart

ALISA

A short time later, I find Brecken sitting at a picnic table in a scenic, tree-filled canyon. His bike is parked in the nearby parking lot, and his helmet rests on the bench beside him. With a hanging head, he props his arms over his knees. He looks miserable.

As well he should.

I sit next to him, not knowing what to say. I glance around. A stream runs through the center of the peaceful mountain park, and picnic tables are strategically placed throughout with fire pits close by. Green and refreshing—it is the first place I've been where I feel comfortable. "Wow. I love it. What is this place?"

He pushes away from the table and sits farther away on a large boulder. He runs his fingers through his dark hair, making the sun glisten against the silky strands. "I can't do this," he says, ignoring my question.

"Thank heavens," I sigh in relief. "That was terrible."

He rubs his hands up and down his face. "I just... I just don't know what to do anymore."

I move over beside him. I can't take his sad expression and slumped shoulders anymore. I place my hand on his arm tentatively. Will he shrug me away? Will he reject me again? He doesn't. He doesn't even act like he can feel me.

Feelings of frustration and hopelessness wash over me, followed by shame and embarrassment for what he's just done. All the heartbreak, the deep sense of responsibility, and hopelessness at his situation crash into me like a wild ocean wave.

I let go of his arm to clear my mind of all the overwhelming grief he's just dumped on me. "Oh, Brecken... I didn't know."

"It's not your problem."

"It is," I say, shaking my head. "I just didn't realize you were so unhappy."

"I'm *not* unhappy. I'm irritated. I need money, and I don't want you following me around, ruining my life. I don't want people to look at me like I'm a freak, and I don't want to start taking my meds again, which is exactly what will happen if you're around, hounding me all the time."

"Don't sugarcoat it or anything." I don't need his permission to be here, but it feels like I do. It's like high school all over again, and a deep ache fills my heart. I hate myself for letting his comment sting. What do I care if he wants me around or not?

Because... just because.

Granted, I watched him do something really stupid and almost get caught. He's embarrassed. Ashamed. He's lashing out. But Raphael should have sent an adult guardian to this damaged kid. I don't know how to handle Brecken, how to influence him, or how to make a difference.

"Hey, don't take it personal," he says, as though he can read my mind. "I don't want *any* of you around."

I turn, angry at his flippant tone. "And how do you think *I* feel? I can't stand guys like you."

"Guys like me? What's that supposed to mean?" He searches the campsite, looking for me.

"Druggies, drunks, grease heads, losers!" I know as soon as the words leave my mouth that I shouldn't have said them. But when it comes to boys, I get offended so easily. I don't trust them, and I refuse to let one hurt me now. "You're all alike!" I blurt. "Perverts and liars." Well, except for my dad and brothers, but they are exceptions to the rule.

He stares at where he thinks I stand, his face a mask of controlled rage. "You don't know me. You have no idea who I am or where I come from. You can't judge me." His eyes narrow, and he calls me a few choice names, then stalks away, further up the mountain path.

He's right, but I'm too angry to apologize. Angry at being dead, angry at Natty for dying and leaving me, and angry that I had to see Mr. Roland again.

Ever since I've been back from my visit to Soul Prison, I can't think straight. Mr. Roland's horrid memory taunts me, always at the back of my mind. The whole situation feels massively overwhelming. I let my face fall into my hands as sorrow washes over me.

A soft hand presses against my shoulder. "Alisa."

I turn to see Gram's warm smile, the light around her, radiant and sparkling. I throw myself into her arms and let my heartache out. She pats my back, murmuring sweet things like she used to. "I know it's hard, dear, but there is a solution."

I pull back and gaze into her eyes. "A solution?"

"Of course, Alisa. There's always a solution. Forgiveness. That is the only way." She nods, smoothing my hair and kissing my forehead.

"Forgiveness? But Brecken didn't really say anything wrong."

She smiles and takes my head. "I'm not talking about your charge, Alisa."

I'm confused for a moment, and then I know who she is talking about. I pull away, feeling betrayed. Why would she bring *him* up? She knows nothing about it. I never confided in her, my closest relative, about the terrible abuse I suffered at Mr. Roland's hands. I'm not about to forgive *him,* and no one who's gone through what I did would tell me to.

She takes my hand again. "You're letting the abuse continue by not letting it go. You *have* to let it go. Once you do, you'll be free. It affects everything, Alisa. *Everything.* This is part of the process."

I yank away. She doesn't understand. She wasn't the one raped by her neighbor, and then locked in the closet while her best friend was raped too. She wasn't smacked repeatedly across the face, or tortured with all the bad things he'd do to her family if she told. She wasn't the one violated and betrayed. She didn't hide in fear under the bed while listening to her dearest friend scream in agony.

"I don't care, Gram! I hate him. I will *always* hate him. I'm glad he's rotting in hell, and I hope he stays there forever. I will never forgive him! Never!"

I stalk away. It's the first time I've ever walked out on my grandmother, but I don't care.

I have bigger problems to deal with.

26

Realization

ALISA

I worry all the next day. Worry about my mom, worry about my brothers, and worry about failing this assignment.

Brecken and I don't speak of the break-in again, although it's always the white elephant in the room. I also worry about the advice Gram gave me at the canyon park. Her words stick in my head like tiny parasites, nibbling away, and I can't get them out. The more I try to ignore the whole thing about forgiveness, the louder it screams in my mind.

How am I going to focus when I can't stop thinking about Mr. Roland? I killed myself so I would stop thinking about him, and here I am, still tormented.

It's Saturday, so I don't have to follow Brecken to school, but to be honest, I would have preferred to be there. Less opportunity for him to get into trouble, or for me to watch him get into trouble.

Thankfully, he slept in and now reclines on the sofa, eating cold cereal. Saturday morning cartoons blare on the TV, and Heidi and Sophie move around the kitchen getting breakfast too. It almost feels like home, and I yearn to taste the crispy sweetness of Brecken's Fruit Loops too.

Crunchy cereal, ice-cold milk. Yum.

"So, what are we doing today?" I ask, my eyes riveted to SpongeBob. "Hopefully not rob the neighbors."

"*We* aren't doing anything. Fun or otherwise."

I roll my eyes at his comment. Like he can do anything about it. "I'm going to follow you wherever you go, so please make the day as interesting as possible." I smile conspiratorially because it's not too bright in the living room. Maybe he can see my wicked grin.

"Huh? What did you say?" Heidi asks, finishing her cereal. "We're going to do something fun? Oh, please yes. I'm so bored."

He glances at her over the back of the couch. "Uh…"

"Can we go to the zoo?" Sophie asks, jumping out of her seat and running over to Brecken. "I haven't been to the zoo in forever!"

Brecken turns to me, or to where I am sitting at least, and scowls. He doesn't say anything, but glances at Sophie's hopeful face. "Let me see how much money Dad left. Okay?"

"Yippee!" Sophie claps her hands and runs to her room. "I'm going to wear my new pink shorts," she calls over her shoulder.

"Can I invite a friend?" Heidi asks. "It's boring with just you and Sophie."

She is obviously growing up, and I don't blame her for wanting to bring a friend. I would have wanted that at her age too, and the zoo sounds like a fun, safe place to hang out for the day.

"I'm not paying for anyone else," Brecken answers. "She'll have to bring her own money, but I guess I don't care."

"Cool." Heidi hurries to the phone and begins punching numbers as she walks down the hall to her room.

"That was really nice of you." I recline, laying my arm on the back of the couch. "You're a really good brother."

He snorts and looks away. "And mother, and father, and babysitter."

"Where *is* your dad anyway?" I haven't seen him since I arrived.

"He works. A lot. And he's out of town at the moment." Brecken grabs the remote and starts flipping through the channels.

"My dad works a lot too, but he is always home at night. I miss that—seeing him come in and plop down beside me, asking me about my day. What does your dad do?"

"What does *yours* do?" he counters, avoiding my question. Very clever.

"Um, my dad is an accountant. Pretty boring, but he likes to take us rafting and camping and stuff like that." The more I think about it, the sadder I feel. I'll never go camping again. I'll never sit by a smoky fire making s'mores, or get to sleep on the hard ground in a tent again. I turn away even though I'm pretty sure he can't see my sorrow.

"You were lucky. We never do that."

"Why not?"

With a sigh, Brecken answers. "Because my dad can't take time off. We're still paying tons of medical bills from my mom's hospital stay. We don't have insurance. Dad runs his own business and... why am I telling you this? It doesn't even matter." He throws the remote down and stands up.

"Who are you talking to?" Heidi says, returning from her bedroom.

"No one."

She stands before him, her arms crossed, her hip jutted to the side. I almost laugh. She looks just like me with my brothers. "Are you taking your pills?"

I can tell Brecken is tempted to say something rude, because there's nothing more irritating than a little brother or sister telling you what to do, but to my surprise, he says nothing. He turns and pounds down the stairs to his bedroom.

Heidi frowns and goes into the bathroom. The shower turns on and music blasts. Since I don't want to sit in the living room alone, I head downstairs and walk into Brecken's room right as he's taking off his T-shirt. His arms are in the air, the shirt wrapped around his wrists.

"Ahh!" I scream, taken by surprise and turning away. "Get dressed!"

He laughs. "What? You've never seen a guy's chest before?" He flexes his arms, proud of his bulging biceps. "One as awesome as this?"

My automatic reaction is not what he expects. Nor what I expect either. It's not that I'm unimpressed, or even shy. The problem is that when I see nakedness of any kind, I think of Mr. Roland. It makes me sick, and even though it's not fair to Brecken, that's how it plays out.

Gram is right. I'm letting the abuse continue. I've never had a normal relationship with a boy during my life, and the fact that I keep reliving those horrible moments with Mr. Roland, prove her point. I can't even look at a hot guy like Brecken without getting upset. I need help, but where do you get it once you're dead?

"Get dressed!" I command again, jabbing my finger at him.

"I am," he says, clearly disappointed. "You're the one who's not supposed to be here. What do you care anyway? Don't guardian angels get to see everything? There are no secrets, right?"

"Oh, I hope not," I say, waiting outside his door. "And I already told you. I'm not an angel. Just a guardian. And speaking of that, can you please tell me what the big obstacle is that you're facing, so I can help you overcome it and get out of here?" I rest my head against the cement wall, waiting.

When he doesn't say anything, I sneak a peek into his room. He sits on a chair, his dirty T-shirt wadded in his fist, lines of worry etched on his face. His lips pulled down into an anxious frown.

"What's wrong?" I ask, forgetting myself and hurrying over to kneel beside him. As soon as his eyes lift to mine, I sense the overwhelming feelings of stress and exhaustion. I place my hand on his and say what I've never said to any other guy in my whole life. "It's going to be okay. I'm... here for you."

Just then, darkness envelops the house.

The power has gone out.

27

No Confession

ALISA

My eyes adjust instantly to the sudden darkness, and I can see perfectly, but I freeze, kneeling beside Brecken. He jumps up and runs right past me to the stairs.

I hear Sophie crying. "The microwave won't work," she sniffs, holding an uncooked bowl of oatmeal.

Brecken puts his arm around his little sister, and then glances at me. "I told you so."

"You did?" Sophie answers, wiping her wet cheeks.

"It's still no reason to resort to crime," I mumble.

"Not you, honey. I'm talking to my... my imaginary friend," Brecken says, consoling his little sister.

Heidi walks in, shaking her head in disgust. "I'm so sick of this. I'm calling Dad."

"Maybe he'll wire us some money." Brecken heaves a heavy sigh and falls onto the couch, his legs draped over the side. "This is so stupid!"

Brecken's dad promises to send enough money to pay not only their power bill, but to buy groceries too. There is even enough to go to the zoo. But while we wait to hear back from the bank, Brecken and I visit in living room. The girls play outside.

"Now do you understand the situation we're in?" Brecken says. "My dad can't always send money when he's gone." He leans over his knees, his hand shielding his eyes. "And the bank's only open in the morning on Saturdays. I hope they hurry."

"Yeah, I get it, but it doesn't change the fact that if you'd been caught, you could have gone to jail," I say. "Would that be better for Heidi and Sophie?"

Silence fills the room and Brecken refuses to answer. He knows I'm right, but doesn't want to admit it. My heart softens and I lean forward, sure he can see me.

"It worked out this time." I pat his hand, not sure if I should continue where I left off downstairs in his room. Against my better judgment, I do. "I meant what I said before. You can trust me. I can be a friend." I don't know why I promise this. I hardly like him, and I can't wait to leave. I have no patience for his life of crime, but the words come unbidden from my heart, so I let them spill like cool water over parched earth. They have the desired effect.

He gazes softly into my eyes and smiles. "You know, I don't have any regular friends who are girls."

"Why?"

He looks away and rolls his eyes.

"I've never had any guy friends either."

He glances at me, surprised and suspicious. He wonders if I'm lying. I can feel it, but he laughs and shakes his head.

"Nope. Never," I say, reinforcing the truth.

"Why?"

"Uh... " I'm not about to tell him the truth, that a lot of my hang-ups are connected to Mr. Roland, who has infiltrated my personal life. Since I died, I've learned that many of the decisions I've made were tainted because of him.

A rush of hate barrels through me. I stamp it down, trying to concentrate on Brecken instead of myself for once. Brecken looks vulnerable, and I have an overwhelming feeling of compassion for him—a result of my job as his guardian, I'm sure—and I really do want to help him, but my secrets are my own, and I'll keep them that way.

"Are you gay?" he asks, trying to playfully shove me. Instead, his hand goes right through me. "Are there such things as gay angels?" A wry smile appears on his face.

"No, I'm not gay, and I already told you. I'm not an angel." I move over to the door with my arms crossed over my chest. "Plus, being gay doesn't stop you from having friends of the opposite sex." I shouldn't have said that. Now he'll ask what my reason is, and I don't want to tell him. Maybe this is a good time to leave and be by myself. I'm not supposed to do that, but it's what comes natural.

"Alisa, wait."

With pursed lips, I turn, looking straight into his eyes. They seem so deep and black in the dim light. Something flutters in my chest and the urge to touch his hand pulls at me. Scowling, I push those weird feelings away.

"Tell me how you died."

I stare at him for a long moment, my mouth frozen, my mind blank. I don't want to admit the truth. That I'd been so weak, so depressed and lonely, that I couldn't hack it. It seems like a pathetic excuse now. All people have problems. All people struggle. Most don't go out and end their lives because of it.

He walks forward, his hand reaching out. It goes right through mine, but the sensation shakes me like an electric shock. Compassion, caring, and understanding warm through my soul, softening my resolve, melting my determination to leave.

He feels these things for *me*.

I study his face, his eyes—his unruly bangs that flop over his forehead. Who is this guy? He doesn't seem like an unfeeling/ druggy-loser to me anymore. He doesn't *feel* like a boy who sleeps around, gets drunk, or beats people up. Brecken—despite his wild behavior and appearance to the outside world—is kind, generous, and loving. If I can help him clean up his act even more, he'll be amazing.

He leans forward, his face serious. He really wants to know my story. "You can tell me, Alisa. I'll understand."

He might, but I can't risk it no matter how much I want to help him, no matter how much I want him to trust me or like me. Shaking my head and giving him a look of apology, I blink my eyes and disappear.

28

No Relief

ALISA

Once again, I flee home. I curl up on my bed in a ball like I used to when life seemed overwhelming. Gram's words come back to me again. Mr. Roland interrupts my life. How can I forgive someone who did something so heinous that my every waking moment is torment and my every nightmare carries his face? I don't know how to let go. I don't know how to heal.

After a while, I sit up. The house is quiet, so I peek into my parent's room, and then check Ty's room, two doors down from mine. All empty. I debate floating through the floor to Derek's room, but I'll just find the same thing. Nothing.

I have to get back to my work, but for a moment more, I bask in the familiarity I miss so much, floating to the living room, and running my fingers across the ivory keys of our grand piano. I come to rest on the hard, black bench, all the music I've memorized rushing to the forefront of my mind. I yearn to hear that music streaming from my fingers again... but I can't press the keys. I can't do anything without a body. I threw mine away, and now more than ever, I wish for it back.

Wallowing in self-pity, I drown in my misery until I can't stand to be with myself any longer. I have to do something. In the past, I would have called Natty. Where is a heavenly phone when you need one? As soon as the thought crosses my mind, the unnerving tug and pull of spirit travel pulls me from my house in an unwelcome flash of energy.

A moment later, I find myself in the all-too-familiar living room of Natty's old house. The house that has become a memory of torture for both her and me.

For a moment, I stand frozen, anticipating hyperventilation. Memories whirl in a tornado of confusion. Why did I come *here?*

I search the room. Very little has changed. The same flower-print couch rests against the back wall; the same matching end tables hold the same brass lamps. The painted walls now sport a lighter shade of brown, and there's hardwood where carpet used to be, but that is the only difference.

Some strange force in the pit of my soul pulls me down the long hall toward Natty's old bedroom. I stand in the threshold and peek in, seeing light blue, newly painted walls with baseball posters tacked up. There's a toy-box in the corner. The unmade bed screams this is no longer Natty's room.

I back up and glance toward the kitchen—sick curiosity taking hold of me. There's a door in there that leads to the basement, and like all horror movies, all the bad stuff happened in the basement.

I can't stop myself even though every fiber of my being cries out for me to turn around and run. The brass door handle is locked. Has that lock always been there? It's been years since I've been down there, and I certainly don't want to go down now, so why do I feel compelled to descend these stairs?

Pushing through the door, I take that first step. Darkness envelopes me, but I see with perfect clarity. Spider webs hang from the rafters with eerie daintiness—their delicate threads decorating the ceiling with scalloped dust. I enter the room of horrors—a ten by twelve area of cement and two-by-fours. Memories smash their way through my brain, forcing me to re-experience those tortured moments with stunning accuracy.

I'm twelve years old, wearing a pink and white sundress my mom sewed for my birthday. I sit on a wooden crate down in the basement where Mr. Roland led me. I watch him approach, a sticky-sweet smile on his puffy, flushed face.

"I'm so glad you came over today," he says. "Natty gets so lonely." He moves closer and squats before me, his hands resting on my bare knees.

Vomit rises in my throat, but I'm too afraid to cry out or show my fear. My breathing hitches, and I hug my arms close to my chest.

Maybe he won't hurt me today. Maybe he's just being friendly. Maybe he'll take my hand and lead me upstairs into the safety of the afternoon sunshine.

"I get lonely too," he says, his hand sliding up my leg.

Instantly, raw fear, so powerful I can't control it, takes over. I come back to the present, screaming with feral terror, falling to my knees. Dry sobs wrench violently through my mind. I can hardly think, can hardly stand to relive it.

"Help me," I whisper to whoever is listening. In the blink of an eye, I materialize back in *Idir Shaol*, rocked to the soothing tones of Gram's voice.

"Shh, darling. Everything will be all right."

I don't know how long I sit there, wrapped in the comfort of Gram's arms, but after a moment, I pull back and gaze into her bright blue eyes. "I'm a basket case," I say, feeling like I should be wiping tears from my face.

"No, you're perfectly normal."

"Now you're lying." I smile and look down at my hands clasped in my lap. "I don't even know what normal is."

"It's you," she says, smoothing back my hair.

"I think you're right, Gram. About Mr. Roland, I mean."

"I know," she whispers, squeezing my hand. "You'll get there. Don't worry."

I'm not sure I believe her. I don't know if I'll ever get there; if I'll ever be purged of the hate and anger I feel toward that vile man. "I should get back. Brecken probably needs me."

Gram faces me with a proud grin. "Yes. That is exactly what you should do. I'm so proud of you, Alisa. You've grown so much."

"You think?"

"Oh, yes. You're doing wonderfully." She takes my face in her hands and kisses me, then draws me in for a hug. "I'll see you again soon."

I smile and squeeze back. "I love you so much."

29

New Resolve

BRECKEN

Brecken stares at the empty space where Alisa just stood. She's gone. Just like that. Just like always.

Somehow, she has gotten under his skin, and his desire to make her leave is wavering. And then what does she do? She leaves of her own accord when he *doesn't* want her to. He kind of likes having her around... just to hear her sarcastic comments that make him laugh, not that he would ever admit it to her.

But he can tell she is holding back, not wanting to share her story. He understands. He feels the same way most of the time. The less people know, the easier life is. But Alisa makes him want to talk, to share. He wants to unburden his heartache, his worries, to her. He feels she might understand, that she'll be there for him, just like she said. Can he trust her? He wants to.

He thinks back to their last moment. The sadness in her eyes and the slump of her shoulders as she disappeared. She's hurting. He can feel it, and he wants to help her to heal.

A part of him forgives her for leaving when things get uncomfortable. But another part of him grows irritated. It seems that leaving is her answer to everything. For once, he'd like to see her be strong, the way she always nags him to be.

The hypocrisy of their situation slaps him hard in the face. She wants him to turn his life around and be a "good boy," yet she has some serious issues she won't admit or confront either, let alone talk to him about.

The more he thinks about it, the more frustrating it gets. He'll tell her exactly what he thinks when she comes back. But right now, he needs to focus on his sisters. He doesn't want to ruin their day with a bad attitude. His mother's sweet voice and calming words come to mind. "Wherever you go, no matter the weather, always bring your own sunshine." She'd heard it somewhere and had loved it, repeating it to them daily. He couldn't forget the quote even if he tried.

He forces a smile and calls to his sisters. "Get your stuff, guys. It's time to go." They'll go to the zoo, eat hot dogs, watch the elephants, and have a wonderful time. Brecken intends to force himself to have fun, to be fun, to laugh and act like he hasn't a care in the world... for his sisters.

30

A Day at the Zoo

ALISA

With a sigh, I appear in the backseat of an old Ford Taurus. Their mom's old car. I sit beside Sophie as she holds a doll and whispers to herself as she plays. Heidi and Brecken sit in the front, neither saying much. After a few minutes, we pull up to a beautiful, red brick home with three white gables and a black front door that gleams in the sun. Lovely shrubbery decorates the yard and walkway. The house oozes money. I almost expect a doorman to appear.

"Just one sec," Heidi says, jumping out of the car. "I'll get her."

A moment later, a girl Heidi's age bounds out the front door, her blonde A-line surrounding her creamy-white face. She wears expensive clothes I recognize. The kind I *used* to wear. Sketchers, Abercrombie and Fitch shorts, an Aeropostale T-shirt. A cute little clutch hangs over one shoulder.

I miss clothes like that.

"Hi Madison!" Sophie calls from the back seat.

The door opens beside me and Heidi slides in, pushing me to the middle, letting Madison sit in front beside Brecken. The girl stares at him, and I can't help but giggle at her obvious infatuation.

Brecken's head whips around, searching for the creator of that giggle. I duck down, not that it matters. It's too bright for him to see me. Although I'm pretty sure he senses me in the back seat.

"What's the matter, Breck?" Heidi asks. "Who are you looking for?"

He catches her eye and shakes his head. "Just thought I saw...

a car coming. No big deal."

Heidi turns and looks out the back window. "Well, let's go before it gets too hot."

A fresh breeze blows softly as we meander along the Zoo's winding paths. I stay behind, following in Brecken's wake, watching the dynamics of this little family. Tall trees sway and aromatic flowers grow with abundance. The reptile building smells musky, the sour odor surrounding us like a cloud. Even in my spirit state, I can smell it.

I watch Brecken, amazed at the way he treats his sisters—so patient, so... nice. Granted, my brothers mostly treated me the same way, but Brecken... well, he just doesn't look the type. He looks like the guy who will snarl and hiss if you get too close.

I step close—so close I can smell his cologne. I take a deep whiff, liking whatever it is he wears, wishing I could smell it better. He turns, hearing my inhalation, but doesn't say anything.

I can still hear Heidi saying, *"Did you take your pill?"*

I'm relaxed and playful here at the zoo and I begin to wonder what Brecken would do if I teased him like I used to tease my own brothers. I miss that lighthearted bantering and want to have a little fun. I place my hand on top of his head and try to ruffle his hair. I can't really mess it up. I don't know how to move objects—if that's even possible, but Brecken knows I'm there.

He swirls around, dropping Sophie's hand, accidentally smacking Madison on the arm.

"Ow!" she howls. "What are you doing?"

He searches the area, smoothing his hair. "Nothing. It was... my hair's messy."

"I don't think your hair could get any messier," Heidi says with a derisive chuckle.

"Very funny," he says.

"I like your hair, Brecken. I think it's cool." Madison grins up at him with eyes of adoration. She sidles up, standing closer than necessary.

Once we start walking again, I take Brecken's hand in mine. This was my favorite thing to do with my older brother, Derek. He'd always try to shake away, irritated. I loved embarrassing him. Just like I suspect, Brecken jumps and tries to shake me away. I laugh in spite of myself. He dances around looking like an acrobat.

The girls stop and stare.

When Brecken realizes he is the center of attention, he stops, taking a deep breath. "I'm going to the restroom. I'll catch up to you at the giraffes."

The girls scowl and walk off without him. Madison is clearly disappointed.

"Oh man. That was funny!" I laugh and slap my knee. "You should have seen your face." I do my best impression of him, dancing around, shaking my contaminated hand.

"Cute. Real cute and very mature." He walks the other way, a few four-letter words drifting on the air back to me.

"Oh, come on, Brecken. I was just playing."

"No. You're trying to make me look stupid, like I really *do* need medication, and I don't like it." He stares hard in my direction.

I stick out my chin. "Fine. Be a baby. Whatever."

Brecken's eyes squint and he walks away.

I follow. "Geez. I just wanted to have some fun. I miss my brothers. That's all. I didn't mean to make you mad."

He stops abruptly and turns. "You have brothers?"

"Uh, yeah."

"Really?" He crosses his arms over his chest. "What are their names?"

Does he not believe me? Does he think I'm lying? Why does he even care? These aren't questions a charge is supposed to ask their guardian. Charges aren't even supposed to *see* his guardian! This whole thing isn't right.

"Tyler and Derek," I say, finally.

"Uh huh. Older or younger?"

With a sigh, I say, "Ty is twelve and Derek is eighteen. There.

Happy?"

He smiles and continues up the trail. "For the moment."

"So, there are three kids in your family?" I ask, wanting to learn as much about him as I can. Siblings seem like a safe place to start since he asked about mine.

"Yep."

"And your mom died?"

I'm rewarded with a nod.

"I'm really sorry, Brecken. My mom almost died the other day too. If I hadn't been there to—"

"What? When? Before you died or since you've been here with me?"

"Uh, since I came to be with you," I answer honestly.

"Wow," he says. "I never thought about you people having families. Weird."

"Well, I did have a life before you, you know. We don't just sit up there on pink clouds playing harps."

A wry smile slides onto his face. "Good thing. All us mortals would go deaf."

"Hey!" I say, laughing. "I took piano lessons my whole life. I rock on the piano." I fold my arms across my chest, daring him to argue.

"I'd like to see that," he says softly. "Really."

The mood changes so quickly that I'm at a loss for words, but I want to share my latest dramas with someone. "Oh, Brecken. It was so cool seeing my family again. I miss them so much, but they're really screwed up, and I think it's my fault." I shouldn't share these things, and there's nothing he can do to help anyway, but I'm so lonely for a friend who might understand.

We stop under a gnarled tree and sit on a bench at the gorilla's encampment.

"I can see you," he says, in wonder reaching out to touch me. "Tell me about your death, Alisa. Please. I want to know." It's the pleading in his voice gets me. But does he want to know about *my* death, or death in general? I figure it's death in general. Because of his mom.

Facing him, I study his features for sincerity and place my hand on his. His concern washes over me. I've never felt these emotions from anyone besides my family and Natty. How wonderful it is to feel it from him too. It makes me careless and I decide to confess the truth.

"Well... I guess the only way to say it, is to say it right out." I take a deep breath and jump, figuratively speaking. "I killed myself."

"You... killed yourself?" He leans away in surprise. "Why would you do that?" He frowns, his expression going from astonishment, to horror, to anger. "So many people with horrible diseases are fighting to live. How could you do that to your family?" His expression turns from anger to disgust. Shock zings through me, and I can't think of a thing to say. This is not the reaction I anticipated.

"I thought you'd died of cancer or something." He lurches to his feet and paces in a circle. "I can't believe it."

"My best friend died of cancer a few months before me. My Grandmother, who I was super close to, died before that. I couldn't deal with it. You don't know." I plead for him to understand, my arms outstretched.

"That's just... selfish."

He stares at me in astonishment, and I stare back, unable to move. The rejection burns like hot wax, slowly melting my confidence. Any feelings Brecken and I have developed up to this point are gone, and what I get from him now is contempt. I have no words for how much it hurts.

"I can't have a guardian angel who committed suicide," he whispers angrily. "I'm barely making it as it is! What help could you possibly be? You couldn't even handle your *own* life."

He's right. I don't know anything. I hadn't known how to live myself. I'd copped out. Given up. I'm a failure, and now I'm supposed to show Brecken the way?

"I... I'm sorry," I murmur.

He jerks away and storms down the path without looking back.

31

Running Away

ALISA

I don't go home. I can't. No one is there anyway. I'm not sure where my brothers are, but I don't feel like looking for them. Instead, I picture Gram—her blue eyes, her white hair, her loving face. But instead of appearing at her side, I appear in *Idir Shaol*. Back to the place I most want to leave.

I hurry to my cottage, wondering if they've given my bed away. As soon as I see my familiar blue and white quilt, relief floods through me. I fall onto the bedspread, hiding my face in its downy softness.

It isn't long before I feel a warm hand on my back.

"Alisa?"

I'm so embarrassed to be caught blubbering once again. "Shana?" Her soft expression and loving concern do me in and emotion gets the better of me. I start to cry.

She puts her arms around me and pulls me close. "What happened?"

"I can't do this. It's too hard. You have no idea. It's impossible. There's no way I can help him. I can't even help myself. Plus, he can *see* me and hear me too. Can you believe that?" I ramble on, complaining, crying, and generally feeling sorry for myself. When I finish, Shana brushes my hair back and smiles.

"He can see you? Wow. That's not normal, but... cool."

"It's *not* cool. It makes it really hard. How am I supposed to influence him when he can ask me questions right back? He asked me how I died."

"He did? What did you say?" Her face lights with interest and she slides closer.

I take a long breath, searching her eyes. "The truth. I told him the truth. I thought we were becoming friends. That he would understand. He didn't."

"Oh, Alisa. I'm so sorry." She hugs me again. "But you haven't failed yet. It's not uncommon for guardians to come back to *Idir Shaol* for various reasons during their assignment. Sometimes guardians need help or advice from Raphael."

"Really? How come no one ever told *me* that?" I can't believe they'd leave me in the dark about something so crucial. I thought I was totally on my own, and now betrayal hovers around me like an itchy blanket even though I try to push it away.

She laughs and socks me gently in the arm like Natty used to. "Anaita talked about it during class. Remember?"

No. I don't remember. What a surprise.

"Come on," she says. "Let's go see Raphael."

Raphael reclines in his office chair, his fingers intertwined over his stomach. His serious expression does little to help me feel better, and he doesn't say anything. Just waits for me to talk.

"I didn't realize I could come back if I needed to. I must have missed that part in class." Nervously I pick at my white robe, brushing off invisible dirt. "And uh, I want to talk about my charge. Um, I'm not sure I'm a good fit for this assignment."

"Oh?"

"Yeah, because he can see and hear me."

"Yes. I told you he had special abilities. Remember?"

I clear my throat and continue. "About that. I must have dozed off in our interview or something."

"Spirits don't doze off, Alisa." He leans forward on his desk, gazing intently into my eyes. "They may tune out, not pay attention, or even ignore you, but they don't doze off."

"Right." As embarrassing as it is to admit I hadn't listened to him, it's worse to admit that I failed my task after only a few days. I can't go back anyway. Brecken knows I killed myself. He won't let me help him even if I hold him at gunpoint.

With an audible sigh, Raphael shakes his head. "I admit it seems daunting, but that's all part of overcoming impossible obstacles. Did you think it would be simple? That you'd walk in and Brecken would turn his life around with a snap of your fingers?"

Actually, yeah. That's kind of what I thought. "No, I didn't think that. It's just that he knows I committed suicide and now he won't listen to me."

"How could he possibly know that, Alisa?" He gazes at me with a knowing smile, and I wither before him. If he is trying to make me feel stupid, he has succeeded on a grand scale.

I stand up. This is getting me nowhere. I'll just go back to my cottage and wait out my sentencing. Maybe I'll get a soft spot on the grass next to Mr. Roland. As I open the door, Raphael calls out to me.

"Alisa. You haven't failed yet. In fact, you're doing wonderfully. In a case like this, you have to let a friendship grow. You have to get him to trust you, to trust that you know more than he does, so he'll listen to you. He's hurting and knows his words were wrong. I'll tell you one more thing. His mother died of breast cancer, fighting to live, fighting to stay with her family, fighting for each painful breath. The fact that you so casually threw away your life was more than he could comprehend at the time. Go back. He'll forgive you."

I nod and walk out the door. I know that taking my own life was wrong, and I totally understand about his mother. I would have felt the same way in his shoes. I'll tell him I'm sorry. I'll beg his forgiveness and prove I can be humble, no matter how much it hurts. I'll go straight back to Brecken because Raphael is right. I can't give up yet. I've tormented my brothers for much longer than I have Brecken. I still have fuel inside me.

32

Fury Unleashed

BRECKEN

She killed herself. Killed herself! Ended her own life. Her words pound through Brecken's mind over and over and over. He can't stop them. Can't get her voice out of his head, the way she said it... as though only admitting she ate the last cookie. She doesn't seem remorseful at all, and she expects him to tell her it's okay?

Isn't she sorry? All she has are excuses and he refuses to listen to those. He can only think of his mother lying in that hospital bed, the beeping machines surrounding her. Her face so pale, her eyes so sunken.

She fought to live for two years.

With every surgery, the doctors cut a little bit more of her away. She didn't want to die. No one in that hospital did. To think of all the patients he'd grown to know day after day. All those people praying, crying, and trying to live.

How could Alisa have done this to her family? Brecken clutches his face, wanting to rip all thoughts of his guardian out of his head. He hates her. Hates her with herculean fury. He won't let her stay now. There is no way he will tolerate her presence, and if she ever comes back, he'll tell her to go to hell!

33

Silver Teeth

ALISA

I close my eyes, picture Brecken, and try to block out the pain-filled expression I last saw on his face. A smile flits across my lips as I appear next to him on his front porch. He sits in a shady spot watching his sisters play at the park. As soon as I materialize, he stiffens and looks up. My heart softens at the hurt in his eyes.

"You're back." He plucks a lonely sliver of grass from beside the porch and sticks it between his mouth.

"Yep."

"Why?"

"Because you need me... and I need you."

With a snort, he stands up and leans against the cool bricks on his house. "You know, when you first left, I... I was so angry, I hated you. I promised myself I'd *never* forgive you. That if you ever came back..." He shakes his head and looks away.

I hesitate, knowing all of those feelings haven't completely gone away. He's still angry deep down, I'm sure. "What changed your mind?"

He glances at me and throws his blade of grass on the ground. "Because only a few days ago, I felt like ending it all too."

"Oh, Brecken. Please let me explain. You don't know me, but I want you to." I move over beside him, ready to spill my guts, but a sleek, black sports car pulls up to the curb, its engine revving loudly in the quiet afternoon.

And guess who sits in the driver's seat.

"Hey Jilly," Brecken calls, jogging toward the car. She rolls down the passenger side window and he leans in, smiling. He reaches over, pulls her across the seat, and kisses her.

Ack. I'm gonna puke.

When he stands back up, he turns and smiles at me. "See you later, Alisa." He opens the car door and slides inside. Smoke wafts up from the squealing tires as they pull away.

Does he actually think he can ditch me that easily? He just doesn't get it. Moments later, I appear on a soft, brown leather seat. The air conditioning blasts my face, but I don't really feel the cold. I *can* feel its tornado-like strength whipping through the car though.

Brecken stiffens in the front seat, and I decide to be as irritating as possible since he left right when I'd decided to open up to him. "So, where are we going?"

He doesn't answer but turns to Jill. "Hey babe. What's the plan? Something dangerous, I hope?" He leans over and nibbles at her neck.

"Disgusting," I whisper under my breath.

He glances at the back seat and smiles. This is his passive/aggressive way of getting even.

Rude.

Jill flashes a smile at Brecken. "Umm, I have a surprise for you, Breck. Something I've been thinking about doing for a long time. It's something I've been learning about, and I think it would be super special for us, you know? It will bring us closer."

Uh oh. I don't like the sound of this. I can picture all sorts of things that could bring them closer, and I don't want to witness any of them. Leaning forward, I rest my arms on the back of the front seat. "Brecken, whatever this is, please don't do it. I don't have a good feeling."

"Sounds great, Jilly. Can't wait."

We drive in silence to the other side of town. To the side of town where Heidi's friend, Madison, lives. We stop in front of a grandiose home, complete with white marble pillars. The home of a wealthy southern bell.

"Come on." Jill takes Brecken's hand and pulls him out the driver's side door.

Of course I follow, staring at their clasped hands. I stare at Jill's perfect butt, looking for more things about her I can hate. She wears pink flip-flops, white short-shorts, and a pink T-shirt that's way too tight.

She looks slutty, cheap, and desperate.

On the other hand, looking at Brecken sends a ripple of pleasure through me. Maybe it's his edginess, or the holes in his jeans and how they show his tan skin beneath. I like the messy lock of hair that never stays out of his eyes. Even his wily smile is endearing.

We enter the house and Jill pulls Brecken through the foyer, past a beautifully carved mahogany staircase, through an expensively tiled kitchen, to a white door.

"Okay. Close your eyes and promise not to peek," she says. We descend into a cement-walled basement.

This can't be good.

Jill doesn't turn on the lights, so it has got to be dark for them. For me, it's just plain creepy. The wooden stairs creak beneath their feet and the handrail rocks loosely away from the wall. Why is this area of the house so derelict when the rest is so fancy?

Landing at the bottom of the stairs, I realize we aren't in an unfinished basement at all, but a wine cellar. The far wall houses hundreds of slots, each filled with a dusty bottle of wine, and in the far corner, a multicolored blanket hangs, blocking our view.

"Keep your eyes closed," Jill says again, gazing at Brecken's face to make sure he isn't cheating. She takes him to the curtain, pulls it aside, and then ushers him in.

I pass right through the thick fabric and stop in surprise. Four heavy blankets make a square room of about eight by eight feet. Against one quilt stands a low, narrow table filled with tapered candles and tiny, white tea-lights. Jill takes a match, strikes it, and begins lighting the candles. A brocade rug lies on the floor and colored scarves have been draped here and there to give it a gypsy's fortune-telling look. I have to admit, I like it. It's cozy.

Sidling up to Brecken, Jill says, "Okay. You can look now."

Brecken opens his eyes and they widen in surprise. He turns

in a slow circle, taking in every inch of the constructed room. "Wow. This is great, Jilly. I love it. Did *you* do all this?"

"Yep. For us."

He pulls her into a tight hug and kisses her slowly. "It's awesome," he whispers. "But why? If we want privacy, we can find it anywhere." He nuzzles her neck and winks at me. Why is he doing this? He must think it affects me somehow. Boys are so stupid.

She pulls away and socks him in the arm. "This room isn't for *that*, silly. It's for something else. Something better."

"Better? Is there such a thing?"

She laughs and drags him to the center of the rug where they sit down. "This is definitely going to be better." She points to the ceiling and the walls. "This basement is insulated. It's totally private, and I can lock the door at the top of the stairs."

"O-kay," he says, cocking his head, a question in his voice.

Jill's eyes glow with excitement and she reaches out to take both his hands. "Do you ever think about death, Brecken?"

I can't help but frown. Where is she going with this? I suspect Brecken thinks about death all the time, considering his mother recently died.

He gives the makeshift room another cursory glance and nods his head. "Sometimes."

"Me too. *All* the time. That's why I built this room." She slips a book out from under the low table and holds it on her lap, running her hand over its embossed cover. "A friend gave this to me." She lays it between them.

Becoming One, the title reads.

I have no idea what the book is about, but as soon as I lay eyes on it, I take a step back. "I don't know what that book is, Brecken, but I have a bad feeling about it. I really do. I think we should leave."

He glances up, able to see me easily in the dim light of the candles. I stand behind Jill, staring hard into his face.

"Wow. You're... beautiful," he says breathlessly.

He can't be talking to me. He doesn't even like me.

"Thank you," Jill answers demurely.

"You radiate light like I've never seen before." He closes his eyes as though basking in the warmth of my luminescence.

"Are you talking to *me*?" I ask in disbelief.

"Oh, Brecken. You don't know how wonderful that makes me feel," Jill says, scooting closer so their crossed legs touch at the knees. "I love you so much." She runs her hand along his jaw, and I want to smack it away. That's not her face to touch!

Wait. What?

"You don't see it," he says to me, stating it as fact.

"Don't see what?" Jill asks, confused. "I see you, if that's what you mean. I see our love. We can be connected forever, Breck. This book taught me how."

"Huh? What?" He glances at Jill, seeming surprised she's even speaking.

"Breck. Are you listening to me?"

He looks softly into her eyes, and says, "Are we going to have a séance or something?"

"Or something," she says sullenly. "But I don't want to tell you about it if you're not going to listen. This is important to me."

"All right. I'm listening. Go ahead." He holds her hands, staring intently into her shining, blue eyes.

Jill's shoulders relax, and she takes a deep breath. "Okay. Here goes. I've been studying this book. It explains how to fuse your soul with another person's... forever."

"Really? That sounds cool," he answers, looking up at me, all aspects of his teasing gone.

"I know, right?" She rises to her knees, still holding his hands. "It's the coolest thing I've ever read, and my friend has been teaching me how to do it. I want to try it with you."

"Okay. I'm up for it," he says.

"Good. So, I need to ask you a question. Do you know why vampires love to suck the blood of their victims?"

"What?" Brecken pulls back with a frown. "This isn't some Twilight thing, is it?"

"Just listen."

Jill's impatience rises in waves to bathe my face. I'm still behind her because I want to be able to watch Brecken, but I'm tempted to move over by him. Maybe close proximity will help me influence him better.

"One of the reasons they love to suck each other's blood is because it connects them more powerfully than anything else. More than sex even." She stops for a moment and gazes into Brecken's eyes, scooting even closer. "Blood is a living thing, so in that moment they share their blood, they transcend heaven and earth. They become one in spirit, one in mind, one in body."

"That's a bunch of bull crap, Brecken." I cross my arms over my chest and frown. He has to know how stupid this sounds.

"I don't believe in vampires, Jilly," he says with a chuckle. "Those stories are written to give people a good scare. That's all. There's no such thing."

Jill's eyes narrow as she purses her lips. "I'm not talking about vampires like Dracula, who turn into bats, Brecken. I'm talking about real people like you and me who use tools to do it—sharp teeth they place over their own to drink the blood of their lover. It's very primal, very spiritual. I think we should try it." She pulls a small, wooden box with a hinged lid from the table and places it before him. When she opens the lid, two sets of gleaming, silver vampiric teeth reflect in the soft candlelight.

"Brecken, listen to me," I hurry to say. "This is bad. This is *really* bad. You have to know that."

He ignores me and picks up one set of fangs from the crushed red velvet, then touches the tip. "Ouch!" A bead of blood appears. He starts to put his finger in his mouth, but before he can, Jill reaches over, grasps his hand, and draws his finger into her mouth. She sucks his blood with a moan of pleasure.

This is horror film 101, and we are heading somewhere terrible, somewhere I refuse to go. I can't watch, and yet, I can't look away or leave Brecken.

Before any intelligent solutions enter my mind, Jill takes the other set of teeth and stabs *her* finger. A crimson drop of blood blossoms, ready to spill over her fingertip. Before it can drip, she slides her finger into Brecken's mouth.

34

Another Deception

ALISA

I nearly gag. Brecken doesn't think it's fabulous either, because instead of being turned on, seduced, or hypnotized—I'm not sure what Jill is going for—Brecken opens his mouth and pulls her finger out *without* swallowing the bright red liquid that stains his lip. He wipes it away with his arm.

"Uh, Jill?" he says kindly. "I don't think this is for me."

"Brecken." She leans forward. "You have no idea how good it can feel. She presses him back until he lies on the floor. She moves over him slowly, bringing her lips to his. He doesn't push her away.

It's like he has forgotten I'm even here. Why won't he listen? A cold ball of anger wells up inside me. If I could rip her hair out by the roots, I would. Instead, I clear my throat and squat down beside his face. "Excuse me, pretty boy. But I'm bored with this b-rated romance flick. Can we please get out of here?"

He opens one eye and smiles while continuing to kiss Jill. He even wraps his arms around her waist.

He's at it again. Trying to make me jealous. Why would he even do that? I'm half-tempted to kick him in the head, but I doubt he'd even feel it. "Do you care about me at all, Brecken?" I ask in total seriousness.

He stops his make-out session abruptly. "What?"

"I didn't say anything, baby," Jill answers. She goes right back to kissing his face, his neck, his collarbone.

I look him right in the eyes, trying with all my heart to make him understand. "If you feel anything for me—anything at all, you'll leave with me now. Please."

He searches my face, and then his eyes close for a moment,

as though in pain. He gently pushes Jill away.

She sits up with a confused expression. "What's wrong?"

He gazes at her, a frown forming as he studies her at arm's length. "Jill. Your aura. It's... muddy."

"My aura?" she repeats. "So what?"

"It's just that it's a brown color." He pushes her back further to scrutinize her face.

"What's that supposed to mean?" she says with a glare, her jaw clenching.

He squints as though trying to get a better look, as though trying to clear up a puzzle. "I've never seen it like this before."

She shakes her head. "Don't start with that crap again, Brecken. You know I don't believe in it."

"We've talked about this before, Jill. It's not like you don't know I see it," he says. "It helps me know what people are feeling, what *you're* feeling."

Anger radiates from her. She's ready to explode, but instead of screaming, she smiles. "You're right, Brecken. You're always right. You're obviously not ready to embrace this, so we'll do something different instead. Okay?"

Brecken releases a breath and nods. "Sure. But I really should get going. I don't like leaving Heidi and Sophie for so long."

"Yeah, I know," she says. "Will you do me just one favor before you go? Close your eyes for one second."

With a reluctant sigh, he says, "All right, but this has to be quick."

"Oh, it will be."

Jill takes her fangs and dips them into a shallow bowl of liquid that sits on the table. She blows them dry, and before I can blink, she places them in her mouth, bends forward, and sinks the needle-like fangs deep into Brecken's bicep.

His eyes fly open and he shoves her away. "Ow! Damn it, Jill!" He stares at the puncture which blossoms red on his arm. His eyes flick to mine in confusion.

Jill steps away.

After a few seconds, Brecken falls forward, one hand reaching out for balance, his other hand rubbing his glazed, sleepy eyes. With a moan, he lets himself fall all the way to the floor, his head bumping against the carpet-covered cement.

Jill is motionless, staring at Brecken's prone figure, a serious expression on her usually dim-witted face. She says nothing.

Kneeling at Brecken's side, my hands flutter desperately as my mind whirls, searching for a solution. I come up with nothing. I'm horrified that Jill would hurt someone she supposedly loves. What kind of a person can react so coldly, with such calculation?

After a moment, she wraps her long, white fingers around his wrist, checking his pulse. She shows no sign of worry. Only the frigid expression of an ice-queen. She lays Brecken out flat and adjusts his arms. Then, instead of bandaging his seeping bicep, she pulls his arm out to the side and lays her head on his chest. She wraps his arm around her, and places her lips on the delicate skin around the wound.

And sucks.

35

Her Darkness Revealed

ALISA

There is no way I can sit back and watch Jill drink Brecken's blood. And even though I've never tried to force my will on anyone, I know my mind has more power in one square centimeter than she has in her whole body. At least, that's what was told in *Idir Shaol*. I can supposedly make things happen by sheer force of will, but I've never tried it. I've never felt a need to.

With my hands fisted, every bit of fine matter in my spirit is focused on Jill. Narrowing my eyes so I can see only her, I picture a white-hot dart of fury, flying like a bullet from my mind into hers, exploding in the soft recesses of her buttery brain.

Nothing happens.

She continues to suck, a serene expression gracing her blissfully oblivious face. I can't even describe how she sickens me. I close my eyes, forcing a calm to come over me, forcing my mind to slow down—this time without the interference of frustration or anger—and send a silent message into her mind.

"Stop."

A strange expression comes over Jill's face, and her sucking slows. Her brows knit together in question, she sits up, wiping her mouth with the back of her hand. The sudden burst of energy I'd used is gone, and I fall forward onto my hands, fatigued, limp, and mentally exhausted. I can hardly move as I watch the scene unfold in slow motion. Jill grabs a Band-Aid and unceremoniously rips it open, slapping it down on the white skin of Brecken's inner arm. She lies down next to him, snuggling close to his side while the candles burn, flickering lower and lower, their melted wax making a thick puddle on the table.

Dark shadows dance on the heavy quilts, and no sounds filter down from upstairs. Where are her parents? Doesn't anyone care where she is or what she does? When I was alive, my mother knew everything that went on in her house, where each of us was, and what we were doing. I swear she was psychic. I figured all moms had that gift.

After a moment, Jill falls asleep on the hard ground, a blanket spread over them. I kneel before Brecken and smooth my ghost-like fingers down his cheek. He looks so peaceful, like an innocent little boy, like he must have looked as a child. Then I remember his sisters. He needs to wake up! He needs to get out of here. "Brecken! Wake up!"

He doesn't respond. He breathes in and out, his chest rising and falling, his lashes fluttering against his pale cheek. I'll have to wait for him to wake up on his own. Time slides by at a snail's pace. The one lone window across the room is small, and creates shadows that pass over us with the setting of the sun. Still, there's no movement or sound from upstairs.

Finally, Brecken begins to stir. His eyes flicker, an agonized groan escapes his lips, and he turns on his side, waking up Jill. He blinks repeatedly, his hand raised to his forehead.

Jill sits up in a hurry, fully cognizant. "Brecken? Are you okay?" She's full of concern as she brushes his hair from his forehead.

Oh, to stomp on her, to rip her hair out. To bite *her* arm!

"Baby. I was so worried!" She leans forward and kisses his lips tenderly, then traces them with her long, white fingers.

Seeing her touch him, lie to him, does something to me, and I snap. An uncontrollable righteous fury rises up inside me, and the only thing I see is her neck squeezed by my unrelenting fingers. I spring for her, determined to take her down, to pound her face into the cement floor.

But in spite of my indignation, I fly right through her and the quilt that hangs as a makeshift wall. I roll to a stop next to the wine bottles that line the basement shelves.

Rising, I stare at the blanket I barreled through. It sways back and forth. For a moment I'm mesmerized, watching the to and fro vacillation of the quilt. I made it move. I affected something in the physical world. Feeling stronger and even more determined than I had a moment ago, I stomp back inside the comfortable, candlelit room to witness Jill helping Brecken to a seated position. With her arm around him, she whispers words I can't hear.

I don't have time to figure it out. Brecken needs to wake up and get out of here before Jill decides she's hungry again. I kneel before Brecken, placing my hands over his, staring straight into his eyes. "Brecken, can you hear me? Can you see me?"

"Huh?" His head lolls with dizziness. "What happened?"

"You tripped on the rug and fell." Jill's explanation is ridiculous. He'll never believe it. He's not an idiot. "You hit your head pretty hard."

"I did?"

"Yeah, hun, you did, and if I hadn't been so worried, I would have laughed. You looked so funny at first, but you were only out for a minute. Everything's all right now. Can you get up?"

"Yeah. Sure." He shakes his head and tries to stand but loses his balance and stumbles forward, his hand catching on the low table. The candles sway, spilling their melted wax. Jill is quick to slip under his arm, taking his weight.

"Ow," he groans, noticing his bandaged arm for the first time.

"You cut yourself," she said. "You don't remember? Wow, baby, you must have hit your head hard."

That lying, sneaky, little... I bite my tongue and my chest heaves. Can't he see through her? Boys are beyond stupid. Dead or alive. My temper boils and there's nothing more frustrating than being helpless.

"Brecken, can you hear me?" I ask again.

He takes a step up the stairs. "Yeah." He answers with slurred detachment. His hands slide along the walls, grasping at the loose railing that rocks under his weight.

"You need to get home as soon as possible. Your sisters need you." He's not really clear minded enough to listen, but maybe thinking of his sisters will get him to move faster. He has such a soft spot for them. "You're dad's working late and they're getting scared. We have to hurry!"

"Yeah, okay. Hurry," he says, stumbling on the top stair.

"What?" Jilly turns to glance into his eyes.

"I need to get home."

She helps him to a chair at the kitchen table where he plops down, his elbows resting on the tabletop, holding his head. Rocking back and forth, he groans looking like he might pass out again.

"I'll make you some herbal tea before you go. How does that sound?" Jill says.

"My head is killing me."

"I'm not surprised with the thumping you gave it." She smiles at him, then takes a cup from the cupboard and drops a dry teabag in. She fills it with water and places it in the microwave. "This will be done in one minute." Taking down a bottle of Ibuprofen, she shakes out two white tablets. "Here. These should help." She sets a cold glass of water before him.

Brecken takes the pills without question.

What an idiot.

36

Stupid Boy

ALISA

The pills don't kill Brecken so they really must have been ibuprofen, but I'll never trust Jill again. She's not who she appears to be, her pretty face and perfect body covering up a dark and putrid heart. I know what her future holds if she doesn't do some drastic changing. She'll get a condo complete with a lava-filled hot tub right next to Mr. Roland.

After Brecken finishes his peppermint tea, she drives us home. I sit in the backseat and fume. Brecken's eyes are still slightly glazed even after she dumps him onto his living room couch. He lies there exhausted while she kisses his forehead.

"See you later, Breck. Hope you feel better."

"Yeah," I murmur as she closes his front door. "Later."

The dark circles beneath Brecken's eyes give him a hollow, ethereal look in the dim light of evening, and he probably won't remember any sort of conversation, but I can't wait any longer. "Brecken. We need to talk."

"Huh? Where are you?" He lifts his head and searches the living room. His sisters are nowhere around.

"I'm sitting in the tan La-Z-Boy." I move closer to sit right in front of him on the coffee table. "Can you see me now?"

"Uh... yeah. Kinda." His head falls back to the couch cushion. "Man, my head is killin' me."

"That's because she drugged you."

He squints and turns to his side, his cheek resting on his hand. "What?"

With a loud sigh and rolling eyes, I try to control my irritation. All sorts of sharp remarks are on the tip of my tongue, ready to spill over in a polluted downpour. I should wait to have this conversation, but I don't want to. He needs to know who Jill really is. "Jill told you that you pricked yourself with those stupid teeth things. Remember?"

"Yeah, and that I tripped on the carpet."

"Well, you didn't. She drugged you, and bit your arm, then sucked your blood like a freakin' vampire. I watched the whole thing."

He says nothing for a moment. "That's stupid."

"No kidding."

"Jilly would never do that."

I scowl at his stupidity. Never have I met anyone so blind or dense. "Why would I lie? I'm here to protect you."

He starts to nod, and then a sly grin spreads across his face. He wags his finger in my face. "You're jealous, aren't you? You're trying to make her look bad so I won't like her anymore."

Oh. My. Word. "You're an idiot."

"You think I'm se-xy. You want to kii-iiss me," he sings, the asinine grin still on his face. He falls back to a velvety pillow and chuckles.

My mouth opens and closes. Nothing witty springs to my mind. How dare he accuse me of... of... liking him!

"I knew it," he says. "It's cool. I get it. Lots of girls like me." He smiles stupidly, and his eyes close like he might fall asleep.

Fury burns in my chest and I let the flood spill forth without censor. "You really are dumb, aren't you? And just so we're clear, I *don't* want to kiss you, I *don't* think you're sexy, and I *don't* like you. Do you know why?"

"Why?"

I lean forward so he can see me clearly, our faces only inches apart. "Because... you're an idiot!"

I leave Brecken on the couch and reappear at the hospital next to my mother's bed. I have to get away from him, from his crooked smile and condemning words.

My mom sits alone, staring out the window. The TV is on, but she's not paying attention to it. Neither my brothers nor my dad are here to keep her company. I take her hand and brush it with my cheek. "You look better, Mom." She can't hear me, but maybe she can sense me like she did at my funeral. "You gave us quite a scare," I whisper.

She turns, a thoughtful expression on her face.

"Yeah, I'm here. Don't ever take those pills again."

She takes a deep breath, and tears fill her eyes.

"Oh, Mom. It's okay." The sting of invisible tears burn my own eyes as I climb onto the bed next to her. I lay my head on her chest with my arm around her waist like I used to when I was little. Memories rush to the forefront of my mind, memories that carry scents of cookies, Christmas, and bedtime stories. I close my eyes and breathe her in, hoping never to forget this feeling... just in case I never get the chance to be with her like this again.

I used to come home from school or a night out with Natty, and get in Mom's bed to tell her all about my day. She'd stroke my hair, nodding and commenting. That's how it feels now. Like she'll place her hand on my head any minute and wrap my hair around her fingers... like she used to.

She begins to speak, as though she knows I'm there, and her voice grows in strength. "Oh, Alisa. Where are you?"

Her question fills the silence and then she says, "You were so beautiful. I miss your smile, your beautiful brown eyes." She sighs, and a pregnant tear drips down her pale cheek. "I'm so sad all the time," she whispers to the wall.

"It's not your fault, Mom. It's no one's fault." My words sound empty. Even to me.

37

The Oldest Emotion

BRECKEN

*I*t takes a while for Brecken's head to clear, and the headache that pounds inside his brain keeps sledging away. He reclines on the couch with a package of frozen peas pressed to his forehead and tries to remember his conversation with Alisa.

He vaguely remembers arguing with her, but that is nothing new. He remembers her accusing Jill of drugging him, but he can't quite get it straight, because Jill wouldn't do that. She loves him. In fact, she has loved him for a long time, and he loves her too. But since Alisa arrived, some of his feelings for Jill have changed. He still cares about her, but it isn't that powerful rush of passion like before. Jill is beautiful, a close friend, comfortable and easy to talk to. Someone he shares a past with.

He's not certain what Alisa's problem is, but he's pretty sure it revolves around jealousy, and that changes everything. At least for him. He's mad that she left again, and he'll give her the cold shoulder when she comes back, just to make her squirm, but then they'll get over it.

He has felt drawn to Alisa from the beginning. There has always been something different about her, something intriguing, and thinking that maybe she's jealous of his closeness to Jill...Well, that is just plain interesting.

38

First Touch

ALISA

"You were gone a long time," Brecken says as soon as I show up. He's on the couch watching TV, staring straight ahead so he doesn't have to look at me. From the tightness of his shoulders and the set of his jaw, I can tell he's upset.

Not wanting to argue, I plop down in the La-Z-Boy recliner with a heavy sigh. "So, how are things?"

"Don't you think it's kind of rude to just leave like that?" He crosses his arms over his chest and glares at the TV.

"Umm, no. You were totally out of it."

"No?" He sits up and peers around the room, his eyes finally finding me. "You say all those... things, then disappear, and you don't think it's rude?"

A prick of irritation stabs at me, but I rein it in, not wanting another uncomfortable confrontation. "If you want to talk about rude, how about we refresh *your* memory, Brecken." I march over and stand before him with my hands on my hips. "If I recall correctly, you basically called me a liar."

"I did not!"

"Yes, you did. You didn't believe one thing I said about Jill, and I *wasn't* lying."

"Who are you talking to?" Sofia asks, sauntering into the room. She goes straight to the fridge and stares into its vast emptiness.

"No one," Brecken answers, sullen.

"I heard you," she says, going back to her room with a yogurt cup. "Are you sick again?"

With a tired sigh he tells her no, and then lies back down, turning toward me.

I feel sorry for him. It would be terrible having your family think you were psycho when you weren't. I sit on the coffee table before him. "Brecken?" I resist the urge to brush his hair from his forehead, not that I can, but I want to. He seems vulnerable, a little boy. His eyes search mine, their deep blue enhanced by the lamplight. His lips part like he's about to speak, but he doesn't. I find a yearning in his eyes I don't understand and can't explain. I want to pull away, to run like normal, but I force myself to stay seated on the table. "I'm sorry," I say. "I didn't mean to hurt you."

"You didn't," he whispers. "It's just that I know Jill, and she wouldn't do that. We've been dating a long time. She loves me."

I can't hold the question back. I want to know. For some reason, I have to know. "Do you love *her?*"

"Sure," he says, flicking of particle of lint from the couch. He doesn't meet my gaze. But his words make my chest ache. I pull back. He's wrong to love her. She *doesn't* love him. *I* do.

"Ahh!" I scream, jumping back. I can't believe I just thought that! What a terrible thing to cross my mind. It's not true. I do *not* love him. He's the last person I'd love. I pace the room, rubbing my head, thinking, thinking, thinking. Did I say it out loud? No. I don't think so. Oh, please. I hope not.

"What's wrong?" he asks, sitting up straight, his gaze piercing me.

"Uh... uh." Nothing intelligent comes out of my mouth. What can I say? I hardly know him. I don't even *like* him. I care about him, of course, but only because he is my charge. I have to. It's a requirement, I think.

"Alisa, tell me." His whisper is barely loud enough to hear.

"I can't talk about this."

"Why?" he asks, standing up. We face each other, almost nose to nose.

I feel his aura radiating around me. Its static warmth pulsing through me like a soft breeze. For the first time, I reach out and stroke his cheek, standing closer than I normally would have ever dared.

With a sharp inhalation, his eyes widen at my touch. He reaches up, placing his hand over mine, his mouth opening in a surprised "O."

"Brecken, please believe me. I'm telling you the truth. I would never lie to you. I... uh."

"I know," he says, a soft smile forming on his lips. "I get it."

He does? I don't. But standing this close to him, I wish I did. In that moment I want a real body so bad, to really feel his hand on mine, to feel the pressure of him next to me, to feel his lips—.

I pull away suddenly, astonished at the path my thoughts have taken. He reaches out quickly to slip his arm around my waist, to pull me back, but it goes right through me as I float out of his grasp. I move back, one step at a time, my mind racing. This isn't right. A guardian cannot fall for her charge. It is wrong, wrong, wrong, and I'm sure to get in trouble as soon as Raphael finds out.

Will he pull me from my job? Will I be punished? Strangely, I *want* to be Brecken's guardian now. More than anything. I can't imagine not seeing him ever again. But am I such a silly girl that I can develop a crush on a boy so quickly?

I step back again and Brecken steps forward.

"What are you doing?" I hear through the fog of my mind. I look up at the same time as Brecken to see Heidi and Sophie standing next to the table, an empty yogurt cup in Sophie's hand. The two of them stare, wide-eyed. He glances at me, then down at his outstretched arms. He lets them fall to his sides and then turns to his sisters with a chuckle. "Uh, there's this play at school that, um, I'm trying out for."

"A play." Heidi cocks her hip, a knowing look on her face. "You're trying out for a play."

"I am," he states. "You don't know everything about me."

"I know enough to know you've never even *seen* a play at school, let alone ever tried out for one." She smirks and shakes her head. "You really do need meds." Her laughter follows her to her room. She slams the door behind her.

Brecken's expression hardens at her remark.

Sophie stares up at him from behind the couch that separates the kitchen from the living room. "I think it's cool. I'd come see you."

"Thanks, Sof," he says, sinking back down on the couch. He pats the spot next to him and looks up at me.

Is he insane? "I can't."

"Why not?" he mouths.

Good question. Why not? It's not like we can do anything. With a sigh, and against my better judgment, I sit beside him. He rests his arm on the back cushion, almost around my shoulders. I shiver and turn to him, our faces inches apart.

Brecken glances over his shoulder at Sophie.

She watches him closely.

"I'm going to practice the kiss that's in the play. You tell me if it looks real," he says to her.

"Umm. Okay."

"What!" I screech, leaning back.

He leans forward, a playful glint in his eyes. I lean back more. He inches closer. I recline against the arm cushion until I'm almost flat on the couch. He chuckles and gives me a lazy half-smile. Is he really going to do this? Should I let him? I kind of want to.

The world stands still. There is nothing but us. No TV. No little sisters. No disruptions. The warmth of his breath mists on my face, smelling of something sweet I can't place, and his aura surrounds us, encasing me in light. He stares into my eyes, his face suddenly very serious. I don't move or push away.

I close my eyes just as his lips brush past mine, like a soft feather tickling my mouth. A tingling thrills through me, and I want him to keep kissing me, to press closer. But that feeling won't come, that hard, physical pressure of a body, holding another physical body. I ache with a need I can't explain.

His eyes widen and he leans back, a look of surprise on his face. "Alisa," he whispers breathlessly.

"Wow. That looks real to me," Sophie says, jumping down from her chair. "You'll do well in that play."

39

Evil on Another Level

ALISA

This is bad. Very, very bad. I have to make it stop. But to make it stop, I have to quit thinking about his incredibly blue eyes, his wide, muscular shoulders, the beauty and passion of his spirit, which has totally taken me by surprise.

I run without thinking.

Once I stop, I search my surroundings. Nothing looks familiar. I'm not in my old neighborhood, nor am I anywhere near Brecken's house. But something has drawn me here. That's how it works.

I stand in front of an old, run-down house. Its haunted, dark windows and warped gables eying me like an intruder, glaring, demanding I leave at once. A chill slithers down my back. Yellow-brown paint peels from the wood siding, and the worn front porch sags from years of use.

Something pounds inside me. Heart-thumping fear. It slithers over and around me like a deadly Black Mamba. I want to leave, but there is something in that house I need to see. I know it as well as I know my own name.

Tentatively, I enter the house and find myself in a dirty, garbage-filled living room. Old hamburger wrappers and used pizza boxes lay scattered on the stained carpet. Unnerving quiet follows me like a ghost as I head deeper inside, toward the kitchen. My eyes pierce the darkness, drawn to an open door with stairs that lead down into a basement.

Another freakin' basement.

I stop on the stairs, wary, yet wanting to get this over with.

As I move down, I hear voices, muffled by a closed door at the bottom of the stairs. Automatically I tiptoe, trying to be quiet even though no one can hear me.

Stepping through the closed door, my eyes grow wide, and I'm ready to bolt. A large group of people sit on the floor on blankets and throw pillows. Candles glow around the perimeter of the room, creating deep shadows. The tang of lamp oil as well as sweet perfumes drift toward me.

Someone must have drawn me here, so I search each face, each expression, recognizing no one until I came to the dark, heavily lashed eyes that matched my own, as if he were my twin. Derek?

He reclines on a red velvet pillow, a brunette-haired girl beside him, stoking his cheek. A dark bottle dangles between his fingers, from which he takes a swig every few seconds.

My heart, figuratively speaking, flips at the sight of him, but that ache is quickly replaced by anger, per normal. I stomp straight toward him, my hands clenched and my teeth grinding. "Derek. What are you doing here?"

He doesn't answer and doesn't acknowledge that some invisible force is raining fire and brimstone down on him. He never used to drink. He spent most of his time at the school track, training for the cross-country team. He'd always gotten good grades and is a straight A student. He has a girlfriend, but it isn't this floozy who has draped herself all over him.

Disappointed, I can't even think straight. "Get up!" I demand, standing behind him, and trying to lift him to a standing position. He doesn't budge. It's not until I turn around that I get my next heart-stopping shocker.

Jill.

She sits on the other side of the room, intertwined in the arms of some guy, her vampire fangs twinkling bright in the candlelight. Dread spreads through me, its dark claws pulling me down, down, down. Feelings, similar to the ones I felt in Soul Prison, wash through me, and I nearly sink to my knees in despair.

I didn't even realize we all lived in the same city.

I stare, rooted to the cement floor, as Jill leans forward and sinks her fangs into the bicep of the guy she lies beside. He moans as the needles penetrate his skin, then wraps his legs around Jill and rolls her over so he is on top. That's when I notice he sports his own set of shiny, new fangs.

He bites into her skin, just below the collarbone.

The hot, acidic memory of vomit rises in my mouth. The response is automatic. I turn, horrified, to Derek. He watches Jill, his eyes wide, but not with a disgusted grimace, like I have.

More terrified, yet fascinated.

I have to get him out of here, and I have to do it now. "Derek. Please listen to me. You have to leave. This is dangerous. People could really die. Don't you get it? What if one of those fangs punctures an artery?" That has to happen once in a while. They aren't always careful, are they? "Derek. Get up!" I scream at the top of my voice.

Nothing works. He can't hear me. He doesn't want to. I remember being told in *Idir Shaol* that guardians aren't able to influence everyone, that some people refuse to listen. People have to be open, their souls somewhat receptive.

Derek takes another swig from the bottle in his hand, then lies back and closes his eyes. I watch him, a smile flitting across his mouth. In sorrow, I turn away.

"Dude, wake up," a boy sitting next to Derek says. "It's gonna start."

"Huh?" Derek responds, sleepily.

A woman enters the room. Tall, regal, proud. She glides toward a table at the front of the room, her long black cape trailing behind, a cowl covering her head. She holds a tapered black candle in her slim fingers, and the only thing that shows of her shadowed face are her ruby-red lips, which glisten in the dim light.

All eyes turn to her. Including my own.

I watch her, riveted. Something about her captures me in a wonderful, yet terrible grip. Part of me wants to fall at her feet and beg for attention. Another part recoils with such revulsion that I desperately want to flee.

That is when I see it. A dark shadow clinging to her skirt like a cloudy sheath of silk. It slithers around her legs, its grasping hands holding onto her with parasitic strength. It glances up and catches my eye, the darkness of its gaze drowning me as though I've fallen into a deep, polluted cesspool.

I pull my gaze away, the awful smile of the shadow fiend still in my peripheral vision. Who *is* this woman? What is she doing here? And who is her sticky friend? The one thing I do know is that whoever she is, she's dangerous.

And evil.

"My children," she says lovingly as she gazes at each member of the room. "It is right that you are here. I'm proud of you all. Especially our newest members." She glances at Derek and smiles seductively.

My soul recoils just a bit more. The candles in the room flicker and the walls that surround us glow with dark heaviness. Grim foreboding drifts over me like tiny poison snowflakes, stinging my soul where they land. The longer I'm here, the worse I feel. I have to get out, but I can't leave my brother!

"When I first came here," the woman says. "I worried we wouldn't find the numbers we required, but we have been rewarded by the diligence of our initiates in this city." She smiles, grasping the edges of her cowl and sliding the hood back, letting it come to rest on her slender shoulders.

Long, white-blonde hair falls around her cheeks and her light blue eyes glisten with heat.

I can't look away, though I want to. She holds me spellbound just as she does the others in the room.

"Tonight we have two who graduate to the next level of ordination."

She stretches her arm out to Jill, who steps forward. Jill kneels on a pillow at the woman's feet and bows her head. The woman takes Jill's hand.

"Rise," she says to Jill. "This initiate has completed her requirements in the Order and will now become an Adept." The woman reaches for a folded black cloth that lies on the table behind her. Holding it up, the cloth unfolds into a long, silky robe, identical to her red one. She places it over Jill's head and lets it fall around her shoulders.

With a slow sigh of satisfaction, the woman turns Jill to face the others. "Jill will complete her next assignment this coming week. Not only has she reached the level of Adept, but will also become the chief custodian of this chapter, being the first in this area to accomplish the tasks placed before her."

Silence fills the room as everyone watches. My eyes burn, yet I can't take my gaze from her. Jill radiates confidence, her chin jutting out, her chest raised in pride. She searches the small congregation, catching each person's gaze and holding it.

That's when another ghostly being of wispy, gray smoke appears. It weaves a web around Jill's feet and gazes up at me with a smile that splits its faceless visage as it slithers up to her waist.

One by one, the people in the room rise and approach Jill to congratulate her, including my brother. He steps forward as a receiving line forms. When Derek arrives before her, Jill takes his hand, her fingers threading with his. "May the dark one grant your desires," she whispers, her eyes riveted to Derek's.

He answers like everyone else has. "Likewise."

I reach out one last time and place my hand on his arm. Derek's fear and uncertainty ooze into my mind, and something else... something that alarms me to my very core. He's angry. He wants to lash out, to hurt someone.

Me.

I let go in surprise. This isn't my Derek. He's not vindictive or a grudge-holder. Doesn't he understand what I went through? Can't he forgive me? He can't pin his bad choices on me. His being here isn't my fault.

Anger, like I haven't felt in a long time, well, for at least a few hours, erupts inside me. How dare he use my death to justify his joining this... this satanic fraternity! I take one last look, and leave.

40

Running Away, Again

ALISA

I don't have anywhere to go, and I don't want to go all the way back to *Idir Shaol*. So instead of appearing in some strange place like Egypt—which is tempting—I decide to go back to Brecken.

The mere thought of being in his presence twists my mind into knots of anxiety. Our last moment together had been a kiss. He'd *kissed* me. And the ache that kiss creates in my heart... It all rushes back—the light, the heat, the wonderful magic.

And, heaven forbid, I want it to happen again.

Questions ramble around inside me. Why did he kiss me when he has a girlfriend? Does Raphael know? Will he send for me? Will I lose my post? It's not like I instigated it, but I didn't stop it either.

I like Brecken. *Really* like him. There is no way around it. I didn't plan this, but I don't want it to end yet either. Secretly, I wanted that kiss, and now I have to suffer the consequences. I have a job to do after all. This isn't just about life and death. This is about redemption and eternity... and a timeless existence in Soul Prison—surrounded by evil—if I don't succeed. And what will happen to Brecken? What is his destiny if I fail? I can't bear to think of it.

Brecken, when I find him, is in the process of grabbing his gym bag and running out the door. "Where're you going?" I ask as he runs past.

He stops abruptly and stares straight ahead. "Lacrosse practice."

"You play lacrosse?"

He turns, facing the direction of my voice. Sunshine spills through the window, casting long shafts of light across his face. I'm pretty sure he can't see me, but he faces me square on, only a foot away. "I used to. There a problem with that?"

His angelic-ness vanishes and his tone rocks me back on my heels. The force of his anger is like a physical blow. "No. I just never pegged you for a lacrosse player."

"Really? And just what sport *do* you think I'd play? Or am I such a loser that all I'd do is sit around like a pothead all day?" He smirks and walks out the door, leaving me alone in the kitchen.

"Uh, well." I can't think of a single sport I think he'd play. Not that he isn't athletic. He just portrays himself as the bad boy in a *leave me alone* kind of way. He doesn't scream sports. I follow him to his mom's car. He pulls out of the driveway, the tires shrieking.

"Why are you driving so fast? Are you trying to kill us?" I hate it when people let their anger determine their driving. My brother does that.

Brecken doesn't answer.

I watch the road, one hand on the dashboard, afraid we'll crash. Not that I'd get hurt, but he would. "Why are you so mad?" I still haven't figured it out and can't seem to get past his porcupine bristle.

With an audible sigh, he glances my way and then back to the windshield. "It's just... you took off. *Again.*"

The look of hurt on his face and the guilt of my constant running is beginning to haunt me. "Oh. I'm really sorry about that."

"Was it that bad?"

"What?"

His lips tighten and he shakes his head slowly back and forth. "The *kiss.*"

"Oh, Brecken, no. That's not it at all. The kiss was... well, it was... freaking awesome." I turn away, embarrassed to admit my feelings, and watch the trees zip past in a blur. "There's just the whole thing about me being dead that kinda puts a crimp in it."

"That's a minor detail," he says, a slow grin spreading across his face.

"Yeah. Minor."

"I thought maybe you were... disappointed." He stares at the road stretching in a straight line ahead of us. "That seems to be what I do best lately."

"What? No." I place my hand on his arm. "Not even close. And why would you be worried about disappointing anyone? I haven't seen you do that since I've been here."

"Oh really?" He glances toward me. "You've *never* been disappointed in me?"

I think back over our time together, the constant arguments, the constant frustration, the break-in, Jill. "Oh. Well, as your guardian, there are times when I'm disappointed, but then we work it out. You're totally not supposed to even know I'm here. It kind of messes everything up. It's much easier to influence people when they don't know you're around. As for the other stuff, well..."

He glances at me again, rolling his eyes. "Well what?"

"Never mind," I say, suddenly shy. How can I discuss this? It's too new, too crazy.

We pull up next to a cemetery.

"What are we doing here?" I don't like cemeteries. I don't like dead bodies or the idea of people decaying under my feet.

"This is where we practice."

"You have *got* to be kidding." I follow him to a wide grassy area where no headstones have been placed yet. Fifteen other boys are there, tossing a lacrosse ball to one another. Some wear protective pads over T-shirts. Others wear their pads directly over their skin.

"We tear up the park's grass too much so we practice here half the time." He proceeds to take off his shirt and put on his shoulder pads.

"I had no idea you were part of a team," I say with an amazed chuckle.

"I'm not. I don't play in the games. I don't have the money for dues, new gear, or any other fees. We're too poor," he says with a sneer. "But the team feels sorry for me, and I'm pathetic enough to still want to come once a week."

The hardness in his eyes doesn't dispel the hurt in his voice. I hadn't realized how much he'd had to give up when his mom died. My heart breaks just a little bit more for him, but I can't stay in that aching place long. It brings up too many memories of my own. Instead I stare at his half-naked body, his muscles rippling as he fastens his gear.

Surprisingly, his body doesn't disgust me like before. I don't know what has changed or is different, but his bare skin doesn't elicit feelings of revulsion. I don't associate the tanned skin of his chest with Mr. Roland or feel the need to hide. Maybe I am healing. Maybe Gram is right after all.

And Brecken is beautiful.

I've never seen him like this in broad daylight—his chest, muscles sculpted like a Grecian statue, his dark hair, glistening with streaks of auburn in the dense summer sun.

I take a place on the sidelines and watch him stretch out with his team. Their goalie leads them around the cemetery in a brisk jog. After a couple of laps, the coach waves them in. They divide into two teams. Skins and shirts.

Lacrosse seems like a game I would have enjoyed... with a body. It's fast paced, intense, and full of constant action. An idea blossoms in my mind and a smile grows on my face. I close my eyes and re-appear beside Brecken.

"Hey," I say, floating next to him. A sheen of sweat dots his brow, but he isn't out of breath. He also doesn't answer me. I crouch next to him as though I am about to run the next play, which I am.

He whispers, "Go away!"

"No way. I'm gonna to help you get a goal." I don't know a lot about lacrosse, but I saw a couple of games at my old high school. How hard can it be?

The play begins with two guys in a face-off. The skins win the ball and it flies from stick to stick. Brecken guards the goalie, helping to protect him and the goal. A guy on the other team catches the ball and searches for a teammate.

I sidle up next to him. "Pass it to the kid by Brecken."

A frown creases the boy's brow, but he throws the ball to the appointed player. It passes in front of Brecken, who intercepts it with lightning speed, tearing off toward the other side of the field. He throws the ball to a teammate, who scores a goal. Cheers erupt and I dance over the field, monumentally proud of myself.

"I told him to do that," I call out as Brecken runs past me, back toward his goal.

"What?" he says, almost stopping.

"Nothin' man," a teammate answers. "Get over by Dodson and we'll run that play again!"

"Okay." Brecken ignores me.

I stay beside him, trying to influence one player after another. Not all of them listen, but most do, and by the end of practice, Brecken has made four goals. His team has eleven points all together. The shirts can't keep up. I giggle with glee the whole way home. "That was so fun!"

"You didn't do all of that." He faces forward, his expression grim.

"Most of it. All I had to do was whisper in their ears and they obeyed. It was fantastic."

His frown deepens and he grips the steering wheel tighter. "That isn't right. You shouldn't do that."

"Why not? It's why I'm here," I say, returning Brecken's frown. "That's what guardian's do. Influence. I'm one of the good guys. Geez."

He glances at me, his eyes squinting. "Do you even know who the bad guys are, Alisa?"

I ponder his question. "What do you mean? Bad guys are murderers, rapist, and child molesters. Yeah. I know who the bad guys are." I can't help but think of Mr. Roland or his tortured expression as he reached for me in Soul Prison.

"That's not what I'm talking about."

"Then what *are* you talking about?" I don't understand why he's trying to ruin my good mood. I'm not ready to argue again. I want to go back to the fun, happy, romantic Brecken.

"There are bad guys out there that are spirits like you... or something."

I laugh, shaking my head. "There are no bad guys like me. If they're truly evil, they're in Soul Prison."

He shakes his head. "You don't get it. There are other beings out there. Bad ones." He glances at me again, his expression wary. "Don't tell me you haven't seen them."

Uh, no. I haven't. There are evil spirits around? Doing what? Doing what guardians do but in reverse? Trying to get people into trouble? I'm not sure I believe that. Then I remember the ghostly beings that had swirled around Jill and the lady in red. But those weren't real spirits, actual people, like me. They were more like slithery demons.

"I haven't seen any spirits like me... who are bad," I say hesitantly. I don't want to scare Brecken into thinking bad things might be lurking. He has enough problems as it is. "Bad spirits are held prisoner. They don't get to come here. I've seen it myself."

His snort tells me he can't believe I'm so naïve, and I don't correct him. "Hey, I'm just telling you how it is," he says. "I've seen them. They're around." He pulls into his driveway and gets out without saying another word.

I follow, sullen and thinking.

He throws his bag by the door and rummages for food in the kitchen, finding crackers and cheese-wiz. He sits on the couch and flips on the TV. I think about what he said, and about what I've seen, but he can't be right. Spirits would be aware of each other. Wouldn't I know if there was an evil minion trying to influence my charge? "So do you see evil ghosts? And if so, how often?" I sit down on the couch beside him.

"Not as much as I see *you*," he says, teasing and crunching loudly on a cracker.

"Very funny."

"Well," he begins. "They're more like shadows. They're dark. They don't glow like you, and they don't ever talk. They just watch me."

I ponder this. They sound just like the strange spirits I saw in the basement of that old house. They hadn't spoken either. They were just kind of there, seeming to silently suck the life force out of their host. "It doesn't make sense," I say finally. "Who are they, and what do they want?"

He glances at me, still chewing, and shakes his head. "I don't know."

41

Life Isn't Fair

ALISA

The fact that Brecken is seeing other weird beings throws me for a loop. Totally confused, I know I need outside help with this one. Taking a mental breath, I close my eyes and picture Raphael's glowing face. A moment later, I stand outside his office door. The quick trip between worlds leaves me dizzy and for a moment, I rest against the wall. Then, before I lose my nerve, I rap on the wooden door three times.

Raphael greets me with a smile and a hug. "Alisa! How good to see you! How is everything?"

As if he doesn't know. "Fine."

"Good, good. Have a seat." He walks around his desk and sits in his chair, facing me. "So, you have some questions?"

I have tons of questions. And I decide to get one off my mind that's been there since I saw my brother at that old house. "Yeah. First off, why doesn't my brother, Derek, have a guardian? Or anyone else in my family, for that matter? Aren't they just as important as Brecken? Isn't everyone? Why haven't I seen any other guardians since I've been on earth?" I stare him down, daring him to say my family doesn't matter.

"Ah. Right to the point as always. How shall I explain?" he says mostly to himself as he steeples his fingers. "Everyone is watched over. Everyone. No one is left out until they are past feeling. Past hearing. Too closed."

"My brother is not closed!"

"I never said he was. Let me finish, Alisa," he says with a sigh. "Your job is different than a guardian angel's. You are in the processes of paying back a debt. You don't get to fraternize with other guardians, nor do you get to see other guardian angels. You have to do this on your own, like penitence. Understand?"

I nod slowly, starting to see the picture, but it isn't clear yet.

"Since you are in the general area, we thought we'd let you help watch over your family a bit. I knew you'd want see them, and honestly, I don't see the harm in it."

My heart warms toward Raphael just a bit more. "Thank you."

"As far as your brother goes," he continues. "We are aware of his situation, but there are valuable lessons for him to learn. If he doesn't respond to our influence, there isn't much we can do. He'll have to learn the hard way."

I don't want Derek to learn the hard way. He deserves to have a wonderful, happy life with as little stress as possible.

Raphael seems to read my mind. "You can't force people to listen, Alisa. Haven't you noticed?"

A sarcastic chuckle escapes my mouth and I sit back, my arms crossed over my chest. "Nope. Haven't noticed that."

"Any other questions?" he asks with compassion.

Letting out a long breath, I sit back up, facing Raphael fully. "Yes. Brecken says he sees dark spirits. They don't talk to him or anything, but now I've seen them too. What are they? *Who* are they, and what do they want?"

"Hmm." He flicks invisible dust from his desk. "I'd hoped we wouldn't have to have this conversation, but our luck hasn't held out." He glances at me, his mouth drawn, his eyes sad. "But you should know since they *are* showing themselves." He stops speaking for a moment and swivels in his chair to stare at the wall. "They are damned souls, Alisa. Souls that have never been born and never will be. They have been cursed to roam the earth forever because of the evilness of their hearts—because of evil choices they made long ago." He turns and watches me with no emotion marring his expression, waiting.

Damned souls? Cursed? Evil choices? "But who are they?"

Raphael shakes his head slowly. "It doesn't matter. You have more influence than they do—more than they could ever dream of—because of the goodness inside you."

"But they *can* influence people?" I ask to clarify.

He nods. "At times, yes. At other times, fully. They can possess the bodies they cling to if their host is weak."

"But why? What do they want?" This is a whole new world of information I have to sift through. It's confusing, and I don't like surprises. I don't like learning there is an enemy team I have to fight against.

With a heavy sigh, he explains further. "They made a pact of sorts, eons ago, so they could experience the physical world. They acquire souls in trade for... well, the body."

"Acquire souls? Like steal them or something? Who would make a pact like that? Not God." I don't want to believe in a god who would promise someone's body to an evil being.

Raphael chuckles. "No. Of course not. Someone else. Just do your job and worry about Brecken."

"So they possess bodies?" My mind automatically goes to all the horror movies I've ever seen, like *Exorcism* or *Twilight Zone*. I don't want something like that to be real. It feels unsafe, making all humans vulnerable and unprotected.

"In a manner of speaking, but not like you're thinking." He sighs and leans back in his chair. "It's not something you need to worry about right now as you aren't a guardian angel. These are things guardian angels deal with. You only have to accomplish your one assigned task, and then someone else will be permanently assigned to Brecken if there's a need."

I hadn't thought of anyone else guarding Brecken. I know I'm not an actual guardian angel, but the thought of someone else taking over for me leaves me aching and speechless. Then Raphael's last words filter through my mind. "Wait. If there's a need? What's that supposed to mean?"

For a moment, Raphael's mouth sags, his brow furrowing, as though he is reluctant to admit he's made a mistake in saying anything at all. I can tell he doesn't want to answer, so I quickly reach over the desk and grab his hand. Flashes of light, scenes of Brecken's life, explode in my mind, painful and overwhelming.

I push away, gaping at Raphael. "What was that?" I lean against his desk, my chest tight.

"You shouldn't have done that, Alisa." He stares right back, his jaw clenching. "It's not for you to see."

"You can see the future? Do you already know what's going to happen to Brecken? To... me?"

"It's not like that. Nothing is set in stone. What you saw," he says with a sigh, "is what will happen if circumstances don't change."

I back away toward the door, never taking my eyes from his face, shaking my head. "You're the only one who knows all the rules, aren't you? There's no such thing as free will. No one really gets to choose, do they? It's all just a game."

"Alisa, no. That's not how it is."

"I don't believe you." All I can see is the heart-wrenching image of Brecken lying on the ground. Broken, bloody... and dead.

42

Procrastinating

BRECKEN

Alisa is gone, but she hasn't actually run away this time. Brecken isn't sure what she is up to, but it's the perfect moment to call Jill. He still cares about her even though his feelings have changed, and he doesn't want to end their relationship cold turkey. Not having her in his life would be strange and lonely, but he can't in good conscience date her any longer.

He doesn't know what the future holds with Alisa, but he can't keep stringing Jill along, letting her think they are a couple when they aren't. Even if Alisa never comes back, he just doesn't have those feelings for Jill anymore.

He picks up the phone.

Jill's voice, smooth and sweet, like warm lemon taffy, soon answers. His heart warms at the smile he hears in her words.

"Hey, Breck. I hated not being with you at all this weekend."

He sighs, not knowing how to continue the conversation without it ending in a huge argument. "Yeah. Me too. You always cheer me up." His comment sounds selfish to him. Has he only kept her around because she makes him feel good? "I wanted to talk to you about something, but not over the phone." This was going to be hard. How can he break up with her when she cares so much about him? Maybe he should wait longer. It's not like he's in a hurry. It's not like his relationship with Alisa will evolve that much in the next day or two.

He'll take his time. Next weekend would be better for a breakup.

"Hmm. That doesn't sound good, Brecky. You sound so serious. What's wrong?" she asks, a pout in her voice.

"Nothing. It's just something we need to talk over, you know?"

"Is this about your medication? Because it doesn't bother me. I know you're taking those pills again. I saw them on your dresser. You know I'll stand by your side no matter what. I don't care what anyone says about you, baby."

Irritation stabs at his heart. What people say about him? No one even knows about his pills except his family and Jill, and she wouldn't say anything to anyone else, would she? Jill cares about him.

43

Fighting Destiny

ALISA

I have to get back to Brecken fast—to protect him. I'll never leave his side again. If there is anything I can do to change the future, I'll do it.

Then another chilling thought hits me.

If Brecken dies, he'll be with me.

⁂

It's Wednesday morning and I haven't shared my vision with Brecken yet. I've been back with him for three days but haven't dared communicate the awful truth. I don't know if I can hold out much longer.

He sits in his history class, his legs stretched out before him. I couldn't be more bored, yet my mind races, trying to understand how he is going die. I didn't exactly see that part when I touched Raphael. Will some drug dealer do the deed? Will he be hit by a drunk driver? Will *he* be the drunk driver? Am I supposed to protect him from himself? Someone else? I just don't know, and the energy it takes to figure it out leaves me testy and exhausted.

I sit in an empty desk halfway across the room, picking at the hard, plastic desktop. Pen marks and old gum have hardened there, and memories of my own math classes resurface. I glance over at Brecken, remembering my conversation with Raphael, and notice that his black combat boots are untied again. I hate that look. I can't understand why he dresses this way. There isn't a goth bone in his body, so who is he trying to deceive?

I know who he really is inside—compassionate, caring,

lonely. And I've memorized every feature of his face, from his curly, mussed hair, to the twitch in his lip. I love watching him, love the way he takes care of his sisters. He isn't fooling anyone with this bad boy facade.

Especially me.

My heart warms, and it puts me in a less anxious mood. "Let's get out of here, Breck," I say, knowing no one else can hear me. "I want to talk to you and it can't wait. It's important." I try to make my voice pleasant, yet serious.

He sighs and the two kids sitting beside him look up. His silent glare is enough to discourage their interest. His finger taps a rhythm on his thigh.

"I spoke to someone in charge and there are some things you should know," I say from across the room.

"Shh," he whispers, a little too loudly. Other students turn and glare at him.

I can't help but giggle. "You're so cute when you're angry."

"Be *quiet!*" he spits, not thinking, obviously.

"What did you say?" the teacher asks.

Brecken closes his eyes and shakes his head. "I didn't say anything."

"Oh, really?" Her right eyebrow lifts into a thin, angry line.

"He told you to shut up," the kid next to him offers with a grin.

"I think it's time for a trip to the principal's office," the teacher quips.

Even though this is a serious event, I can't quit giggling. Mostly because Brecken sits in the chair across from the principal scowling, and the angrier he becomes, the funnier it seems. Maybe it's my way of coping.

"So, Brecken. What can you tell me about this incident with Mrs. Beecher?" the principal asks. He doesn't look or even sound mad. I don't think Brecken is in any real trouble.

"Yes, Brecken," I mimic. "What can you tell us?"

Brecken looks up slowly. "It was nothing, Mr. Cheney. I was just thinking out loud," he says.

"You were thinking the words, *shut up* and then accidentally said them out loud?" he asks, his voice incredulous.

"No, not exactly."

"Let me clear this up for you," I answer. "Brecken is very upset at me so he lashed out, unthinking, and told his teacher to shut up." I chuckle to myself.

Mr. Cheney releases a slow breath. "I'm not going to suspend you even though this isn't the first time you've been here, but you really need to watch yourself." He takes another breath, and hesitates as though disinclined to go on. "Brecken, I want to help you. I know you struggled last year with the death of your mom... and that you were diagnosed wi—"

"Stop," Brecken says abruptly. "Just stop. There's nothing wrong with me." He stands, his hands fisted, his face in an expression of anguish.

"I'm sorry. I didn't mean to imply there was," Mr. Cheney says, also rising. "I'm just concerned. I know it must be hard with your dad gone so often and... "

"I'm fine. Everything's fine." Brecken turns, but before opening the door, he asks, "Can I leave?" He stares at the floor, not making eye contact.

"Yes," Mr. Cheney answers.

I follow Brecken out. He walks down the hall, but doesn't go back to class. Instead, he swings his backpack up over one shoulder and goes outside, leaving the school behind.

"Brecken?" I screwed up, teasing him that way, getting him in trouble. My heart aches watching his sagging shoulders, his drawn expression, and I'm so embarrassed. I feel so stupid.

He just keeps walking.

"I'm really sorry," I say. "I didn't know this would happen. I was just—"

"Teasing. Yeah, I know," he says, finishing my sentence.

I don't know what else to say or how to finish this

conversation. I walk a few steps behind and watch his head tilt toward the sidewalk. What is he thinking? It wouldn't be hard to find out. All I'd have to do is reach out and place my hand on his shoulder.

So I do.

Just as I thought, his feelings are those of embarrassment, despair, hopelessness, and last of all, loneliness. As far as his actual thoughts go, I'm still in the dark, but this gives me a pretty good idea about how he feels. I could have figured it out without touching him though.

"Can we talk?" I ask finally.

He turns to me on the sunny, public sidewalk. Only a few people are out. An old man across the street edges his grass, and a lady on the other side of the road walks her dog. They pay no attention to him.

"What is there to talk about? I don't think this is going anywhere." He continues walking, leaving me behind to stare in confusion.

What is he talking about? "Uh, you lost me there," I call to him.

He doesn't stop to explain.

With a grimace, I follow him down the sidewalk, across a grassy quad where the soccer team practices, and through the tree line into a small, forested area. He stops at a low-branched tree, drops his backpack, and swings up to the first thick branch.

I like the spot. If we walk twenty feet in any direction we'll be back on the street, but this patch of woods feels private, secluded. I float up to the branch beside him and sit with my legs hanging down.

"This is a cool place." I take in the birds that fly between the trees and moss-covered ground. "Do you come here a lot?" It's just shady enough that he can probably see me.

"No," he says with a sigh. "It's usually full of students."

I wait for him to continue. When he doesn't, I figure he's waiting for me. "Please talk to me. Tell me what's wrong."

His expression is full of longing, yet resignation. He hesitates.

"I really like you, Alisa, and I want more than anything for you to feel the same." He jumps down from his branch, still pacing.

"I just don't think... " He stops, looking up at me. "Dammit Alisa, what's *wrong* with you? Why did you do that to me in class today? Why did you try to get me in trouble? I feel like you don't even care about me. You always get mad, you're way over sensitive, you say mean things, and then don't act sorry... "

I'm stunned. This is not what I'd expected. I pull back, as though taking on a barrage of bullets. "Wow, Brecken."

"I'm sorry, but if we can't even communicate without fighting..."

"Okay. Wait," I say, floating down from the branch to stand beside him. I can do this. I can have a normal conversation with a boy without screwing it up. I take a deep breath trying to think of something to lighten the mood. "I'm sorry, Brecken. Really. I always do this. I don't know how to act around guys. If they like me, I screw it up, if they don't, I make it worse."

"It's okay." He relaxes. Even chuckles.

I shake my head and try for an easier topic. I come up with, "Does your girlfriend know you're dating someone else?" I always turn to jokes. They're safe, but from the look on his face, he doesn't think I'm funny.

But then his eyes warm and the tenseness in his shoulders eases. "She suspects I'm seeing someone else."

I can't help but smile. The moment turns quiet and it's time to broach the subject I fear most. "Brecken, I... I'm not sure how to say this," I hedge, trying to clear my thoughts.

"I know what you're going to say," he says, leaning toward me.

"You do?"

"Yeah, and honestly, I feel the same way."

I frown. "What are you talking about?"

"What are *you* talking about?"

"About why I'm here. About your future." I am unable to get the picture of him lying dead out of my mind. The blood that pools around his body.

"Oh."

"What did you think I was going to say?" I ask, even though I already know. He wants me to say I love him, that I want to be with him forever, that I can't stand for us to be apart, but I can't say that... for a million reasons, even though I want to.

Taking a deep breath, he cocks his head. "You look speckled where the sun filters through the branches." He reaches out, his hand only inches from my face.

The yearning inside pulls me deeper into that ocean that will never be mine. "I wish I could have met you a long time ago." It's true, and since I don't know how much time we have together, I want him to know this. I don't want it to end without him understanding my feelings.

"Me too, Alisa."

For that space in time, I soak him in, like a sponge dying on a blistering, sandy beach.

"Speaking of that," he leans back and pulls another twig from the tree, "there's something I've been wondering. Where did you live when you were alive? Where are you from?"

I laugh, amazed at the coincidence in my circumstances. "Actually, I'm from here. I didn't realize they'd sent me to my hometown at first, and I don't know why they did, but I'm glad."

"You're from *here?*" He leans forward. "I don't remember you from school."

"I didn't go to your school. I didn't live on this side of town," I say with a chuckle, surprised I could grow up in a city and not even recognize it when I came back.

"This side of town? What does that mean?"

"Umm, just that I lived in the Fruit Heights area," I explain.

"Oh. You were a rich kid." He sits back, a strange expression masking his features. One I've never seen before and don't recognize.

"Well, I'm not rich now. I don't even carry a wallet," I joke, trying to bring back the lightheartedness of the previous moment.

"I don't know why I thought this would work," he mumbles, his face becoming a mask I can no longer read. He stares off into space, lost in his thoughts. "I can't do this."

"What do you mean?"

"It doesn't matter," he says, looking right into my eyes.

What just happened? "Brecken!" I call as he walks away, discouraged at the chasm that just opened up between us. "How about we go to Canyon Park? I really like it there, and there's something I have to tell you and then, I promise, after that, I won't bother you anymore. I'll leave you alone... if that's what you really want."

He watches me silently and wants to refuse. I can feel it, but for a moment, he softens and his jaw relaxes. "Why not right here? Right now?"

I look around. The school bell will ring any moment. Classes will be over. I don't want any interruptions. "It will just be better. Please?"

He hesitates, shifting his weight and looking down the street. Finally, he says, "All right."

I sigh with relief. Maybe I can still fix this. Because if I want Brecken to know me, there is one conversation that has to happen... as much as I dread it.

44

Confiding a Deep, Dark Secret

ALISA

We arrive at Canyon Park on his motorcycle just as the sun begins to set. A stream bubbles past, tripping over stones in its way, singing a cheerful tune, oblivious to the roiling feelings inside us. I sit at the edge, wishing I could dip my feet and feel its cold current pulling against my ankles. Brecken sits next to me.

"I'm not sure where to start." I sigh in mental exhaustion. After all I've gone through, I just want to rest. I gaze at his beautiful face, determined to memorize each line, the way his eyes crinkle when he smiles, the way his lip twitches when he teases me, the way his mouth moves when he speaks. I can even smell him, like pine trees and Lever soap, a memory I never want to forget.

He watches me, curiously.

"What I'm about to tell you I've never told another living soul. Ever." I search his face for any sign of sarcasm or impatience, but find none. My mind races and my chest tightens in dreadful anticipation. Can I really do this? Can I confess my darkest secret to him, all in the hope that he'll trust me? Understand me? Want me?

"Okay. Go ahead."

"I... want you to know me better. You know, before you decide to..." I can't believe I am about to have this conversation.

He gives me a funny look and shakes his head at my silliness.

"Okay. So here goes. When I was eight years old my best friend's dad started sexually abusing me." I glance at his sunset-lit face to gauge his reaction.

He studies me, his mouth dropping open. His brow creases

into a frown and he actually reaches out to me. "That's not what I expected you to say."

I nod. "He abused me for years, and my friend Natty too. Sometimes both of us together."

"Oh, Alisa..."

"Yeah." I stand up and wrap my arms around my waist. I step into the middle of the stream, wishing it could carry me away like the dying leaves that float along its edge.

Brecken beckons me to come back, his arm out, his hand open, and I glance into his beseeching eyes. He meets me on the muddy bank, his body barely brushing against mine, the wonderful tingle of his aura surrounding me.

With a hesitant sigh, I whisper. "It lasted a long time. Forever, it seems like."

"I'm so sorry that happened to you."

"It was my brother, Derek, who finally figured it out." I shake my head, wanting to clear it of the horrible memories, but they flood back, like roiling tidal waves on the ocean, tossed back and forth with the force of the storm.

"I'd accidentally left my clothes in the bathroom after a bath. My underwear had blood on them. I wasn't old enough to have periods, and I guess my brother knew it. I remember him coming into my room, holding my dirty clothes. He stared at me, like he wanted to kill someone. I'm not sure how he figured it all out, because I wouldn't talk about it, but he must have told my parents, because a few days later, Mr. Roland was arrested. I never opened up to Derek, even after that. Mr. Roland died in prison a couple years later. It was Natty who testified against him. I couldn't do it. "

Brecken's eyes squint shut, his lips drawn back like he is going to be sick. "I'd kill anyone who did that to my sisters."

"I know. That's how Derek felt. Your sisters need you so much. You have to protect them. There are other bad people out there like Mr. Roland!"

"Is that why you killed yourself?" he asks me softly, his eyes round and glowing in the sunset.

I sigh and step back. How do I explain my tortured life? I don't think I can do it accurately. "Partly. My life was complicated.

When my grandmother died, I was so unhappy, so lonely, but I kept going. I began healing. But when Natty, my best friend, got cancer and died, I died with her. I couldn't deal with anything anymore. I didn't care anymore. My one confidant who'd understood my hidden pain was gone. My parents got me antidepressants, but after I started taking them, I felt even worse, like a black hurricane constantly surrounded me, heavy and polluted. I ached with despair all the time. I can't explain it, but I had to make it stop. I just needed it to stop."

Brecken nods. "So then what?"

"So then... I drove into a tree. I got what I wanted, except I didn't. Nothing is what you imagine it is after you die. You don't get to rest. You don't get wings. You don't get to be with loved-ones, not if you kill yourself. You do get to work though. Dead people work all the time," I say with a sarcastic laugh.

Brecken chuckles as though he understands what I mean. "You poor thing. And then you were sent here to deal with a loser like me."

My heart fills with something I can't explain. "You're *not* a loser, Brecken. You're the furthest thing from it." I have come to understand this boy, and now, hopefully, he can understand me. I step closer, aching to feel him for real, to feel the heat of his breath on my face, the warmth of his hands on my back.

"I... " My unsaid words drift on the soft breeze, and I wonder for a moment if I can really say them out loud. I don't want to keep my feelings to myself anymore. What if I never get the chance again to tell him?

"Brecken, I... love you," I whisper. I would never normally tell a guy I love him. In fact, I would have rather died—figuratively speaking—than tell a guy I even liked him, but I have a feeling my time with Brecken is drawing to a close. I want to tell him what's in my heart before it's too late, before I'm snatched away and never get the chance.

"I'm still not sure how this all works," I hurry to explain. "But I might not have a lot of time left with you, and I just want you to know... or whatever." With a nervous laugh, I step back. "You know what I mean." My heart lies open at his feet. Never have I felt so vulnerable, so fragile.

"Wow..." He smiles, warmth curling his lips into a grin. "Thank you, Alisa. I... don't know what to say."

"This is the point where the boy usually says, 'I love you, too.' " The fact that he hasn't leaves a raw spot in my chest that threatens to rip deeper, depending on his next words.

"I'm..." He glances quickly into my eyes, and then back down at the stream.

Rip. Like a blade of grass on an early winter morning. One wrong step and I'll be completely smashed. I stand on the border of rejection once again. "I thought you'd say..."

His hands rake through his windblown hair, making it even messier. "I want to, but... I don't know if it's a good idea," he says in frustration. "Here's what I *want* to say." He turns to me suddenly. "*Yes,* I feel the same way. Yes, I want you. But it won't be that way. I'm pretty sure about that. It doesn't seem to matter what I want. I never get it."

"Then *take* what you want!" I yell back at him. "You're still human. You have a physical body. Do you even know what that means?" My chest heaves even though air is not being sucked into my lungs, even though my words make no sense. He can't have me. What am I thinking? I'm a ghost.

"You don't understand, Alisa. You can't. And it doesn't matter anymore. I'm *tired,*" he says. "Can you see that?" Anguish coats his face and he turns to trudge back up the hill toward his motorcycle.

"Brecken... please don't go. Please—"

"I'm sorry, too." He watches me silently for a moment before continuing up the path, the gravel crunching beneath his feet.

"I thought sharing my past with you would make a difference," I yell at his stiff back.

He stops, but doesn't turn around. The soft, afternoon breeze lifts his hair and it stirs around his neck. "It did. It does. I... I just... need time."

I watch him grow smaller as he guns his bike and peels out of the parking lot.

"You don't have time," I whisper to myself.

45

A Broken Heart

ALISA

I've never been dumped before. If that's what this is, and a raw, open slice through my soul has left me unsteady and aching. I don't know how to fix this.

Brecken obviously needs some time alone, and so do I, but the longer I dwell on my situation, the worse I feel. I decide to look for my brothers. They need me too, and if I can help fix their screwed up situations, maybe it will take my mind off of mine.

I picture Tyler's face in my mind, the light brown of his milk-chocolaty eyes, and his dusty-blond hair with the cowlick in back that makes it always stick up. My heart aches for him, all alone with no one to support him.

Ever since he and Derek walked out on my mom, things have felt disconnected. Where did Derek take Ty, who still needs his mother? He is too young to hang out with Derek's friends, too young to sit in on grownup conversations, and too young to be exposed to whatever Derek has started with his new rebellion.

Tyler needs someone to hold him when he cries, to ask about his day, to comfort him when hopelessness surrounds him like a pack of ravaging wolves, and I don't trust Derek to do that anymore.

Within seconds, I appear at Ty's side. He sits on the back porch of a house that seems vaguely familiar to me, but I can't place it. I sit next to him and gaze at his drawn face, but I'm unable to tell what he feels just by looking at his somber expression, so I place my hand over his.

Feelings of loneliness drift over me, but aren't overwhelming. Ty is sad, but not despondent like before. With a sigh, I look up at the blue afternoon sky. This peaceful moment, holding my brother's hand, is just the medicine I need, and hopefully what Ty needs too.

After a moment, the glass door behind us slides open. A woman I recognize as Derek's best friend's mom steps out with two full glasses of lemonade.

"Here you go, sweetie." She hands one to Tyler.

"Thanks," he answers quietly.

She sits on the step next to him and sips her drink. "It's a nice day, isn't it?"

"Yeah."

She looks into his eyes. A sparkling love radiates there. "I spoke to your Dad today. He says your mom is doing great and getting better fast. He's glad you're here with us, and so am I."

"Yeah, me too," Tyler answers. "But I miss my family."

"I know," she says, nodding and staring out into her backyard. "It's hard, but you'll get through it, Tyler. You're a wonderful, smart boy. But it will take time."

"I guess." He bows his head. "I wish Alisa were here."

His comment pierces my heart like an arrow, and I put my arm around him, willing him to know that I *am* here, loving him and missing him too.

"Yes," Mrs. Reynolds said. "Alisa's death is a terrible thing. I'm so sorry it happened."

"Me to," Tyler says, staring at his untouched lemonade.

I hate hearing this. I can't seem to escape the repercussions of my terrible decision. Oh, to go back in time, to change the course of events, to be with my family. And yet, I take each guilt-ridden barb into my heart. I deserve to hear this—deserve to feel the pain I've caused. I welcome the torture of Tyler's words. Maybe saying them out loud will help him heal. If I can suffer that for him, even for a moment, I will gladly.

"Didn't she care about me?" he asks suddenly. Tears well in his eyes and threaten to spill over his reddening cheeks. His voice breaks and he tucks his head into the circle of his arms, hiding his face.

"Oh, honey." Mrs. Reynolds sets her glass down and takes him in her arms. "I'm sure she did, but from what Derek said, she was taking medicine that made it hard for her to feel good or to think things through."

A sob escapes him and he leans into her, still hiding his face. After a moment, Ty's tears slow, and he sits up, wiping his face.

Mrs. Reynolds gives him another squeeze, then picks up her drink and takes a sip. "It'll all be okay," she says. "Your mom is getting help, and everything will go back to normal."

Tyler glances at her and nods, but I can tell he doesn't agree.

Things will never be normal again.

46

A Bad Plan

ALISA

For two weeks, Brecken and I hardly speak. He is on his best behavior: no stealing, no smoking, no swearing. He doesn't even go out with Jill during that time. I have no reason to lecture him, influence him, or correct him on any bad behavior. I don't do much but follow him around. I start wondering if maybe there is nothing left for me to do here. Maybe my job is over. If so, why am I still here? Why hasn't Raphael pulled me back to *Idir Shoal*?

I flit back to Tyler often, and he begins to improve. A smile returns to his face, and he becomes friends with Mrs. Reynolds other son, Gavin, who is only a couple years older.

I visit my mom as often as I can, and one time I overhear the doctor say she can go home soon. Everything seems to be turning around.

One evening, as twilight approaches, I sit on a park bench with Brecken, watching Heidi and Sophie play on the swings. Dramatic brush-strokes of pink and orange paint the sky as the sun sets behind the rounded hills, and a soft breeze blows. Relaxed, I find myself releasing the tension I've been feeling around Brecken.

Things have come to a place where we can communicate again. Kind of. Which is good because I still haven't told him about the vision I saw in Raphael's office. The time is just never right. But I have high hopes that we'll soon broach the subject.

Like right now.

"Can we please just sit without talking," he says before I can get one word out.

For a moment, I almost acquiesce, but the time for

procrastination has passed. It's now or never. "Isn't that what we've been doing for the last two weeks?"

He doesn't answer.

"Breck. We need to talk." I scoot closer to him, within touching distance, because being close to him somehow soothes me—and I hope him too.

He glances over and shrugs in a *whatever* kind of way and goes back to watching his sisters.

I take a deep breath and clear my throat. It's an old habit. "You need to know that something really bad lies ahead and I'm worried."

"Something bad always lies ahead." He stares right through me, his gaze hard, cold, and frustrated. "That's just a given for me."

"Is it?"

He shakes his head, his jaw flexing. "Of course. Why else would you even be here, Babysitter?"

I turn to watch the girls, mulling over his statement. Why is everything so hard with him? Why does everything feel like a battle? Why is it I can't get through, can't explain my feelings, can't understand his?

I shift uncomfortably.

He seems to sense my frustration because his eyes soften and the sun sparkles in his eyes, deep and unfathomable, like a bottomless ocean abyss. "All right," he whispers. "Let's talk. You go first."

"Chicken," I say with a chuckle. At least he is warming up. It is a step in the right direction. If he is willing to forgive me for running away all the time, I am willing to forgive him for stomping all over my heart. Over and over again.

"Let's go inside so I can see you better." He holds out his hand and I take it, the tingle of his touch tickling my fingers. Even though I'm sure he can't really *feel* me, I enjoy his fingers brushing through mine. I follow him inside to the living room.

One lamp glows in the corner and the TV is muted. The drawn curtains block the evening sun, and darkness blankets the room. We sit on the couch and face each other, my mind racing.

"I see you," he whispers, inhaling deeply. "And I love the way you smell. Like cinnamon rolls on Sunday morning." Back to the old Brecken I love. He tries to take my other hand unsuccessfully, and clears his throat. The smile he beams at me fills my heart, and I can't stop smiling either. "Alisa, I've changed my mind. I want to go first. Okay?"

I nod, wondering what he feels compelled to say to me after two weeks of self-inflicted solitary confinement. I pray it isn't something that will ignite another argument.

"I've been thinking pretty seriously about something. I know I've been weird these past two weeks, but I've been trying to decide what to do."

"Okay."

"When you came, something inside me clicked. I didn't want to admit it, and I'm still not sure what it is, but I'd lived without it for a very long time. It's hard to change and I have reflex habits that are difficult to let go of, but I want to try. *Finally,* I want to try, if you can be patient with me."

His words send a thrill through me, tingling from the inside out. The zing feels undeniably wonderful.

"My life... this life I'm living, seems like a dream, and sometimes a complete waste of time, especially with all the other guardians they've sent, but you are different than any of them. I felt it immediately." He tries to squeeze my hand, but his fingers pinch together instead.

I squeeze back.

"I have an aunt who lives an hour away. I'm going to take Heidi and Sophie there. She'll be a great mom to them and will really love them. She has wanted us to come live with her for a long time."

"Oh, Brecken. That's so great! I'm so happy. The girls need a mother and with your dad gone so much... not that you aren't doing a great job, but, you know."

"Yeah. That's what I thought, too. They'll love it there. She even has a swimming pool."

Brecken scoots closer and puts one arm around the back

of the couch so I am enclosed in his arms. It feels so right, but a battle rages in my heart. No matter how much I pretend, I can't have this boy. No matter how much I wish it, he can't have me. I'm dead. He's alive. This little play we're enacting will end.

He leans forward, the shadows of the room playing across his face, his eyes appearing like dark, glossy pools of mystery. "Alisa, I want to be with you. I know I was mean when you first told me about killing yourself, and I'm sorry, but it got me thinking. Dying can be fast and over quickly. Families move on in time. I've seen that firsthand. What I'm saying is... well, I have everything planned, and I want you with me the entire time."

I lean away to better read his expression. "Wait. What?"

He continues in a heated rush. "We'll have to wait until we get back from my aunt's, but tonight's the night." He smiles, his eyes filled with hope as he watches me.

"Maybe I'm slow," I say. "But are you telling me you want to kill yourself?"

He sits back, his brows pulled together, the corner of his mouth lifting in question. "You, of all people, should understand."

His comment stings just a bit. "You can't do this. Why would you? Especially when you were so awful to me about it? You can't really mean to..."

"Why not?" He gets up and walks around the table, his hands gesticulating as he paces. "We would be together. There's nothing here for me anymore. I'm tired of trying to hide who I am. I want—"

"Brecken. Stop. You *can't* kill yourself!" I jump up and hurry over to him. "It doesn't work like that. We'd *never* get to be together. Ever." I stare hard into his eyes, holding both his hands. "And what about your sisters? They need you."

He backs away. "No they don't. They don't even like me. They pretty much ignore everything I say. It wouldn't disrupt their lives in any way."

"Oh, Brecken, it would. You have no idea how much your life impacts theirs. And what about your dad? He needs you. Do you have any idea what this would do to him? First he lost his wife, and then you?" I can't believe these words are coming from my mouth. They sound so mature, so responsible, tumbling from my hypocritical lips.

He plops down onto the La-Z-Boy, his hands cradling his head. "I'm just so tired."

I kneel before him, wishing more than anything I could take him in my arms and make him forget his misery. I wish so much I could have met him long ago when I was still alive.

So much opportunity wasted.

"I know, Brecken. I felt the same way once. I truly did." I try to smooth back his hair, but my fingers brush right through the silken strands, impotent.

He gazes at me, wearing an expression of hopelessness. "I need to go." He stands, walks to the table, and grabs his car keys. "My aunt is expecting the girls by five."

47

Determined to Die

BRECKEN

Brecken can't believe Alisa's reaction to his plan. He thought she'd be excited, that she'd want to be with him too, on a *heavenly* plane. But maybe she's right. Maybe it doesn't work like that. But it doesn't make him feel any better. In fact, he feels stupid and embarrassed about the whole thing. He shouldn't have told her. He should have just gone done it and let it be a surprise.

They drive in silence to his aunt's house, Sophie, babbling to herself as she plays with little animal toys. Heidi mostly stares out the window—like always—with a bored expression, ear buds in her ears, music blaring.

"You should turn that down," he says, waving his hand in front of her face to catch her attention.

She glances at him and shrugs, ignoring his suggestion.

It's typical of the way Heidi treats him. She acts like she doesn't like him. She'll be glad he's gone and won't care at all. Sophie is the only one who might feel bad, and he'll miss her *and* her cute, childish imagination, her sweetness.

Alisa sits in the back with Sophie, not saying anything. What does she know anyway? She can only judge from her own experiences. She has no idea how he feels, what he is going through, what his outcome will be.

He still hasn't broken up with Jill and if he takes himself out now, he won't have to. That would solve one problem. It just doesn't seem important to continue on. His dad doesn't care—as far as he knows. His mom is the only one who truly loved him, and now she is gone.

She never came back to see him after her death, and he fully expected her to. It's a huge disappointment. She knew of his "gifts" and he'd thought for sure, she of all people, would come back. Maybe she *didn't* love him like he thought. His heart aches with that possibility.

Everything is just too hard. Every morning when he wakes up, it takes monumental effort to get out of bed. His life is falling apart and he's starting to have nightmares again, just like he had as a child.

In these terrifying dreams, he is always on a fiery battlefield, surrounded by hellish fiends, fighting with them, and then fighting against them. He doesn't understand it and his heart is torn with guilt—as though he has betrayed his friends. And the fear...

He doesn't know what he's done to warrant such feelings. He wakes up exhausted and terrified. Brecken hasn't told anyone about the dreams, and he isn't about to. People think he is crazy enough as it is.

No. Suicide is his best option.

His miserable life can end, and Alisa will forgive him just like he forgave her.

48

Forever Battling

ALISA

Brecken doesn't say one word to me after we drop off the girls. We come straight home, and he jumps out of the car, storming toward the house.

"Brecken, wait!" I stand in front of him. "I thought we decided suicide wasn't an option." I walk toward him as he fingers his keys. His eyes are wet, red, and horribly sad.

"That was your conclusion. Not mine."

He barrels through me. The rush of *him* fills me for a split second, but it's long enough to take my breath away, figuratively speaking. Every bit of matter—or whatever souls are made of—melds with him. For a moment, we become one, and that rush consumes my entire being. It's over too quickly. I can't help but gasp and fall to one knee. I want to cling to that moment, but before I can even blink, he moves on, and I'm left empty. A vacuum.

Did he feel the same surge? The same emotion? The same... merging? Did he feel anything at all? Dizzy, my mind spins in a million directions.

"Brecken," I gasp, pulling myself up to face him, feeling like I will hyperventilate at any moment. "I want you to be happy. Of course I'd love to spend forever with you, but the only way to make that happen is for you to live your life and die the right way."

He searches my face, looking breathless himself. His chest heaves and the pain in his eyes beseeches me to understand. "Maybe this *is* the right way... for me." He reaches out, but there is nothing for him to hold but thin air. His hands fall to his sides. "Maybe this is my destiny. Maybe it's supposed to happen like this. Just like you dying was meant to happen so we could meet."

"Brecken. Listen to what you're saying. I wasn't meant to die. I was meant to *live,* to get married, and to have a family. I screwed it all up. One-hundred percent. We weren't meant to meet like this."

His expression falls and he turns away. "Then maybe *nothing* is meant to be. Maybe there's no purpose and everything's just an accident. If that's the case, what's the point?"

I don't have an answer. I'm still confused myself. How can I possibly explain life and death when I am just as lost as he is?

Before I have a chance to say anything else, Brecken's cell phone rings. It doesn't take a genius to figure out who it is. I hear her pouty, falsetto voice clear over on the other side of the room.

"Hey, Jill," Brecken says when he answers. After a pause, he glances over at me. "Uh, I don't know. I'm kind of busy tonight." He's quiet for a moment. "Yeah, I know. Okay, I guess."

More jabbering from Jill.

"All right. But only for an hour. Yeah. I think so too." He holds the phone to his ear with a pained expression, and then glances at me. The conversation continues to drag on.

"No, everything's fine," he says. "Yeah, okay. Six o'clock. I'll be there. Bye."

I try not to glare, to not feel jealous or hurt, but if he thinks he can just leave me behind and hang out with his girlfriend...

"So," he says, glancing at me. "Jill wants me to come over for a little while." He takes in my expression and hurries to add, "I think it would be a good time to tell her my feelings have changed, and to... break up."

I cross my arms over my chest, and continue glaring. I agree it's time for him and Jill to break up, and it has to happen sometime, just not tonight. After our conversation earlier, I want to make sure he doesn't do anything stupid. And if he is with Jill, only stupid is possible.

"Come on, Alisa. It will only be an hour at the most. Don't be mad. I'm tired of fighting."

"I'm not mad."

"Right."

Sighing, I turn to him. "Fine. You're right." I lean my head against the back of the couch, closing my eyes. So tired. So drained.

"After I come home, we'll have the whole evening to talk."

"After *you* come home? You honestly think I'm going to let you go alone?" I watch him incredulously. He really thinks I'll just sit here and wait?

"Well, it's kind of a private conversation. No one wants to get dumped in front of an audience." He walks back out to his car and gets in. I stand beside his window—having followed him like a lost puppy, ready to jump inside too.

"I promise to come home as soon as I can, and I'll tell you all about it. Please let me do this alone."

A storm rages inside me. All the reasons I should say no are forefront in my mind. I don't trust Jill, and I can't trust Brecken not to be sucked in by her lies. How can I let him go alone? Yet I want him to trust me. There can never be a relationship between us if I don't start showing him that I trust *his* judgment too.

With a sigh, I agree. I'll let him dump his doofus girlfriend in private, but then he is all mine.

49

Beginning to Heal

ALISA

I sit alone, staring at the white, pictureless walls in Breck-
en's living room. With the girls and Brecken gone, the
quiet soon becomes tedious and lonely. Rather than
waste time, and since I haven't seen her in a few days, I decide to
visit my mom.

A moment later, I'm at her side. She's content, in her bed,
her blankets fluffed around her, looking through a photo album.
Dark hair hangs lustrously about her shoulders and she wears my
red-plaid pajama bottoms with a white tank top.

My clothes.

She robbed my closet, and a warmth I haven't felt in a long
time gratifies me. I sit cross-legged next to her on the bed and
lean near to see the pictures she's focused on. They are from the
last campout we went on the summer before I died. Stately pines
make the perfect backdrop to the mountain lake scene. I can
almost smell the scent of wild flowers on the remembered breeze.

Most of the photos are of my brothers and me. In one, I
hold a trout I caught. It dangles from my fingers, its gills spread
wide in death. There are a couple shots of us laughing in a canoe.
Two seconds after that picture was taken, Derek tipped us over. An
unforgettable water fight had ensued. Such happy memories. Had
I been depressed then? I'm not sure, but it doesn't look like it.

My mother probably wonders the same thing. She doesn't
look sad though, and she isn't crying. Her clear eyes shine, and
her skin glows a healthy pink. She runs her fingers over our faces
and smiles.

"I'm here, Mom," I whisper, touching her shoulder. I want so
badly for her to know I'm with her, that I understand, that I don't

blame her for anything.

Hearing the sound of feet on the stairs, I turn. Mom's bedroom door bursts open. Tyler lopes to the bed and jumps on, rolling right over me so he can sit next to Mom.

"Hi!" He hugs her waist. "Whatcha lookin' at?"

I pull back, staring at him in surprise. He seems a completely different kid than he was just a few weeks ago.

Mom wraps her arms around him and kisses the top of his head. "Just some pictures. Remember this one?" She points to us in our sleeping bags. "It was such a fun trip."

A sad expression comes over his face, and his smile turns into a frown. "Yeah, that was fun." He grabs the remote from the nightstand and flips on the TV. "Want to watch a movie?"

"Sure," Mom answers.

He searches the list of recorded movies and clicks on the most recent Transformers film. One I'd thought was monumentally stupid, but I snuggle in to watch anyway. Not ten minutes later, my dad comes in carrying my favorite treat in the world.

Hot buttered popcorn.

"I come bearing sustenance," he exclaims dramatically, and plops down on his side of the bed, placing the giant bowl on Ty's lap. I wish I could smell its salty-butteriness as strongly as I used to. I can sense its wonderful aroma, but it's different from when I had a physical body. In *Idir Shaol*, I can smell everything—the flowers, trees, shrubbery—but here, my senses are dulled, and I distinctly feel the lack.

For the next two hours, I bask in my family's company and wish Derek were here too. I snuggle by my dad, garnering strength and confidence, and then I move to lean against my mother's shoulder to feel her spirit. She seems happy now, relaxed. Maybe they are on their way to healing... finally.

When the movie ends and Ty has been sent off to bed, I realize how late it is. I jump from the bed, giving my parents a quick peck on the cheek, then focus on Brecken's house. He is probably waiting for me.

I appear at his house instantaneously.

He isn't there.

50

Blocked

ALISA

I check the clock. It's been three hours since Brecken left. Plenty of time to tell her she is wacko and get back home. I should have been here earlier, waiting. I shouldn't have spent so much time with my family.

I focus on Brecken, concentrating on him and only him.

I anticipate re-appearing at Jill's house, but instead I materialize in front of the old rundown house where I saw the unearthly fraternity meeting. He can't be here. I frown and step forward to go through the closed front door.

As soon as I step onto the porch, I smack into an invisible barrier and ricochet back, tripping on the bottom step and falling. This is disturbingly like trying to go over the diamond bridge. The similarity is not lost on me. I try again, but the same thing occurs. An unseeable force blocks my way. I can't go in. Plain and simple.

This has never happened to me on Earth. If Brecken is here, I should be able to go to him. Nothing should stand in my way. My spirit prickles at this new development.

I close my eyes and think of Brecken's face, focusing harder this time, concentrating on the deepness of his eyes, the softness of his full lips—things I shouldn't be thinking of—and close my eyes. I don't feel the familiar tug and pull in my belly, yet I open my eyes, fully expecting to be by his side.

Nope. Nothing.

A deep foreboding fills me. A dark fear. The heaviness of failure.

A sense of urgency stabs at me, and I wrack my mind for a solution, but the harder I try, the emptier my mind becomes, like a sieve losing sand. There has to be a way.

But what?

I'll go straight to the source and find out for myself. Moments later, I stand at Raphael's office door, panicked, pounding on the hard wooden surface.

For the first time, the door doesn't open.

I stare, stunned. A vast, black hole opens inside my chest, and all feelings of hope are sucked into a void of nothing. In despair, I sink to my knees, my hands covering my face, each breath slow and filled with desperation.

Then I feel a hand on my shoulder. I turn to see Anaita's brilliantly blue eyes.

"He's not here," she says. "He won't be back for quite a while. I'm in charge for the time being." She doesn't smile or offer any other information. Just stands with her hands clasped before her. Cold. Rigid.

She could offer to help, but from the tightness of her lips, the narrowness of her eyes, I know she won't. Brecken could die because of her haughty selfishness. I hate her more in that moment then I ever have before.

"I need Raphael *right now!*" I cry, feeling pathetic under her stare.

"Sorry. Nothing I can do about that." Her eyes do not invite me to confide, but who else can I turn to? I need someone, anyone, who knows how things work.

"I can't get to Brecken," I hurry to explain. "For some reason, I'm... locked out. I need help." I watch and wait for her to express concern or worry.

She gives me a cold smile and sighs. "Come to my office."

I follow her down the hall, wishing she'd move faster, but she continues as though we have all eternity to solve my problem. Her office, which is half as big as Raphael's, is much more plush, with fluffy, white pillows sitting on a red velvet couch, and multicolored candles burning on every surface. She walks behind her desk and sits down, ushering me to a chair across from her.

I balance on the edge, ready to fly back to Brecken. "We

need to hurry, Anaita. I think Brecken's in serious trouble."

"Indeed, he is," she says, not seeming the least bit worried.

I don't have time for niceties. I'm done pretending. "Well? What are you waiting for?"

"You seem to think there's something we should do." She reclines and steeples her fingers in her lap.

I tamp down the desire to scream, to rip out her condescending eyes, her full, pouty lips. I've already wasted too much time. What if Jill is drinking his blood at this very moment? What if, heaven forbid, he's going forward with his plan to kill himself? What if he's dead already?

"A month ago, you didn't care one whit about his boy. What could possibly have changed?" she asks with a sly smile.

I lean forward, my hands white-knuckled. I refuse to be embarrassed or ashamed. "Please. *Help* me."

"First, tell me the truth," she demands, grinding her teeth and leaning forward also.

"What do you mean? I don't have time for this!"

"You do know what I mean, but please, waste time asking stupid questions."

Her words bite, but I can only think of Brecken. I'll go through any humiliation to see him again. "Fine. I love him. But I'm sure you're already aware of this. *Now* will you help me?" I drop my hands from the desk and stand straight, my shoulders squared.

With a tired sigh, Anaita leans back. "Sit down, Alisa. There's nothing you can do for Brecken at the moment."

"What do you mean?" I sit reluctantly, my heart aching. Why is she stalling? What is wrong with this woman?

"There's a reason you were sent to help Brecken, and it wasn't so you could fall for him, although most bad boys are alluring, aren't they?" She smiles, but it doesn't reach her eyes. "I've always been drawn to them myself."

"I'm not like you."

"Hmm. Be that as it may, you have broken the rules. What would you say if I told you, that because of your behavior, you have been removed from this assignment?" Her eyes narrow and she leans forward as though she morbidly anticipates my misery.

My heart sinks in disbelief. She can't pull me from my guardianship. She isn't in charge. It's up to Raphael.

"Nothing to say?" She sits back, relaxed. "No crying for another chance? No begging?"

"When will Raphael be back?" I'm done playing cat and mouse. I don't have to be here, and I don't want her help anymore. She's not a good person, angel or not, and I refuse to bicker back and forth anymore.

"I already told you. I don't know. But I will tell you this—it's already too late."

I stare at her, shaking my head. I look straight into her eyes. "You're a real piece of work, lady." Full of disgust, I turn for the door. "I'll find a way to help Brecken myself."

"You do that."

Looking back over my shoulder, I give her my best glare.

She doesn't seem fazed.

I run as soon as the office door closes behind me.

51

A Nice Surprise

ALISA

I will myself to appear in the basement of the old house—not on the front porch, not in the filthy living room with pizza boxes, or anywhere else. I have to get inside. I have to see for myself that Brecken is all right.

Still, to my dismay, I cannot enter. Whatever barred my entry before, bars my way still. Frustrated beyond belief, I do the only thing I can think of.

I go home.

To my surprise, my parent's house bustles with activity. Long time neighbors are in the kitchen washing dishes, chopping vegetables, and visiting. Others sit at the kitchen table cutting out pictures and scrap-booking. In confusion, I hurry to the living room to find my Aunt Karen sitting on the couch drinking peppermint tea with my mother.

They laugh, their eyes sparkling with happiness as they reminisce about their childhoods. The sunset gleams brightly through the large, front window of our spotless house.

This is how it used to be.

An indescribable ache stabs at my chest as the realization of what I've thrown away is displayed before me. If only I'd understood, if only I'd known what I was giving up. If only some wounded soul like me had come to me beforehand and warned me of the danger of taking my own life, I wouldn't be here like this.

Trapped and miserable.

I float up through the ceiling to Ty's room, wondering if he is home. Sure enough, he's at his desk, working diligently on a model airplane. I've never understood how he can sit for so long, so focused, his fingers steady.

After giving Ty an invisible hug and kiss, I push back down through the floor, glancing at the ladies in the living room and continue on to Derek's room in the basement. As I suspect, he isn't there. Dust motes float in a single ray of sunlight that filters through the small window. His bed is made—Mom must have done that—and a newly folded pile of clothes lies next to his pillow.

How long has he stayed away? Does he even know Mom is home from the hospital? Does he ever come back to get clean clothes? I let the anger at his cruelty to our family filter through me. He should give our mom another chance. He shouldn't hold a grudge for so long. His refusal to forgive is hurting our whole family.

As soon as I think this, guilt nags at me.

I am doing the same thing in a way.

But I am holding onto hate for Mr. Roland, not someone in my family, and what he did was worse. He deserves my hate. He deserves to rot for eternity. How could I possibly forgive him? Wouldn't that be like saying what he did was okay?

I can't do that.

But Derek *should* forgive our mom. She wasn't in her right mind when she hurt Tyler. She shouldn't be held accountable. It wouldn't be fair.

Tired of analyzing, and missing Brecken like a crippled bird yearning to take flight, I go in search of him. My family is okay, on the road to healing, and I can concentrate on my new love—I mean my new job.

I close my eyes and shimmer out of sight, my spirit tingling in anticipation. I pray it will work this time, pray I'm not too late. I appear in Brecken's kitchen. He walks in at the very same time, a look of irritation plastered on his face. He slams the door shut behind him, not even realizing I'm there.

"Where have you been?" I demand out of frustration, sounding overly parental. "I've been looking everywhere for you."

I stand with my hands on my hips, like my mom used to. I rush to drop them.

He looks up in astonishment and searches the room for me. "I've been trying to console Jill. She's been crying all evening. I couldn't leave her alone like that. I feel terrible." He drops down on the couch and rubs his face, deep lines creasing his forehead.

"You feel terrible? For *her?*" I fairly scream. "I've been all over the place looking for you. I was so worried. I even went back to *Idir Shaol!* For some reason I couldn't get to you, and I tried over and over, and I agonized over all the things that could have happened to you! Then I went to that old house, but something kept blocking me from going inside, and all I could think was that Jill had hurt you, or you'd killed yourself, and that I'd failed, and would never see you again, and—"

He looks up, his eyebrows creased. "You looked for me in *Idir Shaol?* Where's that?"

"It's... like Heaven. And I knew you weren't there. The point is that I thought Jill had done something to you." I can see by the look on his face that he still doesn't completely believe the story I told him about Jill drinking his blood.

"I'm sorry you were worried, but you didn't need to be. I don't actually *need* a guardian. And... that's where I was," he says listlessly.

I fall onto the couch, holding my head in my hands. After all I've been through, the heartache, the worry—and he was with Jill the whole time. He doesn't even act like he cares. That is the worst part.

"Okay. I just... I was just so worried and I don't like you being with her."

He snorts and shakes his head. "I've also been trying to ditch *him.*" He gestures over his shoulder to the lazy boy recliner. "He has followed me all night."

I don't see anything. "Who?"

"The gray guy."

The gray guy? "What are you talking about?" Did he mean one of those dark evil spirits? A shadow fiend or dark minion, like the one Jill and the Lady in Red have? But I can't see it.

I have the sudden urge to back up.

"I used to call him the Shadow Man when I was little. He scared the crap out of me back then. Especially since I sleep alone in the basement. He's not *always* around, but when he is, he watches me and never speaks. I've started seeing a new one too. One with a darker color. Almost black. But that's only been recently."

My mind whirls with the implications, and I pace the room, adding it all up. "A dark spirit has followed you since you were a child. Another has come on the scene just barely... when you started... dating Jill?"

He turns, and throws me a warning glare. "Lay off it, okay?"

"Hey, I'm just sayin'." I continue to search the room and wonder why I can't see this mysterious being. "Can it see *me*?"

"I don't know, but he gives me the creeps." Brecken shivers and walks into the kitchen. "And he never leaves when I tell him to."

"Then *I'll* tell him." I storm over to the corner and scream, "Get out of here! As Brecken's heavenly guardian, and in the name of the god I serve, I order you to leave!" I point to the front door and wait in silence. "Well? Did he go?"

"He's looking at me funny. I don't think he can... hey, wait! He's gone! He just disappeared. Alisa! You did it. Do you know what this means?"

"Uh, no. What does it mean?" I ask, suddenly exhausted.

He hurries over to me, his face glowing with happiness. "It means he has to obey you! You told him to go and he did! You really are my guardian angel." His eyes soften as his arms reach out. I can sense the gentle tingle of his hands trying to hold me.

I step forward to make it easier for him.

"Thank you, Alisa." He gazes into my eyes, and it feels like sunshine. I can actually perceive my spirit heating up.

I reach out and place my hand on his cheek, slowly running my thumb over the corner of his bottom lip, imagining what it would feel like if I had a physical body. I lean forward, closing my eyes, yearning to experience more of him than just this glimmer of scintillating shadow.

Our lips meet, our souls meld... but it still isn't enough.

52

Stupid Ex. Always in the Way

ALISA

With closed eyes, we pull apart. The phone begins ringing and rings twice more before Brecken moves away.

"Uh, sorry." He reaches over to the coffee table and picks up the phone, answering the call.

"Hello?" His brows crease and his hand moves over his face and back through his hair. "No. I don't."

I scoot closer and lean in to hear the voice coming through.

"We can't find her. She left just after you did," a male voice says.

"Really?" Brecken answers. "She was sitting on the back porch when I left."

"She looked upset when I saw her," the voice says, "and then she jumped up and ran out the door with her car keys. She's not with you?"

"No sir, she isn't. I'm sorry."

"Could you help us search for her? Please? I'm really worried."

Brecken glances at me, his face drawn and tired. "Of course. I'll be over as soon as I can." He hangs up and sits down on the couch. "Jill's missing. Probably hiding on purpose so I'll go look for her. She's done this before."

"Then why get sucked into it?" It's so obvious he should let her go. Cut those ties once and for all. She's using him, trying to get him to rescue her, worry about her, want her. I shake my head in frustration. Will he ever be free of Jill's manipulating antics?

"Well, let's go," he says.

Rather than argue, I nod. But this will be the last time I let him get sucked into Jill's deep pit of subterfuge. "Fine, but if we can't find her, we're coming right back."

He looks at me, a strange grin on his face. "I know how we can find her."

"How?"

"You."

"Me?"

"Can't you find her? Like you do with me or your family?" His eyebrows raise and he nods.

Ack. I have zero desire to look for her, let alone be her rescuer. With an exasperated sigh, I say, "Fine. I'll see where she is. Then you can call her dad and tell him. That was her dad on the phone, right?"

He nods.

"Okay." Closing my eyes, I picture her face, her ugly, penetrating blue eyes, her maddeningly perfect platinum hair, her horrid, perfect body. Within seconds, I appear beside her in the basement of the old abandoned house.

I made it inside? Figures.

It looks a meeting just ended as there are empty paper cups and melted candles scattered around the room. There are only two people in that chillingly familiar basement room as the moment.

Jill and the Lady in Red.

Let me correct that. Jill, the Lady in Red, and their two evil, gray spirit beings who swirl around their naked feet in a thick, black mist.

At first, their conversation continues in quiet, hurried tones, but then the Lady in Red stills and lifts her head, inhaling deeply, her brows crease as she slowly searches the room.

"I smell cinnamon. Gamigin, who is here with us?" The sharp edge of her voice grates against my soul like abrasive sandpaper.

Chills tingle through me. Her words have a power I don't understand. Like silken chains, I feel bound being near her. Who is this woman?

"A girl," the demon says in a raspy whisper. "A lesser spirit guardian."

"Lesser?" I repeat. "I'm not lesser. If anyone here is lesser—"

"Silence!" the Lady in Red exclaims, standing. "I hear your insolent voice!"

I stop cold, automatically shrinking into a corner.

"Come to me, lesser spirit guardian," she commands. "Tell me who you are."

Fear wraps its icy fingers around my chest and squeezes. I don't want to step forward, don't want to confront this powerful woman who can sense me *and* hear me. I'm no match for her, I know. I have a feeling she can crush me into a million little pieces.

Closing my eyes, I will my soul to reappear beside Brecken. No way am I going to stay here, but strangely, nothing happens. I'm still in the room with Jill and the Wicked Witch of the West. Trapped.

"You cannot leave until I allow it," the woman says with a sinister smile. "This is *my* domain. What are you called?"

As though I have no control over my mouth, I hear myself answer. "Alisa."

"Ah," she says, standing. "I am Lamia. Gamigin, who does this powerless spirit protect? Someone important, I hope?" Lamia walks toward me with the practiced gait of a supermodel.

Gamigin floats through the air until he reaches me. He slithers around my feet, slowly making his way upward until his face is before mine.

I stand immobile, stunned that I am so easily overpowered and intimidated.

"Ah, yes," he hisses with glee. "She guards Bretariel, The Undoer."

"Come closer, girl," Lamia commands.

All this time, Jill has remained silent. Until now. "You!" she screams, standing, looking in the wrong direction. "I get it now." She throws her head back and laughs. She glances a Lamia with a look of incredulity. "When were you going to tell me?"

"I knew you'd figure it out sooner or later." Lamia wears a radiant smile, proud that her student has learned something important.

I'm totally lost. I glance at Jill, and then back to Lamia, then back to Jill. I know *she* can't hear me so it is pointless to answer, and I have no idea what they're talking about. I've never heard of this Bretariel guy before in my life.

"He thinks he loves you," Jill sneers. "He wants to be with you. His ghost-lover. Forever." With a menacing laugh, she continues. "I can certainly make that happen now."

"Hush, Jill," Lamia says gently. "I will do the talking." Lamia moves to stand before me. "Thank you, Gamigin."

The demon unwinds itself, floats back to Lamia, and begins swirling about her feet like a slow-moving hurricane. He winks at me and his mouth twists into a heinous grin.

"Unfortunately, I cannot destroy you at this time, Alisa, lesser guardian of the Undoer," Lamia says. "But I can make sure you stay out of my way."

"Oh? And how will you do that? You can't control me or order me to obey like that ignorant, little... whatever it is." I point at her minion.

"Enough!" she yells. Pacing over to the stairs, she turns, and then paces back. Suddenly she stops, a slow smile forming on her ruby-red lips. An evil glint sparkles in her eyes. "I've changed my mind. You may go, guardian."

That's it? She isn't going to threaten me more? Scare me into submission? Torture me with lies and revelations? Fine. I'm out of here. Within seconds, I leave the abandoned house with nothing hindering my departure. I shimmer into view before Brecken two seconds later.

"What took you so long?" He's frantic. Worried about little ole me? "Did you find her?"

His frustration and concern for Jill prick my soul. I want to reach over and smack him, and then tuck him in my pocket to keep him safe. "I missed you too," I tease. "And yes, I found her. But you're not going to like what I have to say."

He waits, his brows raised in anticipation. "Well?"

"She's at an abandoned house with a lady named Lamia. I don't know who she is, but she has her own shadow man that she commands. She's super creepy and kept me from leaving. I think she's what kept me out when I went there before. She's powerful… and frightening." I shiver.

"Then how did you get away?"

"She let me go."

He watches me, his brows knit in confusion, his head cocked to the side. "The lady made it so you couldn't leave, and then the next minute let you go? Just like that?"

"Well, yeah."

"Why?"

Something isn't right. It's my turn to be confused. "I don't know. I don't get it either."

He turns away, shaking his head and pacing the room, his hands stuffed deep into his jean pockets. "She's real. And all this time I thought she was a dream."

"Huh? What are you talking about?"

He looks reluctantly into my eyes, and then sighs with exhaustion. "It started when I was five."

53

The Woman in Red

ALISA

Brecken explains the strange night-visions that began as a child, where a beautiful woman in red came into his room, appearing from nowhere. She would stand by his bed, glaring down at him, never saying a word. He would hide under the covers, shivering, afraid.

Chills cover his arms as he relates his terror.

I can't come up with a single explanation to these awful visitations, but I know when he describes her, that it *is* Lamia. The woman in red.

"Well, at least we know," I say, tapping my chin and thinking. "But what is Jill doing with her?"

"Maybe she's bewitched, or deceived somehow. Maybe I should go find her. She needs to be told, or helped, or something!" Brecken jumps up and grabs his keys.

"Brecken, no! She's there of her own accord. Not because she was forced."

"Why do you judge Jill so harshly?" He says. "I know it's hard, knowing she was my girlfriend and everything, but—"

"Are you accusing me of being jealous? Seriously?" It could not be farther from the truth! I am certainly not jealous of Jill. She doesn't have one quality, not one redeeming attribute, I want. None. "Oh, that's rich."

Brecken's eyes narrow with hurt. "You just don't get it."

I have no idea what he is talking about. "No. I guess I don't."

"Just because you don't like her doesn't mean I don't."

That is a stab through my heart.

"I've been with her for a year and I love her. I know she's not good for me, and that we need to break up, but I'm not going to bash her, ruin her reputation, or criticize her. Got that?" He stands there, breathing hard, his stare turning into a frown.

"Oh, I get it just fine," I say, my hands on my hips. "You can't decide what you want. You can't have me in the flesh so you want to leave your options open. You want it both ways!"

He does not deny it and that cuts deep. I want him to lash out at her, hurt her, like she's done to him. He holds no malice toward her, and I don't understand it.

He takes a step back. Hurt and betrayal etched on his face. "You just *have* to ruin everything. How about you fix your own problems, and stop worrying about mine for a while. You're more screwed up than I am." He grabs his jacket and storms out the door.

54

Forgiveness, a Dish Served Reluctantly

ALISA

I watch him drive away, knowing he's right. I do ruin everything. If something is going great for me, I have to sabotage it somehow. It is a cycle I am very familiar with, but I don't know how to make it stop. It's almost as though I'm not happy unless I'm miserable.

That sounds pretty dysfunctional, and I don't want to be that way anymore. It will always keep coming back to Mr. Roland. I am letting the abuse continue—in my heart, in my mind, in my actions. I'm letting him ruin my life, *and* my death. I am letting him taint my thoughts, my hopes, and my dreams. Even still.

It has to stop.

Now.

And only I can stop it.

Is Gram right? Do I actually have to forgive the devil incarnate to heal? Do I have to let it go? Let go of the pain, the hate, and the shame—to make him go away? Is that even possible? Honestly, I'm not sure.

There is only one way to find out.

It's just like I remember. Dark. Cold. Petrifying. And I am alone. I stand at the gates of hell, the writhing, tormented souls waiting for me in the distance.

I force myself onto the path, force myself to move forward. I watch the ground, not wanting to make a wrong step. I remember how the black grass felt before.

I'm not sure where to find Mr. Roland because he found me the last time, but maybe all I have to do is think of him, focus on him, and I will find him... or he'll find me. The thought sends shivers through my soul, and my mind races in fear. I don't want to see him. Ever. But that is why I am here. To face my fears head on. The crushing weight of anticipation grounds me to fine powder, and threatens to shatter my hope into a million pieces. Will I ever be whole again?

I picture his face. The ugliness of his wicked grin, the roughness of his hands. And then... his eyes. Black holes that sucked my life from me little by little, with no feeling, no mercy. He never cared about Natty or me. I am sure he still doesn't. If he is sorry at all, it is because he got caught.

On and on I walk, deeper into the bowls of perdition, deeper into the darkness, the despair. If I had lungs, I would be gasping for breath. If I could sweat, I would be soaked.

And on I walk.

Pitch blackness coats me, so dark I can't see my hands. I'm afraid to go further. What if I get lost? Would anyone save me? Would anyone care?

I stand on that path, in the dark, surrounded by evil, more terrified than I've ever been before. A foul breeze blows, that eerie, sticky substance accumulating on me like before, pulling me down, weariness draining my energy.

"Mr. Roland!" I scream at the top of my voice. All the anguish, all the hopelessness, all the desperation I feel toward him bursts from my mouth with his name. "Mr. Roland. Come here right now!" I wait, my chest heaving, my heart aching, my mind slowly freezing with impotence.

The darkness presses in on me, forcing me to my knees. If he doesn't come soon...

"I'm here." A dull, raspy whisper.

"I can't see you."

"I am before you," he says, limping forward, beaten, miserable, more decrepit than ever before.

I step back, my eyes adjusting, shocked at the anguish in his eyes. Not because I am afraid, but because he looks so... tortured.

"I... I want to talk to you," I stammer, unable to tear my gaze away from his. I garner what strength I have left, what courage I can. With no one to help me, all the old feelings of insecurity, shame, and worthlessness rush back—everything he ever did to me, everything he ever made me do, every nasty word he whispered in my ear.

I stand straight and search deep into his soul—which I hadn't realized I'd be able to do. Gone is the authority he ruled with, and with that, gone is my fear of him. "What's happened to you?"

"I'm paying for my sins." He sinks to the ground, lying like a dog in submission, waiting for me to kick him in the vitals.

I am sorely tempted. "You've done a lot of bad things."

"More than you know," he moans, rocking to his side.

I want to say, *Good. I'm glad. I hope you're miserable forever.* Instead, I ask a simple question. "Why? Why did you hurt me?"

He shakes his head, filthy tendrils of hair swaying back and forth. "I don't know, Alisa. I was stupid. Selfish. I was an evil man."

"Have you seen Natty?" I ask, curious if she's ever been here to do what I am doing.

"Oh, yes. She comes often," he rasps. He rolls to his knees, his hands grasping his middle.

"She comes *here*... often?" I choke out. "Why would she do that?" She hates her dad. Despises him. More than me.

"She forgave me," he says, bowing his head, holding it like it will explode.

I scowl. That's not right. There is no way she would forgive him.

"Please, Alisa. I'm so sorry. If I could go back and make it right, I would." He sinks to the ground, sobbing. "I surely would."

I kneel beside him, not daring to actually touch him. I have to let go, have to give the burden back, give the shame back, give the guilt back, take my life back. The repulsion I feel—which has drowned me, pounded me, suffocated me—begins to morph slowly into something else. Something that fills my heart with foreign emotions.

I begin to see Mr. Rowland clearly.

Poor, pathetic Mr. Roland.

Pity pours from my soul. This wretched creature is stuck here forever, or at least for a very long time. In that moment, a heavy weight lifts inside me, floats for a moment, then shifts up through my shoulders and neck and exits through the top of my head, taking the impossible burning of *Mr. Roland* with it.

A lightness like I've never felt before mends my being. A joy I can't explain tingles all the way to my fingertips, all the way to my toes. Light explodes from my eyes and I can see everything in that hellish world in grim detail. I feel myself glow, brighter and brighter, and the darkness pulls back, unable to smother me any longer.

I look directly at him. "I forgive you, Mr. Roland. You can't hurt me anymore. You can't hurt anyone, and I honestly hope that someday... someday, you'll be free of your torment."

"Oh, thank you," he cries. Great sobs of released anguish erupt from his twisted lips as he lies at my feet writhing, suffering. "You don't know what you've done," he says. "You don't know."

I suspect I do know, but I don't say anything. Instead, I leave like a wisp of smoke.

55

A Terrible Weight Lifted

ALISA

I make my way back to earth, floating on happiness. I can't wait to tell Gram and Natty about my unexpected experience. A terrible burden has been lifted, and I hardly know how to describe my liberation.

But first, I want to tell Brecken. Warmth and love burst through my heart as I picture his beautiful face, knowing I'll be at his side in only a second. My soul tingles in anticipation.

Nothing happens.

Frowning in confusion, I try again. And again. And again. A familiar clutch of fear begins to worm its way inside me. Over and over, I will myself to materialize beside him, and over and over, it fails.

What is wrong? Am I supposed to visit my family instead? The last time I couldn't go to Brecken, my brothers needed me. But which one now? Figuring Derek is the troublemaker, I focus on him. When I open my eyes, I'm a hundred feet above the ground, floating in the blue, cloudless sky.

"What the—" And then it hits me. "No!" I moan in despair. "Not yet!"

As though an umbilical cord is attached to my belly, I am pulled back to *Idir Shaol.*

"This isn't right! My time isn't up yet!" Impotent fury boils inside me, ready to shoot forth like a geyser of righteous anger at the injustice of it all. They can't do this!

Raphael is back. He sighs and nods his head. "I know it seems unfair, Alisa, but you aren't his permanent guardian, and we feel your attachment to him has become too... serious."

"My attachment?" I scream. "I'm *supposed* to be attached to my charge."

"You know what I mean," he says. "Being difficult isn't going to change anything."

"This isn't right," I cry, beyond frustrated.

"Everything happens for a reason." He carries a white folder over to his desk. "Brecken must make his own choices. He needs to be responsible for his own life. You helped him see that, and helped him accept his gifts just a little bit more. You gave him confidence to be who he is, and kept him from committing suicide. You were a success!" He smiles and leans against his desk. "Now you can move on to the next level."

"The next level?" I ask. "Would that be where my Grandmother is?"

"Uh, well, no." The smile disappears from his face. He sucks in air through his teeth with a pained expression. "It would be to the next level. It takes time to pay for mistakes, Alisa. It's not easy. That's why it's better to atone for our mistakes during life."

"Gee, Raphael. I'm sorry to hear that," I say with a touch of venom. "I didn't realize I had to stop at confession on my way past the pearly gates."

"Now Alisa. There's no need for disrespect."

"Arrg!" I stomp toward the door. "I've had it. I'm done here."

"Wait!" Raphael calls as I am about to slam the office door behind me.

I don't turn around, but I stop, my hand resting on the crystal door handle.

"I know this hurts, Alisa, but there's an important lesson for you in all this. The lesson of letting go."

I pivot slowly, my eyes boring into his like hot coals. "Letting go? The lesson of *letting go?*" I step toward him methodically. "You have no idea what I've been through. You have no idea what I've just experienced. Is anyone actually in charge up here?" I don't care if

I'm being disrespectful or not. I don't care about the consequences. What more can they do to me? What could be worse than being ripped from my family or blocked from Brecken? No other torture can compare. The two things I want most are gone. The fact that I recently visited Mr. Roland in Hell doesn't even enter my mind.

"I think you need some time alone," he states.

Shaking my head in disgust, I flee the room, hot tears that can never fall, burning behind my eyes.

56

Reunited

ALISA

I sit on a lonely hillside outside of *Idir Shaol*, a carpet of soft, green grass surrounding me. Birds flit through the nearby trees, singing gleefully. It is a beautiful spot. Any normal person would be thrilled to be here. But all I want is to be back on Earth.

A sob tears through my throat as I bury my head in my knees. I *have* to get back. I just have to. I can't stay here, knowing my job isn't finished. How can Raphael think it is? Everything inside me screams to go back, that Brecken is in imminent danger.

Not being able to stand the beauty and peace another moment, I picture the park where I used to play as a child. I might not be able to see my family or Brecken, but maybe I can get close.

Luck is on my side. I shimmer into sight next to the park's tall, metal swing-set with the familiar blue plastic seats where Natty and I used to have our best conversations. I reach out and grasp the chain; a million memories fill my mind. I sit in one and imagine myself flying up to the sky and back, my feet outstretched, my stomach doing a roller coaster twist.

The only thing that could make the moment more perfect would be Natty sitting right next to me. A moment later, I hear her soft chuckle.

"I love how that works," I say, knowing she's here, only because I want it so bad.

"Me too."

"You sound content," I say with a hint of jealousy.

"I am, Lis. I'm *so* happy, and it won't be long until you're with me."

"Long in whose eyes?" I shake my head. Time on Earth is nothing like time in the afterlife. The two have nothing in common. Everything takes an eternity now.

"Aw. It'll go by fast. You'll see." She leans back, her short, wispy blonde hair glowing like a golden halo.

"Nat, I need your help." I say, leaning back too.

"I know."

"You do?"

"Sure. That's why I'm here." She sits up straight, and smiles that beautiful, wide smile I love. "Your wish is my command."

"Yeah, right. That's what everyone says. I haven't had any wishes come true so far."

"You haven't?" she asks, perplexed. "What about getting to see your Gram? What about being able to let go of the pain my father caused you? What about finally falling in love?"

"Uh... "

"See?" she says. "Lots of good things have happened to you. But you want me to help you break the rules and sneak back into Brecken's life, right?"

"Yeah." She makes it sound so awful, so illegal.

"Ah, l'amore," she whispers with a sigh. "How often do we find true love? In life or death?"

"It's keeping it *after* death that concerns me," I say. "I can't just leave it like this. Brecken and I parted on bad terms and I really feel I should fix it. I'm sure he's worried and wonders where I am. Maybe he thinks I've abandoned him. Left him on purpose. That I've dumped him. I can't do that. I can't have him think I'm angry for the rest of his life."

"Didn't he say good-bye, Alisa?" She watches me with that gaze again, the one where I can't hide any secrets. Not that I want to.

"Well, yeah, but he doesn't mean it. He doesn't understand."

"I know," she says sadly. "Most humans don't. We don't figure anything out until later, until we're dead."

"Please, Natty," I beg, turning to my best friend in all the world. My sister. My only hope. "There's got to be something you can do."

"Well, there is one thing," she says in a lighthearted, singsong voice.

I jump down and grab the chain of her swing. "There is?" Hope and happiness flood through me. I knew she'd be able to help.

"I can take you one last time to say good-bye. They'll let me do that. At least I'm pretty sure they will."

"Oh, Natty. I love you!" I throw my arms around her and listen to her peals of laughter.

"Come on, before it's too late." She grabs my hand, closes her eyes, and purses her lips. She looks so cute while concentrating. I close my eyes too, her hand tight in mine. A moment later, we are there, at Brecken's front door. His motorcycle parked in the driveway. He's home! I run forward, forgetting Natty is even with me.

"Is someone visiting?" she asks from behind.

I turn to answer and stop cold in my tracks. Parked on the curb is a shiny black Mercedes Benz. "Oh no!" I hurry through the front door, not bothering to wait for Natty. Brecken isn't in the living room. I search the kitchen and even the bathroom, but no Brecken. "He must be downstairs."

I shoot through the floor and straight into his basement bedroom. Only one lamp glows in the corner. Brecken sits on his bed, Jill beside him. He holds her hand as tears course down her porcelain cheeks.

"Oh, Breck," she hiccups. "I'm so... so lonely. Please... I love you so much."

Instantly, my gag reflex triggers and my suspicion of Jill's ability to lie hits the Richter scale. "Please tell me you aren't falling for that," I say.

Brecken's head snaps up and he looks right at me. His eyes narrow as he takes me in, my white dress, the glow of my aura, the pleading in my eyes. I wait for him to say something, but instead of being happy to see me, he seems flustered.

Okay, granted. I shouldn't have started our very last

conversation the way I did, but seeing Jill holding his hand... Jealousy courses through me, her being able to feel the heat of his body when I can't. More than anything, I want it to be *me* he holds and comforts.

I shake my head in regret. "I'm sorry, Brecken. I didn't mean that," I move to sit next to him.

Jill continues to rattle on. I completely ignore her. "I'm being sent back to... uh, heaven. I can't be your guardian anymore." I bow my head, but look up quickly. I don't want to waste the time we have together not watching his face. I search deep into his eyes, deep into his soul, memorizing every line, every crease, every eyelash, and every expression.

"What?" He leaps from the bed, leaving Jill stunned. It's a priceless picture. "Why?"

"Why?" Jill asks. "Isn't it obvious? We're meant to be together, Brecky. Please come with me for just a little while. I really want to show you something."

"Because they said my job here is done. You passed the test, I guess. I tried to talk them out of it, but they won't listen to me."

Brecken's gaze flickers from Jill to me, and then to Natty. "Who's that?"

Jill's face clouds over with darkness. Her eyes close to slits, and hate radiates from her as her lips pull back into a feral snarl. "Who are you talking to now, Brecken? Cuz it's obviously not me."

Brecken turns to Jill, his eyes begging for understanding. "Umm, I need some time alone. Why don't you go home and I'll be over later. Okay?"

"No," she answers. "That's not okay."

"This is my last good-bye," I say, hoping he'll make Jill leave. "I won't ever see you—" A sob breaks from my aching heart and I cover my face with trembling hands.

"Tell me it isn't true," he says, reaching, his hands brushing though me as though I am only made of smoke. My spirit ripples, and then stills. "I'm not ready to say good bye. We need more time."

"I know."

Jill moves so she's standing before Brecken, her hands digging in her pocket, her face a mask of rage, her eyes as cold as lake frost. "This is going to end right now," she says with deadly calm.

Before anyone can move, Jill pulls her needle-like teeth from her pocket and stabs them deep into Brecken's chest.

He screams and pulls back, the fangs ripping out of Jill's hand. He shoves her away, and covers the wound in horror. "What are you *doing?*" He stumbles and falls to one knee, and then to the floor. The surprise in his eyes fades, and then he lies there staring up at me, unable to move.

I kneel by his side, wishing I could staunch the blood that oozes between his fingers. "We have to get you out of here."

"Tell your lesser guardian goodbye, Brecken, cuz it's lights out for you in thirty seconds." She glances at the watch on her wrist.

Brecken's gaze comes back to me, his eyes pleading. Natty kneels beside us. "There's nothing we can do," she says. "I'm so sorry," she whispers to Brecken.

"What's happening?" he mumbles, his limbs flopping like jelly. "I can't... move." His head falls back and his eyes roll under their lids. His fingers twitch.

"Finally." Jill wipes her hands on her denim short-shorts and squats down to look at Brecken. She tiptoes around him and then crouches by his head, staring down into his face.

"What is that?" Natty asks. "Where'd she get those weird teeth?"

"I told you! No one ever believes me! I told Raphael this was happening and he didn't care. He said Brecken had to make his own choices. Well, he can't do that if he's out cold! I'm his only hope now. You've got to help me, Nat."

She watches me with concern, unsure. "I don't know..."

"Please," I beg with all my heart. "We have to help him."

She bows her head. "All right."

57

Kidnapped by Thugs

ALISA

I stand at Brecken's side in the dank basement and watch as Jill pulls out her cell phone. She taps the iPhone's screen and then curses under her breath. "Stupid reception." She stomps out of the room and up the stairs.

"Stay with him," I tell Natty. "I'm going to see who she calls."

"Okay," Natty answers. "Do you think he'll wake up soon?"

"I doubt it." I saw what Jill's drug did the last time. I'm pretty sure we have a few hours before he comes around.

Jill stops in the living room, finally able to make her call. "Hi. It's me," she says. "Yeah. I'm ready. Hurry." She ends the call and glances up at the ceiling, releasing a long sigh. She shakes her head and laughs.

That is when the leech demon appears, a wide smile stretching across his gray, wispy face. He slithers around Jill's ankles and then up her legs until he has wrapped his smoky arms around her neck. He glances at me with a wicked grin. A long, snake-like tongue flicks from his mouth as though he is tasting the air. He licks Jill's cheek.

A chill runs over my shoulders.

She stops laughing, walks over to the window, folds her arms across her chest, and waits. She can't see the gray man. She has no idea he's there, but that doesn't make me feel sorry for her. She chose this road.

Glaring, I stalk over to her, double up my fist, and punch with all my might. My hand goes right through her, just as I knew it would, but what surprises me is that she stops smiling and presses a hand to her face. Her lips turn down into a frown.

A moment later, I hear the squeak of car brakes in the driveway. Instantly, I am out the front door, hoping to influence whoever it is to help me.

I'm soon disappointed.

A silver Jag idles in the driveway, sparkling and beautiful. The door swings open and a long, slender leg steps out. At first, I don't recognize her. She wears a deep crimson business suit, the skirt ending just above her knees. The soft material hugs her lithe figure like spandex, and not one strand of her A-line bob is out of place.

She closes her car door while three goons file out of the back seat, unfolding into giants. "He's in the basement," she murmurs, strutting with the confidence of a super model. Without knocking, she enters Brecken's house.

I watch in open-mouth surprise, and then follow them in, trying to place her identity. Then it hits me.

Lamia. The woman in red. The woman in charge of Jill's vampiric society. How could I not have recognized her? Her hair is different. Shorter. Stylish.

Two minutes later, the thugs lumber up the stairs carrying Brecken. Natty is right behind them.

"I tried to influence them, Alisa, but they wouldn't listen," she says. "They're past hearing."

Brecken's head lolls to the side.

"Yeah, and past thinking too," I answer. "We'll just have to go with them to see where they go."

They load Brecken into the front seat and even buckle his seat belt, then take off down the street. Jill follows in her car. I take Natty's hand and concentrate on that car. Within seconds, Natty and I are sitting in the back seat of Jill's Mercedes.

"I think we need help," Natty says. "You and I can't do this alone."

I'm not sure I want outside help. What if we ask Raphael and he says no? Would he stop Natty and me from returning to Brecken? More than anything, I want to be with him, but I know if he dies now, it will never happen. Not because he would be responsible for his own death in any way, but because he'll probably go to Elysium and I'll still be stuck trying to redeem myself in *Idir Shaol*. "No. I think we should see if we can do this alone for now."

Natty shakes her head. "You're making a big mistake."

"Please don't say that, Nat."

She sighs and turns to look out the window. A heavy stone of doubt fills my heart. *Am* I making a mistake? Why do I feel I have to do everything on my own? Maybe if I'd asked for help during my life, I wouldn't be in this mess. But then, I would never have met Brecken. Then again, maybe I would have. Maybe our destinies are woven together in the tapestry of life, and had I lived, somehow, our paths would have crossed.

To my surprise, Jill doesn't pull up in front of the rundown, little white house like I expected, but at a wide, black, iron gate that leads down a winding drive to a red brick mansion in the distance. The gate opens and we drive up to the front of a beautiful Tudor mansion.

The woman in red steps from her car, her four-inch, gleaming red heals clicking on the paving stones. "Take him to the basement," she commands, sailing into the house, not even bothering to wait.

58

The Auditorium

ALISA

he men drop Brecken onto a narrow cot in a dingy cell down the hall from a basement auditorium. Lamia waits beside him and stares into his sleeping face with hunger. She smooths his hair back. "Almost time, my lovely. Almost."

She steps back and walks into the spacious auditorium. On a raised stage sits a king-sized mahogany monstrosity with brocade quilts. It's surrounded by at least a hundred chairs on risers. The seats start to fill with black-robed patrons. Jill finds a seat on the front row while Lamia walks to the raised stage.

Candles burn in every corner of the room, creating shadows that meld with the ghost-like demons that dance on the edge of reality. One after another, more gray men slither up from an iron vent in the floor. They fill the empty spaces, floating, slithering, and caressing the unsuspecting audience.

A young teenage girl is brought out of a side-room next to Brecken's, and is laid on the king-size bed. Unlike Brecken, she is awake and straining against the ropes tied around her hands. Her eyes are wide with fear, and her screams are muffled by a silk rag stuffed in her mouth.

An expectant hush fills the room.

Lamia turns to the anticipating crowd. "My children. Tonight you witness the union of night and light, deities and daemons. Tonight, the dead rule and command legions. Tonight... we crush our enemy!"

With raised arms, she spins on her heels and ushers in a man who wears a white robe over black silk clothing. He smiles wide at Lamia as he enters, taking her hand and kissing her fingertips. "Beautiful, as usual," he murmurs, grazing her cheek with his lips.

I cringe as an overwhelming blanket of evil permeates the auditorium. It winds around me like a hissing cobra tightening its coils. Whoever this man is, he is evil in its purest form.

Lamia turns to the crowd with a flourish. "May I introduce the original member of our Order? Andras, the Marquis of Hell, the Sower of Discord."

He bows low, his seductive smile never wavering. He watches the crowd, catching the eye of each person, silently commanding their attention.

I move closer to see his face clearer. Natty is still at my side. She holds onto my arm, her hand clasped tightly in mine. "I have a really bad feeling about this," she whispers. "We shouldn't be here and I don't think I *can* stay much longer," she says in a strained voice. "I'm not... a guardian and... something won't let me. I can't... fight it anymore. I'm sorry, Lis. I love you."

She disappears in a glistening mist. Without her at my side, I feel cold and abandoned. Alone and weak. The room seems more vile and dangerous, but I can't leave Brecken in a place like this. Alone. Unconscious. How could I leave him with Lamia, let alone the Marquis of Hell? But can I do this by myself? I scan the crowd, my gaze stopping at a pair of familiar, dark eyes. Eyes I've known my whole life, Eyes that rescued me from Mr. Roland long ago.

Derek.

He wears the same black robe as the other acolytes, and stares straight ahead, his eyes wide, his mouth in a tight, grim line. The fact that he is here makes everything feel more dire and dreadful. I hurry over to him. "Derek? Derek, can you hear me? Please, hear me," I beg, patting his cheek, hoping to wake him up to feeling me.

His brow creases and he raises his hand, but lets it fall back to his lap. Hope flickers through me. "You have to leave. You shouldn't be here," I whisper urgently into his ear. "It's dangerous. *Please* leave. Just stand up and go."

He glances toward the door. It's open, but a large man with

wide shoulders and a jagged scar across his cheek shuts it behind him after he enters. The lock clicks into place with a decisive thunk.

We're locked inside.

A panicked expression flits across Derek's face, but he stays seated, his hands clasped, white-knuckled in his lap. His breathing increases, his heart races. Placing my hand on his arm, I feel a tumult of emotions boiling beneath the surface. Horror, fear, dread.

His panic infects me and for the first time in ages, I turn to that God I have yet to meet, not sure if he'll even hear me, let alone listen. "Please," I beg. "Please make this stop. Don't let this happen. Help us get out of here."

Andras, his shoulder-length black hair falling forward, leans over the girl, who now lies still, paralyzed with fear on the bed. His dark eyes search her face, his long, white fingers stroking her cheek. She writhes beneath him as though his very touch sears her skin. He removes the gag from her mouth and trails a solitary finger along her rosy, trembling lips.

"Please," she begs when her mouth is free. "I made a mistake. I'm so sorry. I won't tell anyone."

"That's right, my dear, you won't," Andras answers in a raspy whisper. "But now you must sleep in the bed you made... so to speak."

Terrified, she trembles, and knowing there is nothing I can do to help Derek at the moment, I hurry to her side. There might not be a way to stop this event from happening, but I can offer this poor girl some comfort.

I slide over the bed until I'm next to her. "Don't be afraid," I say, placing my hand over hers.

Andras leans down, his lips parted, and inhales the scent of the girl's neck, then frowns. He turns his head to the side, his brow creased and his eyes squinting. He takes another slow, deep breath, his nostrils flaring. Slowly he pulls back. "I smell cinnamon."

Andras rises up on one elbow and glares at Lamia. "Have you taken the proper precautions?"

Lamia's chin raises, her eyes narrowing. "Of course. What

do you take me for?"

He glances down at the struggling girl. "What's your name, darling?" he asks, still stroking her cheek.

"Nichole," she whispers, her chest rising and falling with each panicked breath.

Andras begins untying the rough rope around her bound wrists.

"Oh, thank you," Nichole cries with a sob.

He smiles down at her lovingly and takes her left hand, pulling it toward the left corner of the headboard, tying it to a red, satin ribbon that is attached there. The girl yanks on her arm, but the heavy, satin cloth holds fast.

Before she can blink, Andras pulls her right arm and does the same on that side. Within seconds, she lies spread-eagle on the huge bed, the captivated audience watching. Horror fills her eyes and immediately she begins to scream.

I want to scream too.

The audience leans forward, their anticipation palpable. They can't be enjoying this.

"Cease your noise!" Andras commands Nichole, his eyes deep pools of merciless blackness.

I am in way over my head. I can't stop what is about to happen unless I have legions of angels at my back. Helplessness presses against me and more than anything, I feel the need to cry. For this girl, for my brother—who I am sure is about to witness something atrocious—and for myself, powerless to stop it.

Nichole ceases her crying and lies with her head turned away, her sobs almost silent in the hushed, candlelit room.

Andras stands and addresses the audience. "And now we begin." Taking a silver box from a small table by the bed, he opens it. The red-velvet interior glows in the warm light, surrounding a gleaming set of silver fangs, deadly sharp.

He pulls the fangs from the box and places them in his mouth, moaning with pleasure as they slide into place. He turns to the crowd, his lips stretching over his shining canines. "And now my children, I shall become one with this offering, her essence, her soul. I claim her for my own. There is no act more powerful, more binding, or more exquisite."

With a low growl, he swirls back toward the bed, his cape whipping out behind him like silken bat wings. He jumps onto the bed, his knees straddling Nichole's waist, his hands pressing her forearms into the soft mattress.

I blink my eyes, because I'm sure I am seeing things. For a split second, dark, leathery wings spread out behind him, and glossy, ebony feathers coat his raven-like head. When I blink again, he is back to his normal self, the Sower of Discord. But the shift happens again when he sinks his teeth into the hollow of Nichole's neck. His arms slither beneath her, pulling her closer, as he drinks with bloody lips.

Nichole arches, her eyes rolling back, but no sound comes from her dying lips.

I search the room frantically, hoping someone will stand up and fight for this poor girl's life. I even look deep into my brother's eyes, but he sits frozen, dismayed at the sight before him. His hands grip the chair's armrest, his eyes filled with terrified, unspilled tears.

Step by step, I back off the stage, never taking my eyes from the horror before me. Andras moves over the girl until she lays completely still, her blue eyes staring from an ashen face. Finally, he raises himself from the bed, a thin stream of crimson trailing down his chin. He roars in triumph, the muscles in his neck taut and stretched to a grotesque limit.

"What happened?" a small voice says beside me.

My eyes shoot back to the bed to find the source of that high, frail voice. Nichole, a mere wisp, a copy of the body that lies dead, looks up at me expectantly.

"What's happening to me?" she asks, looking right at me, her spirit flickering and dim.

Andras turns. "To whom do you speak, child? There's no one here but you and me." He holds out a hand, looking right at Nichole's tortured soul. "Come."

I look from Nichole to Andras. He can't see me, but he can

see her. She steps forward, unsure, and reaches out to Andras, as though she can't refuse even if she wants to. I watch, completely in shock. Where is her family? Where is the light? Isn't she supposed to walk toward the light?

As soon as she takes his hand, his mouth opens wide—to an inhuman degree—his silver, gleaming teeth appearing even more deadly in this demonic orifice. Her clothes, which are mere rags instead of gleaming robes, whip about in an invisible storm. Her hair flaps wildly about her face as her eyes dart toward mine. She reaches for me, but before I can grasp her hand, her spirit spirals with tornado swiftness into Andras's dark maw.

He inhales slowly, his chest expanding, his head thrown back in ecstasy, his arms out wide. "It is done!"

59

Trapped

ALISA

A collective sigh fills the room.

Jill leans forward in her seat with anticipation, her eyes filled with excitement. I search the auditorium and find the same expression on nearly every person there. But my brother doesn't wear it. He recoils in his chair, repulsed. I make a flash appearance beside him and grab his hand, willing him to erase his open-book reaction. If there is one thing I know, it's that he can't reveal himself without consequences.

"Relax, Derek. Soften your face. Close your eyes. Take a deep breath," I whisper in his ear. "Don't let them know your true feelings."

Immediately he complies, taking a deep breath.

The guy next to him turns and shoots Derek a smile. "Have you ever seen anything like that?" He seems manic, intoxicated, desperate for his turn.

It sickens me.

"Just hang on until we can get you out of here," I whisper, smoothing the stress lines along Derek's brow.

Lamia and Andras stand at the front of the room, smiling and triumphant. They move through the audience with steady, confident steps, shaking hands and receiving congratulations.

When they reach Derek, he takes Andras' hand with a blank stare.

"Smile," I say.

Andras hesitates, and then murmurs, "Yes, indeed. Smile. You mustn't show your true feelings."

Derek's eyes slowly rise to meet Andras' deep, black holes,

which stare down at him.

"Who's your friend?" Andras asks without releasing Derek's hand.

"Uh," Derek starts. "My friend? I don't know what you mean." Derek glances at the kid beside him. "I don't know him."

Andras' eyes narrow and his lips pull back into a snarl. Derek's eyes dart back and forth, then meet Lamia's who has just come over.

Andras turns to her. "This acolyte has a tag-along," he says, a snarl in his voice. "The same spirit who was on the bed with Nichole. I can smell her still," he hisses.

"Really?" Lamia's eyebrows rise to a high, thin line. "Now that's interesting. I haven't sensed it."

Derek pulls back on his hand, which is locked in Andras' grip. "Honestly, I don't know what you're talking about. I didn't bring anyone. I haven't told anyone about these meetings." He glances back and forth between them.

"Take him to a cell," Lamia commands, her arms folded over her chest, her ice-blue eyes, hard and unforgiving.

"Wait! I haven't done anything!" Derek screams as two neanderthals grasp him by the arms and drag him out of the auditorium.

They throw him in a room identical to Brecken's and shut the door with a loud bang. The lock turns from the outside. I stay by his side.

Derek stares at the door, then turns and thrusts his hands through his hair, his breath hissing out. "Oh, no. No, no, no." He paces the floor, sweating like he's run a marathon, his eyes rolling like a dying animal's.

"Oh, Derek. I'm so sorry. I'll get you out of here if I can," I say, trying to send a message of calm, although it flies far from the mark. He continues to panic. He can't hear me. Natty was right. I need help. Even if it means humbling myself and admitting I broke the rules, I'll do it to make things right.

Closing my eyes, I take in the silence, the quiet of this haunted death chamber. I hate leaving Derek and Brecken here, but I have to. I have to go straight to Raphael. I know he'll help.

I picture his face and his office, willing myself to appear there.

I open my eyes.

I'm still in the vampire's death den.

Please no.

I try again with the same results. With a sinking heart and an awful dread, I realize I'm trapped. Hurrying out of Derek's cell and over to a back door that surely leads to freedom, I run my hand over the handle, but of course, I can't turn it, and it isn't even locked. Without thinking, I bang on the door in frustration. My hand *doesn't* slip through like it should have. It stops at an invisible barrier, like the one at the bridge to Elysium.

Leaning my head against the solid wood, I ponder my situation. I'm trapped, like always... on the wrong side, making stupid choices. Just like my brother.

But this time it isn't about me. I've come to save Brecken. He is my whole reason for being here. With a blink of my eyes, I appear inside his cell. At least I'm not trapped from moving between rooms.

Brecken still lies on the stained, bare, sheetless cot, but he has woken up. Kind of. His arm lies over his eyes and he moans softly, as though having a bad dream.

"Brecken, can you hear me?"

He turns toward the sound of my voice, squinting. "I feel like I'm gonna puke."

I kneel at his side so our faces are only inches apart. "I'm here."

"Where am I?"

Placing my hand on his cheek, I say, "You're in the basement of some really fancy house. A mansion. Some really bad stuff is going on here."

He rolls away from me and faces the wall, holding his stomach. "I don't feel good. Let me sleep."

"Brecken, no. You need to get up. We need to get out of here. We can leave right now if you do. There's no one in the hall. All you have to do is open a door." I put all the urgency I can into my pleading, hoping he'll pull out of his drug-induced stupor.

With a long sigh, he rolls over to face me. His bloodshot eyes find mine, and he blinks slowly. "Why can't I sleep for a little while?"

"Because you'll miss all the fun," a voice says from the door.

I whirl around to face Andras in all his demon glory.

"So we meet again," he says, stepping into the darkened room, his eyes darting from corner to corner.

"Do I know you?" Brecken asks, gazing sloppily at Andras.

"You used to," Andras answers. "Who were you speaking to?"

"My guardian," Brecken says, turning over again. "This is a terrible mattress," he mumbles into its bumpy filthiness.

"Ah, yes. But you won't be here long, so don't worry." Andras steps forward and lays his hand on Brecken's arm. "I've waited a long time to see you again, Undoer. A very long time."

At the strange title, Brecken sits up, a frown on his face. He stares at Andras and shakes his head. "Who are you?"

"Ah, you don't remember?"

"Should I?" Brecken rubs his eyes and peers at Andras. "Dude, I've never seen you before in my life."

"We're old friends," Andras answers with a lazy smile.

"I don't remember your face," Brecken says, sitting up straighter, his expression still confused.

Andras takes a step back and cocks his head. "Really? That surprises me."

I'm frozen by the door, observing the exchange. It's like watching an old black and white movie where I expect Vincent Price to step into the scene, and I can't shake the feeling I've missed something.

"You don't remember. I can fix that." Andras begins a slow chant as he moves forward. His lips pull back into a snarl, his words, undecipherable. Before Brecken can react, Andras grabs him around the neck and shoves him hard against the cement wall, breathing heavily into his face. "You know me now, don't you? I see it in your eyes. Or at least the beginning of recognition."

Brecken jumps up, but struggles against Andras' strength, his face growing red as he gasps for air. He presses against the fist at his neck. Andras squeezes tighter, and then his leg rises swiftly, kneeing Brecken in the groin.

The reaction is immediate. Brecken falls to the floor, curled into the fetal position, moaning, and rolling back and forth, his breath coming in ragged hitches. Andras rubs his hand and watches Brecken with unbridled hatred. "You're time is over, Bretariel. You're done. Do you hear me? Done!"

Brecken looks up into Andras' eyes, agony glazing his features. Then Andras flees the room, slamming the door and locking it behind him.

60

Lost and Confused

BRECKEN

Brecken lies crumpled on the cold, cement floor, writhing in agony. Never has he felt such white-hot pain. It fills his belly and spreads out with fierceness to his arms and legs. His whole body feels shattered and broken. He wants to die, just to have the pain end.

When the pain does finally subside, the name Bretariel repeats in his mind, as if he should know it. The familiar cadence of the name wiggles through his brain, but he can't quite remember, can't pull the memory out—like distant answers to forgotten questions on an impending exam.

The man's face floats beneath Brecken's eyelids, a dark phantom that won't disappear. The enraged eyes glowing with hatred.

That face. He knows that face.

But from where? Everything around him feels off, like a nightmare. He can't grasp how he even got here. The last thing he remembers is Jill sitting on his bed, crying. Had Alisa shown up? He can't remember that either.

Brecken begins to relax enough to take a breath. He looks around and doesn't know where he is, or why he's here, but a dark foreboding condenses inside him, coating him from the inside out.

Something terrible is about to happen. He feels it deep in his bones. That man who was here hates Brecken with an intensity he's never felt before. He can't imagine why, but he has a feeling he is about to find out.

61

A Bad B Movie

ALISA

"Wha—what was that all about?" I say, still leaning against the wall, staring into Brecken's luminous blue eyes. I listened to the whole exchange between him and Andras in complete confusion.

Brecken doesn't answer me, but after a few moments, he rolls over and stands up on shaky legs.

"He called you Bretariel."

He falls onto the cot, pulls his legs up, and rolls toward the wall.

"Brecken?"

"Wait... a second," he answers, his breath still catching.

"He acted like he knew you." I stare down at him, waiting. This whole situation is too bizarre. "Brecken. Do you know him?"

"I don't know!" He sits up, his eyes watery pools of suffering. The vein in his forehead throbs as his jaw clenches. "You don't know how terrible I feel," he says, blinking his eyes, and then wiping his face with his arm.

"So..."

"So? What do you want me to say? I have no idea who these people are or what they want."

"Jill's here," I say, frustrated.

"What?"

"You heard me."

"She stuck me with those needles!" he yells into the quiet. His gaze moves around the room but he doesn't really seem to *see* anything. "I remember. She dug those... those things into my chest!" He rubs his hand over the wound.

"She's in on everything. She's bad, Brecken." I stand there, wondering what he'll do now. What will I do now? What can I do?

With a broken smile, he shakes his head and pats the cot beside him. "It doesn't matter. I don't really care anymore. Come here. Sit down."

I don't want to sit down. I want to fight. Not with him, but fight my way out of here, and I want him to fight with me. I have to rescue my brother and find Raphael. The last thing I have time for is sitting and chatting.

I sit down anyway.

My arm tingles when he presses against me and all those feelings of anger and irritation vanish. Oh, how I wish I could hold his hand, run my fingers through his floppy bangs, and brush a kiss across his lips.

Our time is almost over. I'm not even supposed to be here. I'm sure Natty is in trouble for helping, and I've screwed things up royally. No one is coming to help. All is lost, and I bow my head in defeat.

The cell door clanks open. Andras and Lamia step into the room, startling us. They are followed by a couple of their hired thugs.

"Bring him to the bed," Lamia commands. "And tie him tight. I want this to hurt."

As soon as Brecken is laid on the bed, my heart sinks. He struggles in their grasp, kicking his legs, connecting with his fists here and there, but all to no avail. He can't and doesn't get free. It ends up taking four people to tie him down, and even then, it takes Lamia's thugs forever to make the knots hold tight.

I stay beside him, feeling each wave of fury, frustration, horror, and hopelessness that tears through him. Who will do the dirty deed this time? Lamia? Andras? Jill?

How can I stop it? I wasn't able to help Nichole, and now she lies dead, drained, and alone. For eternity. Not even her soul will find peace now.

That *can't* be how Brecken is meant to die.

If Raphael saw this in his crystal ball, why didn't he warn me? This isn't some random drunk driving accident or even a suicide. This is hellfire and damnation spewed up from the depths of the underworld. Demons come alive. Every horror movie made real.

"Brecken! Tell me what to do," I whisper urgently. "Tell me how to help you. It can't end this way!"

He turns his head on the crimson satin pillow, his hair filling with static. In any other situation, I would laugh out loud, but the hilarity of the moment forms a thick ball of tar in my stomach instead. He lies there panting, bare-chested because they ripped open his shirt. A sheen of sweat beads his brow.

"Spirit!" Andras bellows.

I jump and turn to see him looking in my direction. Can he see me? Has something changed? Can Lamia see me as well? I feel exposed all of a sudden, vulnerable. His eyes scan the stage. He searches for me.

"Bretariel should have told you the truth from the beginning, spirit. But as we can all see, he chooses not to remember."

This man is powerful. More powerful that Lamia. I don't understand how the hierarchy works, but somehow, he is the one to be afraid of. He is the one who can destroy me.

"I don't know what you're talking about!" Brecken yells, raising his head from the satin pillow.

I lean over Brecken, my lips brushing his. That's when I realize he's not being completely truthful. I feel it as our lips touch. Something inside him knows the power of these beings. Something in him has begun to remember.

"Don't worry," I whisper. "It will be over fast and then we'll be together, just like we wanted." I don't know what else to say as I gaze into his beautiful face, his terror-filled eyes.

"You have no idea who you're dealing with, Bretariel," Lamia says. "But you will. You will!"

"Go, Alisa," Brecken begs, his eyes filled with such remorse that I can do nothing but break inside for him. "I don't want you to see this. It's going to be bad, whatever they do. I know it. Go back to heaven and I'll find you when I can." His anguish reaches out and wraps around my heart, but I can't leave him.

No matter the danger or outcome, I will stay by his side. I shake my head and stroke his face. "I'm not going anywhere."

He gives me a tragic smile, his gaze never leaving mine. "Everything has finally caught up with me. I'm sure I'm getting what I deserve, but I don't want you to watch me die. Please," he begs.

Returning his tender gaze, I know I will never know anyone like him again, and in that moment, I vow to do all I can to free him. To give him a chance. To give *us* a chance. No matter how impossible that seems.

I turn to Lamia, who slowly makes her way up the stage steps, fury ravaging her fiercely beautiful face. Her confidence astounds me, like a dark queen, sure of success.

I close my eyes, a prayer in my heart for a single miracle— the ability to stop this horrific tragedy from happening. A tingle begins in my fingertips and moves up my arms, like tiny diamonds of light twinkling from the depths of my soul. Energy gravitates toward me, like the bending of light, tightening, expanding, entering my soul.

In that moment, I realize Raphael is right. I *am* strong. I *can* prevail, but only if I truly believe it. Only if I make it so.

I open my eyes.

Lamia stops, her mouth hanging slack for a millisecond. "I *see* you," she hisses, raising her hands like claws.

"Your nails will do nothing to me, demon," I say, recognizing the darkness within her. The soul that inhabits her body does not belong in there and is not its original owner. Where is the true spirit of the woman who stands before me? It doesn't matter now. She let this happen to herself. She allowed evil in. I know it as surely as if I watched it on a movie screen.

"I know you, Lamia, demon vampire, Queen of lies and deceit." I stare her down, no longer afraid. She can't defeat me. She can't obliterate me. Lesser spirit, my butt.

"You have no authority here, guardian," she says, waving her hands in some sort of incantation. "Be gone!"

I can't help it. I bust out laughing. She's so dramatic. And even though I know she can't hurt me, I'm not sure how to stop her from hurting my brother or Brecken.

Their fates seem sealed.

But isn't this why I'm here? My job can't be over yet. No matter what Raphael says. I am a guardian, but I need someone with the power and authority to cast the angels of Hell back to where they belong, past the fiery pit of Soul Prison, into the eternal depths of unending darkness.

"You don't scare me, you vapid blood sucker. Let him go!" I point to Brecken, my eyes flashing hot. Then I hear it. Soft, like the chant of a child. It grows in volume. Undecipherable words, in some unearthly language.

Whirling, spinning, and gurgling away, the power and vitality I felt only a moment before melts into nothing—drained as though some thoughtless moron pulled the plug in the bathtub.

I turn in slow motion and catch Brecken's eye.

"Alisa!" he cries.

I blink, falling to the ground in a heap. The Earth rushes up to meet me and my face slaps against the cold tiles next to Brecken's deathbed.

62

Helplessly Helpless

ALISA

"Your guardian cannot help you," Lamia says, her teeth grinding. "How pathetic—lesser spirit that she is— she'll never get out." Her laughter wafts up like bells gone bad.

I claw back to a sitting position as Lamia bends over Brecken, her arms on either side of his head.

Brecken's response is to spit in her face. I am so proud. She screeches like a banshee, and rakes her nails down his cheek, leaving four straight seeping lines of red.

Lamia turns to the crowd in the auditorium, her lips pulled back into a snarl. "My children," her voice, a growl. "We have a special guest tonight. It will require a special ritual. One you have never seen before and never will again."

She steps down from the stage and moves slowly up the aisle, caressing faces and bestowing smiles. "In fact, you will all have the chance to taste immortality tonight." In a brilliant show of light, she spins, her red cape whirling out like fire, her golden hair, a veil of reflected candlelight. "Behold, Bretariel of the Irin, the great Undoer!"

She holds her arms out toward Brecken as though showing off a fine piece of art. A cheer erupts through the crowd and a hundred hands begin to clap rhythmically, chanting the name *Bretariel, Bretariel, Bretariel.*

I'm so glad my brother isn't participating. He's still down the hall, locked in a cold, dark cell. Although, he might be the next dish served. Grasping Brecken's hand tighter, I squeeze, hoping he can somehow glean courage from me.

When the noise dies down, Lamia continues. "He brings with him his protector. A guardian of the weakest form."

The cheers ring loud.

"Tonight, not only will one of the greatest of fallen angels be sacrificed on the altar of perdition—his damned soul extinguished into nevermore—but his guardian will also be erased from time and existence!"

They're talking about me! But after all I've been through, I'm not about to be erased from time and existence that easily. Without thinking—which is how I do most everything—I raise my hand, palm out, and shove, as though pushing an invisible shot-put.

Whatever force I possess, I throw toward Lamia. She stumbles forward, her red stilettos tangling in her long, silken robes. An acolyte on the isle catches her as she falls.

She turns in deadly silence and locks eyes with Brecken. Not a breath is heard in the whole room. "You'll pay for that," she whispers venomously. "Call off your watch dog, Bretariel, or—"

"Or what?" he spits. "You'll kill me?"

"Oh, I'll do more than kill you," she says, prowling toward the bed where he lies. "I'll rip your soul from your body bit by bit while you live, like you once tried to do to me!"

Brecken chuckles grimly, pulling on his bindings. "That would be a good memory to have back."

With a howl of rage, she springs for him, flying over the edge of the bed on top of him. Her hands grasp his wrists, and her legs wrap around his. When she smiles, it is with the sharp ivory fangs of a monster. Hers are not silver, detachable, or handmade. They are the real thing, the roots embedded deeply into the bones of her face.

I shrink back in horror, suddenly wanting to hide. Before I can move, she sinks her teeth into Brecken's neck. His back arches and his cry rips through the auditorium. Never have I heard anything so feral, so heartrending.

I spring for Lamia, my arms wrapping around her waist as I sail past. Surprisingly, I do not slip through her like a ghost without form, but like a boomerang, yanking her away from Brecken.

With a wild shriek, she grabs at the air.

"Brecken!" I fight my way toward him, hoping Lamia can't grab me as I grabbed her.

"Andras! Stop her!" Lamia screams.

Instead of trying to stop me, Andras, places a white towel against Brecken's wound. "If you want this done right, Lamia, it must be performed according to ceremony. Unless you only want to kill his body?" he asks, gesturing to Brecken, who lies grimacing and groaning in pain.

Lamia wipes Brecken's blood from her mouth. "Fine. Get the book."

63

The Big Black Book of Death

ALISA

One of the acolytes brings a large black and gold book forward. Its gilded edges and vellum pages, musty with age. Lamia takes the book, hefting it to a nearby stand, and opens the weighty cover. It falls back with a heavy metallic slap.

She sifts through the pages slowly, searching for something. I move to her side to see, careful to keep some distance, but close enough to view the devilish pictures and undecipherable words.

Finally she stops, her fingers tracing the words of an unintelligible language written in crimson. Horrifying caricatures of demons and wailing humans decorate the page. Lamia turns, her eyes wide and bright with arousal. She motions for Jill. "Come!"

Jill rises from her seat and walks regally up the steps. At the foot of the bed, she stops and waits, a mixture of excitement and apprehension etched on her butt-ugly face. At least, that's my opinion.

Lamia smiles and motions to Brecken. "Insert your teeth."

Jill doesn't look quite as confident as she did a few moments ago, but she nods, takes a box from her pocket, and inserts her silver fangs. She glances over at Brecken, but hurries to look away.

"As soon as I start reading, you drink. Stop when I tell you," Lamia commands, her voice hard and grinding behind her pearly white fangs.

Jill nods and climbs onto the bed next to Brecken. He watches her, her betrayal burning in his eyes.

"I loved you," he whispers. "I trusted you."

The ache in my chest—when I hear those words—blossoms anew, and I have to look away. How could he have ever given his heart to her?

Jill won't look him in the eye. "I'm sorry. I didn't expect it to end like this."

Brecken turns away, the thick muscles in his neck stretching taut. I can see the pulsing vein beneath his skin, alive, vital. Jill stares at it too. She leans forward and grabs his wrists, then glances again toward Lamia, waiting for the command to begin.

Lamia commences to read. The words, in a strange tongue, are guttural and harsh and draw goose bumps. Her tone—hate-filled as it is—conducts power throughout the room. Dark demons rise up from their hiding places, moaning and tearing at their ghastly faces. Candles flicker and Jill bends down, her mouth opening.

With a scream, I thrust all the power inside me toward her, just as I'd done to Lamia, only this time, it has no affect. Because she's human? I'm not sure. Stunned, I nearly fall to my knees. But refusing to give up, I try again, but Jill remains unfazed. Her lips spread wide as she clamps her mouth on Brecken's neck, her silver fangs sinking deep into his skin.

My soul screams in horror. She'll kill him! How is it possible I can do nothing to stop her?

Brecken doesn't move... or scream... or struggle. He just lies there, staring straight up, accepting his fate. Jill moves over him, gentle as a lover, when in reality, she is nothing more than a murderous succubus.

His gaze catches mine.

Lamia's voice drones on in the background.

Jill kneels there, unaffected by the torture she induces.

I close my eyes, picturing Raphael in my mind. Surely he would help, but my way is barred. He can't hear me. I'm only a lesser spirit after all. No one with any real power. My attack on Lamia had been a fluke.

Unless...

With renewed determination, I push myself up, vaulting through the air. Once again, I grab Lamia around the neck. Immediately, her words are cut off. Somehow, I have power over *her.* When Lamia stops reading, Jill stops sucking and looks up.

"Get her off me!" Lamia screams at Andras. She tears at her shoulders, trying to rid herself of her invisible opponent, but once I realize I pretty much have free reign, I jab at her eyes, pull her hair, and yank her nostrils, anything to disrupt her reading. Just when I begin to feel confident, thinking I can actually prevail, my spirit freezes mid-strike.

"Finally," Lamia growls, turning to Andras who moves behind her, his hand outstretched toward me as he chants.

"Just keep her back," she orders as she smooths her hair back into place. "Jill, stand aside." Lamia turns toward the audience and points at a boy in the front corner seat. "You! You're next. Get up here."

Surprise fills the boy's face as he fumbles out of his seat and hurries up the steps. He arranges his black robe so it won't hinder him, and slides over the bed. He leans forward and waits, a wicked gleam in his eyes.

"No!" I yell, struggling against the invisible force that holds me. Andras stays focused on me and no matter what I do, I can't fight back. In helplessness, I watch Lamia bend over her evil book as the black-robed boy bends over Brecken. As soon as the words pour from her mouth, the boy's lips attach to the thin skin over Brecken's elbow.

One by one, acolytes from the audience come forward, biting Brecken somewhere on his body and sucking his precious blood. I watch the life drain from him, his face growing ashen.

I cry out in despair and helplessness.

Then, when I don't think it can get any worse, the great jaws of hell stretch wide. A large, jagged fissure tears across the room's cement floor with a thundering boom. It widens and the walls shake. A deep black pit looms before us, and Lamia screams in euphoric glee, grabbing the book as a host of dark souls swarm into the room.

"What's going on?" Jill screams, grabbing the nightstand for balance. "Is this supposed to happen?"

"Yes! Oh yes!" Lamia cries out in elation.

The other acolytes in the audience glance around, frightened, and hang onto the seats in front of them, but the floor keeps right on shaking. Andras loses focus for a split second, long enough for me to escape his magnetic grasp, and I run back to Brecken. If I don't speak, maybe I can stay hidden from that heinous man's radar. I vow to keep my big mouth shut.

Close to Brecken's ear, I whisper, "Brecken. Open your eyes. It's me. Please Brecken, wake up." He doesn't respond.

I gaze onto his face, the softness of his lashes lying against his pale cheeks, his lips, once so full and warm, are now parted slightly in a last sigh, and his hair, mussed and damp with sweat. Tiny holes cover his body like he's been attacked by snakes. I lay my head on his chest, hoping it will rise just once with the intake of breath.

It doesn't.

A cacophony erupts behind me, but I don't turn. I don't care anymore. I've failed my charge, my calling, and my mission.

64

Saved by an Angel

ALISA

Darkness fills the auditorium. Demons screech, occupying every corner. The acolytes who remain seated, now wear terror-filled expressions. I don't care. My heart lies at my feet, smashed and broken. Any hope I held dissolves into nothing.

Brecken is dead.

I hold his hand and cradle his fingers. His soul must have risen without me ever noticing. I can't help but feel it is a punishment for my failure as his guardian.

I sit there holding his hand, the darkness overcoming me, until I hear the tinkling of chimes far away. No one else seems to notice. The demons and acolytes continue on in their raucous, manic, and frightening behaviors.

But something *has* changed, like sparkling water poured into me, bubbling and fizzing out to my fingers, energizing me. I sit up straighter and notice others in the room are finally sensing something different.

The shadows begin to retreat into the tightest corners, and a dazzling white light, a sparkling brilliance, appears in the center of the auditorium. A man materializes in glistening radiance.

And he isn't alone.

A host of bright white beings stand with him, their glorious countenances cowing the darkness that threatened me only moments before.

"Enough!" Raphael bellows. He swipes a gleaming sword through the air. Chairs pull from their bolts and fly over the acolytes who cower there. After a moment, a quiet settles in the auditorium, and the last bit of debris comes to rest on the dust-strewn floor. He stands front and center like the avenging angel he is, his dark hair flowing out behind him.

I stare, awestruck.

Raphael turns to Lamia. His eyes, like fire, narrow as he gazes at her. "What is it you think you're doing here?"

She squirms like a mouse caught in a lion's paw. "Only what is deserved."

"I thought I made it clear *eons* ago that Bretariel's soul was taken off the table." He moves toward her slowly, a predator ready to spring. I've never seen him so calculated, so deadly.

"I think," he says, "that you thought you could actually get away with this without anyone knowing. How stupid you've grown over the last ten thousand years."

She withers under his gaze, but plants her feet firmly, trying to appear like an undaunted soldier. "You have no authority over me," she says, her voice shaking with fury. "And no soul is *ever* taken off the table."

"Ah, but that's where you're wrong." He reaches out, slowly his long white fingers wrap around her narrow neck. "I should destroy you right now."

"But you won't, will you?" She smiles. "*You* especially won't re-nig on an oath." She steps back, Raphael's hand slipping away.

. Out of the shadows, Andras springs up behind Raphael, a roar of fury bursting from his mouth as he drives his black sword into Raphael's back. Raphael stumbles forward, falls to his knees, and then to the floor. He rolls onto his back groaning, looking as shocked as the rest of us.

Andras stands over him, his eyes wild, his lips twitching with raw hatred. "You didn't count on *me* being here, did you, Watcher?"

Raphael, although clearly in pain, grimaces up at Andras, signaling for his hosts to stand back. "I'll admit, I'm surprised. How... how did you get free? Only a *Watcher* could set you free." He pushes back with his feet to a seated position, his hand holding his side. "And I know of none who would."

Andras throws back his head and laughs. "Oh, the things

I could teach you, great protector." He leans in close to Raphael, his breath puffing out in a poisonous cloud. "You have a traitor in your midst." His sword drips acid that hisses and spits on the floor. He raises it to strike Raphael again.

The angels who arrived with Raphael don't wait for the command. They swarm, their glimmering swords slicing through the ghostly demons who dare counter attack.

Raphael manages to raise his sword in time to meet Andras. Despite Raphael's injury, he rises to his feet and fights like a wild animal. I watch in dread. How can Raphael possibly prevail when wounded? He holds his side and grimaces at each clang of their swords, yet he seems to overpower the Marquis of Hell, who now has fear etched into the creases of his hawk-like face.

Raphael's angelic army fights at his back, slicing through the demon soldiers who disintegrate in a gasp, leaving nothing on the ground but dust. The fight seems so one-sided, the outcome obvious, the angels winning. Especially when the next wave of angels appears... led by Anaita. Never have I been so relieved to see her.

They swarm into the room, their pale shadows trailing behind them. But instead of raising their weapons with Raphael and his glorious army of light, they fight *against* them. Raphael stares in surprise for only an instant. His shoulders sag, and then he goes back to fighting, resignation marring his features.

I'm frozen with terror, not understanding any of it. The sound of clanging swords fills the auditorium and screams of pain ring in my ears. Angels with auras as bright as the sun are cut down and killed by their angel brothers, their souls sparkling like fairy dust until they disappear.

Then it all becomes clear—her hate for me, her icy demeanor. Anaita is the traitor. *She* released Andras. She planned this all along. But why?

It doesn't take long before her eyes find mine. She doesn't break her gaze until she stands beside me, a radiant sword hanging from her right hand. "Always the guardian," she sneers as she circles the bed. "What a valiant effort you've put forward, but all your labors are in vain."

"I don't know what you're talking about." I search for Raphael who is halfway across the room. No one is close enough to help me, and I am no match for Anaita.

65

Angel of Death

ALISA

Anaita leans forward, letting her sword tip rest on the sheets beside Brecken's still form. "Poor thing. He wasn't as strong as I'd thought. I remember a time when nothing could stand in his way." She glances up and stares deeply into my eyes, just as she did so many times in class. "He played both sides, you know. His heart was as black as that pit you see over there." She points to the gaping crevasse in the center of the auditorium, which is still vomiting up evil spirits for the angels to cut down.

"You're lying," I say, my voice soft, but I know she speaks the truth for it pierces me to the center of my soul.

"Oh, child, he was terrifying to behold, powerful, unstoppable. A general in Hell's army!" Her expression intensifies as she stares into space, lost in her memories. Quickly she looks back to me. "But he was sneaky. A counterfeit. He turned the tables in every battle. Do you understand what I'm saying? Do you?"

I shake my head. Every second that ticks by leaves me more frightened. She's unstable, consumed with fury, ready to destroy.

"What a stupid girl you are." The acid in her heart drenches her words. "That's why you were assigned to Bretariel in the first place, because the great Undoer didn't need a powerful protector. He has powers of his own. Not that he remembered that. All we needed was someone to keep an eye on him. But you went and developed a little crush on one of the most powerful dark souls to ever live." She steps back and laughs, shaking her head, glaring at my stupidity, my foolishness.

Her words sting. "Why do you call him that? The Undoer?"

I ask, trying to keep her distracted so the sword will stay where it is and not become embedded in me.

"Because that's what he is! That's what he did! Every battle, every skirmish for souls, every sneak attack to undermine the enemy... Bretariel made it unravel right beneath their feet. No one saw it coming, no one suspected him of duplicity. It doesn't matter which side he plays for, he is a betrayer! He betrayed his brothers, his people! He will do it to us if given the chance. He deserves hellfire and damnation!" Her eyes slowly find mine again. "It ends tonight, and I will do the deed myself. There's no forgiveness for creatures like him."

She raises her sword over Brecken's body. His head lies turned on the pillow, his arms stretched wide. An open invitation for Anaita to plunge her sword between his ribs.

"No!" I scream, lunging, both hands aimed at her stomach. The shock of sudden contact stuns me, and blazing pain shoots through my wrists.

Anaita stumbles back and drops her sword in an effort to correct her balance. It clatters to the stage steps, glowing with pink iridescence. Her eyes narrow, a feral growl raised between her lips. "You'll pay for that."

Not waiting for my comeuppance, I dive forward, my fingers closing around the hilt of her sword. Anaita grabs my arm and rolls over me, banging my wrist on the hard stone steps.

"Raphael!" I scream, hoping he'll come to my rescue. I shove the heel of my hand into her nose and actually hear it crack.

She whips away, holding her face for a moment. "Well, now. That hurt," she says with deadly calm.

I can't believe I injured her, that I am holding this heavenly sword, which she certainly doesn't deserve. I feel its raw power course through my arm, granting me strength I've never had before. Great waves of energy pulse in my hand and up through my shoulder. I swing the sword back and forth testing its weight, and a small smile forms on my lips. "You made a mistake dropping this," I whisper.

With one swipe, the sword slides through the red satin tie

that holds Brecken's right hand. I leap onto the bed and slice through the other like butter.

Anaita springs for me. I jump back, my feet unsteady on the unwieldy mattress. We slam against the headboard and roll over Brecken in our fight for the sword. I kick her in the face with my foot; she pummels me with her fist. She will soon overpower me. She is a fighter. A warrior. I am nothing in comparison. I have no idea what I am doing, and at any moment, it will end with me as the loser.

The next second, she has me pinned beneath her. She straddles me with her powerful legs, my arms stuck beneath her knees. A smile stretches across her face as she slides a dagger from its sheath on her ankle. "Well now. This is a nice turn of events."

I say nothing, but stare at the knife that matches the sword I just held. With two hands, she raises it high above her head, its razor-sharp edge glinting insidiously. "And just so you know," she says, looking down her nose at me, "this blade is made from sacred samarium for the sole purpose of destroying eternal beings. Once it pierces your soul, you disintegrate completely. Silly little Alisa will exist no more."

I watch her face. There isn't one part of her that will mourn my demise. Not one iota of guilt will wrack her conscience. The only thing I can think of is that I haven't said goodbye to my family. What will happen to my brother still imprisoned down the hall?

With aching resignation, I close my eyes. I will not show Anaita my fear, my utter grief at having lost. I feel a slight breeze as she lifts her arms higher and the rush of wind as she brings her arms down... but nothing happens.

Anaita jerks to the side.

I open my eyes.

Brecken holds her wrist in a vise-like grip, like she is a little bird in the clutches of a tiger.

Despite his lack of blood, he sits there, staring into her face, his jaw clenched, the muscles in his face flexing. He presses her arm to the breaking point... almost. She falls into the soft blankets, her face surrounded by red satin.

"Enough," he whispers, looming over her. The tiny holes in his body still drip with blood. Crimson beads fall from his arms and chest onto her pink robes, the stains growing like rose blossoms as they spread. He can hardly sit up, let alone fight Anaita. "Your time has come to an end." From the look on his face, he seems to know her.

"Oh no," she spits. "It's just begun." Swiveling her body, she twists out of his grasp and knocks him in the face with her elbow. He grunts and falls back, too weak to put up a fight. I scramble over the bed, not quite believing in his miraculous resurrection.

Heaving leaden breaths, Brecken comes up on one elbow, his face devoid of fear. But there is something else. Something I've never seen in his expression before. A power radiates around him, despite his weakness.

"Get away," he whispers.

Confused, I wonder if he's talking to me. Before I can ask, I'm yanked back. Anaita hauls me off the bed and away from Brecken. Her arm tightens around my neck as she drags me off the stage, down the steps, and down the hall to the cell rooms.

My last glimpse of Brecken is of him forcing himself off the bed and falling onto the floor.

Anaita and I reach the first room and she throws me inside, slamming the door shut behind us. "Let's settle this without interference."

Dread entangles me in paralyzing fear. I was at peace when I thought Brecken was dead but he's not! He's alive! I can't let her banish my soul now! But I can't defeat her. I know that. She is too strong, too powerful, too frightening.

"You've learned nothing," she growls, moving forward with precise steps. "You don't get any of it." She throws her head back and laughs. "I guess that's good for me."

She grabs me, yanking me close with one hand on my arm, the other around my neck. She presses me into the wall. I have no need to breathe, but the gritting of her teeth, the hate in her eyes, sucks my life away. Does she really despise me so much? Why?

What have I ever done to her?

Knowing I need to stall for time, I blurt the first thing that pops into my head. "I know the truth."

"Is that so?"

"Yes." My mind scrambles for something that will make sense. And then I have it. A slow smile spreads across my lips. "You loved him. Didn't you? When he first defected, and he rejected you. That's it, isn't it?" I see in her eyes that I have hit a chord.

Her lips purse and she pushes me harder against the wall, her face only inches from mine. "How dare you say such a thing?"

"But I'm right aren't I?"

"No!"

"You said yourself you like bad boys. Who else is there?" I realize my guess is accurate, and even though I am only looking for something to keep the conversation going, I have hit the nail on the head.

"You are so stupid," she hisses, spittle flying from her mouth and onto my face. "I have no idea what he sees in you, someone so weak, so pathetic."

"Admit it," I say, drawing it out.

She stares with hatred into my eyes, her teeth grinding.

"You're forgetting something," I say.

She frowns and her grip on my neck tightens.

"Raphael once told me I am more powerful than I realize, that I can do things that would amaze me, that I have the power to crush evil. Even if it wounds me in the process, I will always prevail if I truly believe it." And even though I am close to death—real death—my mind is clear. Everything is laid open before me like a book, and I know what I have to do. I raise my hand and place it on her wrist, gently pushing her away as though she is only a small child. With my other hand, I take her wrist.

She stares in amazement. I feel her resist, struggling to regain control, but instead of being powerful, overcoming me, she grows weak. Astonishingly weak. More surprisingly, I'm not afraid anymore. I'm not afraid of her, of Andras, or even for Brecken. I know everything will be okay, even though I'm not sure how.

I turn Anaita around so I am behind her, still holding her wrists as though I'm restraining a child, and push her back toward the auditorium. She sputters, curses, and yanks, but she can't break my grip or get away.

Raphael stands at the stage's steps, placing a pair of fiery shackles around Andras' wrists and ankles. "Ah, I see the guardian has returned." His eyes twinkle and he smiles knowingly.

I grin back. "Yeah, she has."

"It's about time," he says, handing me a pair of strange, glowing chains. Two brilliant angels come to my side and hold Anaita's arms as I clasp a shackle around her right hand then another on her left. "Say hi to Mr. Roland for me," I whisper in her ear. "That is, if you're lucky enough to go there."

Her eyes narrow. "Mr. Roland will seem like a birthday party compared to what I'm going to do to you some day."

The power of her words hits me, but I resist those old, familiar feelings of despair and insecurity. I give her my best glare to prove her words have little effect.

The angels lead her, Andras, and Lamia away through a luminescent doorway that stands in the center of the auditorium. A legion of heavenly angels march at their side, their iridescent swords ready to strike with one false move. Raphael follows behind.

"Where are they going?" I ask the angel who is still beside me.

"They'll be taken before a council and sentenced, then locked away for a very, very long time," the warrior says. He smiles and then walks away.

But that phrase: for a very, very long time, does not sound permanent enough to me. I hope they *never* get out, that Anaita will never be able to make good on her threat. She scares me more than anyone else does.

I'm left alone. I'm too nervous to walk up to Brecken, who is surrounded by angels excited to help him walk toward the glowing doorway... to lead him away. They are all so happy to see him, to be near him. He doesn't even seem to remember I exist, and I don't want to demand his attention while he is busy with what must be a long-awaited reunion.

I expect him to look over though, to smile, to wave. Anything.

He doesn't.

I wait, pathetic and rejected, but he steps through the glowing door without looking back. The pain in my heart intensifies as reality hits. He is moving on. I press a fist to my heart, but the ache remains.

Moving slowly back through the halls off the auditorium. I'm not sure what to do now. The battle has ended. The good guys won. We can all go home.

Except for one problem.

I don't have one.

66

No Goodbye

ALISA

I stare at the shimmering doorway as many angels pass through to go home. I turn to one who waits at the back of the line. "So, who is Bretariel anyway?" He smiles gloriously, and I'm reminded of the elves in Lord of the Rings. Funny the things you remember at the oddest times.

"He's the Undoer," the angel says, "Hired—so to speak—by our side, to help defeat Abaddan's hosts. He had only one final task to accomplish for his redemption to be complete. Life. To become human. To place his soul in a body, be born to a family, and prove himself worthy. Now he has done that.

"This above all proves the intent of his heart since he wouldn't be able to remember anything from his past. His memories would all be erased like everyone else's when they're born. He accepted the terms and has been watched over closely his whole life."

I have no reply. I blink stupidly at the man before me. "Oh."

Some of the angels stay to clean up the mess. And although the real instigators have been shipped off, there are still the human acolytes to deal with. They mill around, their eyes glassy. Like they don't remember where they are.

I hadn't paid attention to where Jill went during all the action, but, as I wander around, I find her hiding in one of the back cells close to where Brecken was locked up. She lies curled in a corner, her eyes pinched shut, her hands trembling over her mouth. A shiver of revulsion pulses through me. This is what she deserves. I can tell that madness has taken hold of her. She's gone off the deep end, and for a moment, I feel a tiny bit of sympathy for the poor thing that witnessed and participated in some serious evil tonight. I can't help but wonder if there is a special corner of hell being prepared for her. She stole Brecken's blood, trying to get a taste of immortality after all.

Jill shifts slightly and looks up, her eyes wide and frightened. I don't think she can see me so I stay where I am, staring down at her pathetic form. She searches the room like she knows someone is watching.

She may not have started this whole mess, but she was an obedient little lieutenant, following orders. Orders that she had to have known were diabolic. I wish her a wonderful eternity in perdition.

On my way back down the hall, I stop at the cell where my brother is. He didn't see any of it. Not Raphael, Anaita, or Lamia reading from her satanic recipe book. He missed all the good stuff, and I am so glad. I didn't want to walk in and see him huddled in the corner with his thumb in his mouth, his brain fried from witnessing such horror.

To my relief he sits on the lumpy, stained cot, his knees up, his head hanging. I move through the locked door with only minor discomfort and sit beside him, wishing there was some way I could speak to him. *Really* speak to him. To tell him how much I love him, and how sorry I am for killing myself.

"I can give you a moment if you'd like," a voice says from the door.

I glance up. A beautiful angel with radiant red hair stands in the doorway, her white robes flowing out around her.

"What?"

"You want to talk with your brother, right?" She cocks her head to the side, a smile playing around her mouth. "You can. For a moment."

It takes a second to sink in, but her bright blue eyes confirm my hope. She nods and then leaves the room. I turn to my brother. My big, stupid, wonderful brother. His hair lays matted, and greasy, dark smudges stain his cheek, and a deep sadness wells in his eyes. I place my hand on his and gaze softly at his face.

He turns his head and blinks, his brow furrowing. He tries

to focus in the dim light, and a second later, with a sharp intake of breath, he says, "Alisa?"

I nod, the hot spark of tears behind my eyes. They aren't real tears, but the feeling is the same. My heart swells as I slide closer to him. "We only have a minute."

"What are you doing here?" Then the full weight of his question registers. With shame and embarrassment, he turns his face away and his voice catches. "I'm so sorry."

I smooth my hand over his head with only love in my heart. "I know how hard life can be. I know that it sometimes takes years to look back and see the consequences of our choices. It's all right. I understand. I really do."

Shifting his body, he looks deeply into my eyes, his mouth open in wonder. "You're alive?"

His question, so innocent, so pure, makes me laugh.

"Yep. We go on, Derek. I've been watching over you, trying to figure out why you were with Lamia and Jill in the first place."

He hangs his head, shaking it back and forth. "I don't know. I really screwed up. I just wanted... I don't know what I wanted."

I smile, hoping that he won't ever forget this moment. "Just learn from your mistake. And, Derek?" I want to say something profound, something prophetic, something powerful that he could keep with him always, that will protect him from other bad choices, but nothing comes to mind. So I say what is in my heart. "I love you. I love you so much it hurts, and you don't know how it kills me to see you and our family suffering. I'm so sorry for the pain I've caused. Please... please forgive me. If I could go back— well, I'd give anything to go back."

He stares at me, the wonder of the moment shining in his eyes, his head nodding. "I understand. And I *do* forgive you. I just wish you were still here. All the time, you know? Like before." He looks like he might actually cry. It would be the first time—that I know of—since I died.

"Me too." I lean close, inhaling the familiar scent of his cologne and sweat. "I'll still be here watching, so be good." With a chuckle, I kiss his cheek, bestowing all the love in that one gesture that I can."

"Can I tell Mom and Dad about this?" he asks.

"Definitely. I want them to know I've been here all along, and so has Gram and Natty too. I'm happy where I am. Really. Tell them that." It is a partial truth. I'd much rather be with them in a real body, experiencing life, and not on my way to wherever I'll be sent, but I want them to move on, to release the pain they've been harboring. The pain that I caused. "And tell them I'm really sorry."

"I will." A smile stretches across his face, happier and more content than I've seen him in a long time. The stress lines around his eyes relax and the hardness of his mouth smooths. "They'll be so happy."

"And no more fighting with Mom."

"You saw that?"

"Um, yeah. I did."

He shakes his head, lost in the memory, but not quite as embarrassed as before. The flow has come back, that comfortable camaraderie we shared.

"Well, you better get going," I say, standing. "You should get home."

He dusts off his pants, his black robe at his feet, trampled and filthy. "Where will *you* go?"

"To heaven, of course!" I say with false bravado, a tug in my heart. I'm not about to let him see my anxiety on that topic. "You don't worry about me. Things always work out." I motion toward the room's entrance. It opens without a sound. Derek is free to go even though he can't see the angel who has opened the door.

I kiss my fingers and then wave to him, all the while holding in my true feelings of despondency, loneliness, and uncertainty.

67

In the Nick of Time

BRECKEN

*I*t all comes back to me in a flash—my past, a crystal-clear memory. The angels and demons that had surrounded me so long ago. The raging battles. Anaita, Andras, Raphael, everyone. Everyone who is here now.

My body aches and burns from my murder just moments before, and I can hardly move. The noise and clang of steel swords, the screaming of eternal death ...those cries that I will never forget, are repeated here again. It's almost more than I can stand and the constant thought that pounds through my mind is that I have failed my earthly probation.

I was given this one chance at mortality. Now it's over. I remember the promises I made, that I would choose good over evil, that my damned soul would be redeemed. It seems I made one mistake after another. One failure after another. How could I have ever dreamed I'd get what I wished for in the end? God. Heaven. Angels. Eternity.

Anguish fills my heart and I want nothing more—after all this time and effort—to roll over to give up, but I roll over and see Alisa struggling, like a pinned bug, beneath Anaita's weight.

In a flash, my pain is forgotten as I reach out and seize Anaita's wrist. She turns, surprised, staring into my eyes in horror.

"Enough," I whisper, just as I had on that ashen battlefield so long ago. She'd been at my mercy then as well. I remember her kneeling at my feet as my sword was poised above her. I should have killed her then.

My thoughts shift back to the present. To Alisa. The resignation of an eternal death on her face. If nothing else, I will stop *this,* but will Alisa ever understand? Will she still accept me for who I am once she knows the truth?

Who would want someone so tarnished, so... damaged?

I can't look at her. Not yet. I can't bear to see the condemnation in her eyes. They have to have told her already, and if Raphael hasn't, Anaita surely has.

Anaita steals Alisa away and I can do nothing to stop them from leaving. I fall off the bed in my effort and lie on the floor. I wait, too weak to move, until the angel-warriors I know and remember surround me, buoying me up. I let them lead me away when the battle ends. I let them separate me from my guardian.

68

Alone Again

ALISA

After Derek leaves, I look down the hall to the room where Brecken was held. Just the fact that he is some bigwig demon-turned-angel leaves me reeling. How could I not have known, not have seen it? His aura did tend to shine brighter than most human being's did, but I'd chalked it up to his gifts of being able to see auras and spirits.

I think back to all the conversations we had and how I acted like such a stupid teenager. And I can't help but feel like Raphael used me, and that bit of truth flares hot in my chest like a bad case of heartburn. I hadn't been sent to be a guardian, but a spy.

Brecken knew what I was all along. Maybe he hadn't clearly comprehended it—without his memories—but on some level he knew. It was me who hadn't realized I was a secret agent.

Knowing I'm not needed here anymore, I close my eyes, figuring the only place to go is back to *Idir Shoal*.

How depressing.

I sit on my bed in *Idir Shaol* thinking. How stupid is it to have a bed when I don't sleep? Everything that ever bothered me about this place rises to the forefront of my mind. I hate the fake sunshine, the constant cheerfulness of those who work here, and I *really* hate the pretend sky. Do they think we're idiots? We know it isn't real, and it certainly doesn't make me feel any better.

The other thing is that I haven't seen anyone I care about yet. I *did* learn it was Natty who found Raphael and told his army of angels to save Brecken and me.

Now I am right back where I started, only more bereft, more depressed, and lonelier than ever. I have nothing to look forward to. I lie back and stare at the annoying ceiling, the puffy clouds floating by in the shapes of bunnies, kittens, and baby chicks. I yearn to reach up and rip the heads off all of them.

I miss Brecken with an ache I can't describe. My heart feels hollow, and all I want to do is cry, but no matter how much I try, no matter how much I wish it, those cleansing tears never appear.

I face the wall, scrunching my eyes shut. I'll lie here until I am *forced* to leave. Maybe I'll leave if my old roommates show up, which makes me wonder where they are. Have they become guardians? Even Deedre? I'd like to see *that* on a movie screen.

"No," I hear someone say beside me. "She chose to go to Soul Prison instead."

I turn abruptly to find Raphael sitting on Shana's bed, facing me, looking like my old mentor and not the avenging angel he was only a short while ago. I view him with a whole new level of appreciation. His long, wavy hair falls over his shoulders, and his green eyes regard me with sadness.

"Really?"

He nods. "Some do."

"What about Shana and Cinder? Are they guardians too?"

"Yes, they both are. And doing well." He shifts, placing his right foot on his left knee and leans forward, his eyes intense and seeing right through me. "You did very well, Alisa."

I snort and am tempted to turn back to face the wall. Instead, I bow my head, shame filling me. "You mean falling in love with your charge is condoned now? Good to know."

He chuckles and shakes his head. "Always the joker."

"No. A cynic. So now what?"

"Come. There's someone I want you to see." He holds his hand out. That strong, fighting, powerful, yet gentle hand.

With resignation I say, "I don't know, Raphael. I don't really feel like seeing anyone right now." My head hangs and my heart feels empty. I want to stay here and wallow... and eat Rocky Road ice cream.

"You'll want to see this person."

It has to be Gram, come to say good-bye and send me off to Soul Prison in grand style. I should be grateful and relieved that she would come after the huge mess I made. But inside, I resist. I don't want to see her pitying smile.

Maybe it won't be so bad. Maybe I'll get a spot close to the light, on the edge of tar and mist, away from people like Mr. Roland. I should have forgiven him long ago, but I hadn't been ready. Funny how that works.

"Okay."

Raphael drapes my arm through his and closes his eyes. One second later, we appear in his office, the fictitious light of the noonday sun shining brightly through the wide windows on the far wall.

"Wait for just a moment." He folds his arms over his wide chest and a smile splits his face. He seems inordinately happy.

"What?" I ask with a bit of petulance.

There is a tap on the door and the handle turns. I watch in slow motion as a whoosh of air blows past me, a flash of white appears, then a bare foot steps in, followed by the rest of the man, or should I say, teenager.

"Brecken!" I exhale in breathless surprise. One emotion after another rolls through me. Surprise, happiness, worry, euphoria, apprehension, and then back to happiness and surprise. I want to run forward, to throw my arms around his neck, to kiss him soundly, but I seriously can't move.

"Well, I have some things to do." Raphael winks in my direction, then the door clicks shut behind him and we are alone.

I don't know what to say as I look into Brecken's wonderfully familiar face, the way his eyes blink slowly, his crooked, innocent grin, how his fingers twitch against his thigh—playing a drum tap to some imagined song. He wears a long, white robe down to his ankles, and his feet are bare. He is all Brecken, whole and perfect, and I feel tortured along with my euphoria.

He steps forward, a shy smile playing on his lips. "Surprised?"

I know if he touches me right now he will feel real, not like I'm a ghost and he's a human. My feet know where I want to go and move toward him.

"I asked to see you one last time, before I have go back."

I stop before him, our faces only inches apart. The lump in my throat dissolves. "Go back?"

He measures our proximity, his eyes questioning. "Yes. I wanted to see you."

He is so close. I want to lean forward and kiss him. The thought sends a thrill through me and he smiles as if he has read my thoughts. His hand reaches out. His touch feels real—just like I knew it would—with heat, solid and wonderful. He pulls me closer and his eyes close.

Time slows, and I am surrounded by his arms. I feel the whole length of him—the muscles in his legs next to mine, the hard planes of his chest, the splay of his hands on my back. A beautiful tingle fills my hands as I slide them slowly up and down his neck. I smile in spite of myself. "I can't believe you're here," I whisper into his ear.

"I can't stay long," he murmurs against my neck. "I have to finish my tour of duty on Earth, but then we really can be together, just like we wanted. I don't have to forget any of this. I don't have to forget you. They're letting me keep these memories."

"But why do you have to go back at all? Why can't you stay here?"

"It's my penance, Alisa. I have to complete it. I have to go back and live a normal life as a semi-normal human and try to make a difference." He studies me, the love in his eyes, a gift. "You see, what Lamia said is true. I am a fallen angel. I rooted for the wrong team, and I have to pay for that mistake." He smiles sadly, embarrassed, and I experience those aching feelings through my fingers.

"It was Raphael who saved me. He saw something inside *worth* saving. I was given a chance to start over."

"Wow. That's... just so hard to even comprehend." I look at Brecken, the same Brecken I've known all along, but now, his face glows, shines, and his smile radiates a happiness I've never seen before.

"You'll make it," I say. "You belong in heaven."

He glances at our joined hands, rubbing his thumb over the back of my fingers. The soft pressure creates a yearning inside me, and all I want to do is hold him. I can't bear the thought of releasing him and leaving. Does he know I'm being sent to Soul Prison? How can he think we'll ever be together? I can't be the one to tell him, to disappoint him, so I say nothing.

"I need to go," he whispers, "but I want you to know that every day, every moment, I'll be thinking of you. I'll check in with Raphael to see how you are, and know that... that... I love you."

He's never said those words before, never even uttered them under his breath. Their power distills over me like a warm, humid mist, filling every crack and crevasse of my aching soul, healing my heart, converting my doubt to hope.

He loves me!

My whole life I've struggled to feel loveable—a symptom of my abuse—but Brecken's words, his unconditional love, erases those unwanted memories from my mind.

I throw my arms around his neck once more and pull him close, inhaling the wonderful scent of him. Woods and maleness. I soak him in, figuring it will be the last time. He pulls back to look deeply into my eyes, then leans forward and presses his lips against mine. His hands spread on my back and the pressure of his fingers grip my robe. I tighten my arms around his neck, my hands tangling in the hair at his neck. Never have I clung to anyone this way, with such fervor, such sadness, knowing the magic will soon end.

When he pulls away, the same dread I feel in my heart is on his face. "I have to go."

"I know." My lips graze the soft skin of his neck, the scars from his punctures wounds healed. "You'll wait for me? You won't go off and fall for some other guardian?"

"You need to ask?"

I brush my fingers over his lips, memorizing his face—

the crinkles around his eyes, every freckle, every nuance in his expression. "I'll wait for you forever."

We gaze into each other's eyes, neither of us wanting to let go or look away—our clasped hands, our aching hearts refusing to say good-bye. I yearn to stay in this bittersweet moment, but a knock sounds on the door and Raphael peeks in.

"Time to go, Bretariel."

"Okay." Brecken's lips brush over mine one more time. "And don't forget what I said, and if you're ever in my neighborhood…"

"I will."

He steps back, his arms still reaching for me, this heartache ripping us in two. "I'm not going to say goodbye." His face twists into a grimace as though leaving me is physically painful. How long before we are together again? Will he finish his penance before me? I'm not ready to say goodbye!

Raphael places his hand on Brecken's shoulder, and with a reluctant nod to me, they disappear in a shimmer of light.

And just like that, I am alone.

69

What Future Awaits

ALISA

I stay in Raphael's office, knowing he'll be back. Now that Brecken is gone, I'm ready to go. There's nothing left for me in *Idir Shaol*. There's no one to say good-bye to—no one to miss.

When Raphael returns, he doesn't seem surprised to see me still waiting, but instead of ushering me out or ordering me down to Hell—which is what I suspect will happen, because I did disobey—he comes in and closes the door. Nervously, I await his decision—because I did go back to Brecken when I wasn't supposed to, and I did talk Natty into disobeying as well. The wrong choices I've made are the ones that stick to the forefront in my mind.

Raphael sits down on the couch and pats the cushion next to him. He seems much too calm for a moment like this. The moment of my sentencing.

"I am going to tell you something I haven't said to anyone in a very long time."

I watch him, waiting, holding my breath... figuratively.

He takes my hand and stares into my eyes with an intensity that quickly begins to alarm me. This is going to be bad. Really bad. This is it, and my nonexistent heart pounds in my chest. I can already feel the hot, sticky tar of Soul Prison sucking me down.

"I'm giving you a choice," he says, his stoic expression never changing.

Wait? What? "A choice?"

He turns slightly and exhales through his nose, staring out of the windows that cause the room to glow with glaring brightness.

My heart races faster. I place my hand on his arm, leaning forward. "A choice?" I repeat.

"I think you have earned it."

I stare into his eyes, not daring to hope, and yet, that is all I can do. "You mean?"

"You have proven your worth," he says.

A surge of love sweeps over me like an ocean wave, pounding into my quaking soul. All the fear and reluctance for my future washes away in those few words.

"You can choose to rest in Elysium with your grandmother and your friend, Natty... or, you can go back to Earth. To be a guardian again."

I can't stop the smile that spreads across my face. "Are you serious?" This is too good to be true, and just as I am about to throw my arms around his neck, he stops me.

"Not for Brecken, Alisa. For someone else. Someone just as deserving."

I pull back just enough to study his face, and the significance of his words. How can I go back, and not be with Brecken? For a moment I sit there, immobile, my mind racing to solve this dilemma, and oh, the exquisite pain that pierces my heart, like a dull dagger, ripping and tearing instead of leaving a clean cut. "But why?"

Raphael cocks his head as though confused by my question. "Because he has certain requirements he must meet, Alisa. Without any interference."

"What does he have to do that I can't be a part of?" I'm torn in half. I'm ready to fall down on my knees and start begging. They can't do this to us. There has to be a rule or something.

Just when I thought it couldn't possibly get any worse, he says, "Brecken is required to have a normal human life. To have a family... with a wife and children."

I'm stricken. I can't talk or even think of a coherent thing to say. When I raise my eyes to meet his, I see he is sincere. This is no lie or prank. "You can't be serious," I whisper, pleading. "Please tell me you're joking."

The look on his face says it all. As far as we're all concerned, his verdict is carved in stone. How can I bear this? How could I be a guardian to someone else, all the while knowing Brecken is getting older, getting married, and having children? It's too cruel. To both of us.

"Does he know?" I ask, remembering Brecken's last words, that he'll wait for me—that we'll be together again.

"Not yet," Raphael answers. "But he will. I'll tell him soon, after he's had... time."

Gazing out the window, a million thoughts sift through my mind, ways to circumvent this. Could we run away? Escape? However, I know, deep down, that none of it is truly possible.

"Would you deny him this happiness?" Raphael asks quietly. "The gift of a family?"

I can't answer. I know what he wants me to say, but I cannot say it.

Instead, I do what I do best.

I run.

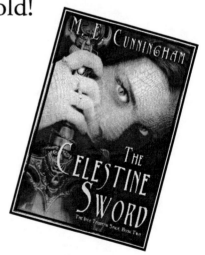

Acknowledgements

I want to give a huge thanks to my rockin' awesome critique group. Without them, this book would be nothing like it is. I love you guys! Renae Mackley, Shannon & Brock Cheney, Richard Johnson and Angela Millsap.

Also, many thanks to the amazing women at Clean Teen Publishing, who took a chance on me. They made this book sparkle, and gave me new hope for a writing career. To Marya Heiman for being so easy to work with on the cover. I was picky, and she bent over backward to give me what I wanted. To Courtney Nuckels, Rebecca Gober, and Dyan Brown for their patient advice and hard work. I love this publishing company!

And last but not least, to my wonderful family, that put up with me patiently while I practiced my craft for the last five years. They've cooked, cleaned, run my errands, and picked up my slack. Bryan, Jacob, Seth, Heidi, Gabriel, and Wyatt. You guys are my life, wholly and completely.

About the Author

Melissa J Cunningham (Also known as M.E. Cunningham) began writing when she was already all grown up and a mother of five. Out of the blue she decided to enter a community writing contest and won first place. From that moment on she had a new love: Writing. Melissa is the author of The Elementalist, Book two in the Ransomed Souls Series, and also the author of the Into Terratir Saga, The Eye of Tanúb and The Celestine Sword.

Melissa's first novel: Reluctant Guardian, was accepted for publication through Clean Teen Publishing in August 2013.

When she is not writing you can find her spending time with her family in Northern Utah, in the country, where she lives among the fields of alfalfa and horses and chickens. Melissa loves all things fiction, from Stephen King to Shannon Hale. She reads it all.

Visit her webpage at: melissajcunningham.com

CPSIA information can be obtained at www.ICGtesting.com
Printed in the USA
LVOW10s0303050216

473814LV00001B/26/P